I0598168

THE "BEST FOR BOYS" LIBRARY.

MAY BE OBTAINED FROM ALL BOOKSELLERS OR POST FREE FROM THE OFFICE.

THREEPENNY COMPLETE VOLUMES.

THE WILD ADVENTURES OF EDDARD & JAM JOSSER ABROAD.

THE WILD ADVENTURES OF EDDARD & JAM JOSSER AT HOME.

THE FURTHER EXPLOITS OF EDDARD AND JAM JOSSER.

THE SLAPCRASH BOYS; THE LIVELIEST OF SCHOOL STORIES.

PLUCKY PHIL FARREN; OR, THE MYSTERY OF BRYTHEWAITE SCHOOL.

HAL O' THE HEATH, THE WANDERING HEIR.

THE BRAND OF THE BLACK STAR.

LIONEL THE BOLD, OR, THE CIRCUS RIDER'S REVENGE.

VALIANT ROY; OR, THE PIRATE'S SCOURGE.

The above Stories were Written by the Best English Authors, and are Handsomely Illustrated and Bound in an Illuminated Cover.

SIXPENNY COMPLETE VOLUMES.

THE VEILED CAPTAIN; OR, THE HERO OF EAGLE CRAIG.

YOUNG CHING AT SCHOOL; OR, HIGH OLD TIMES FOR THE SLAPCRASHERS.

OUR BOYS ABROAD; OR, THE BLACK BANDITS OF THE RHINE

JACK OF THE GOLDEN BELT; OR, STIRRING ADVENTURES IN THE SWAMPS OF CUBA.

DICK STORNAWAY; OR, A HERO IN SPITE OF HIS FOES.

DARING CHING CHING; OR, THE MYSTERIOUS CRUISE OF THE SWALLOW.

GALLANT HAL AND THE CREW OF THE SILVER STAR.

CHING CHING AND HIS CHUMS; A MIRTHFUL, MOVING, AND MYSTERIOUS STORY.

This is a Series of Thrilling Romances, abounding in striking situations and remarkable incidents. They were all Written by Popular English Authors, and are Beautifully Bound and Illustrated.

ONE SHILLING COMPLETE VOLUMES.

HANDSOME HARRY OF THE FIGHTING BELVEDERE. Vols. I. & II.

CHEERFUL CHING CHING; THE SEQUEL TO "HANDSOME HARRY."

TOM TARTAR AT SCHOOL. Vols. I. & II.

WONDERFUL CHING CHING.

YOUNG CHING CHING.—Vols. I. & II.

All Written by E. HARCOURT BURRAGE, and Magnificently Bound and Illustrated.

TWO SHILLING COMPLETE VOLUMES.

HANDSOME HARRY OF THE FIGHTING BELVEDERE.

YOUNG CHING CHING.   TOM TARTAR AT SCHOOL.

THE ABOVE WORKS ARE PUBLISHED BY THE
'BEST FOR BOYS' PUBLISHING CO., 17, GOUGH SQUARE, FLEET-ST., LONDON.

DAUNTLESS DONALD DREW
OR
BESET BY BITTER FOES

No. 17.   "BEST FOR BOYS" LIBRARY.   6D.

DONALD DREW

Or,

PRESSED FOR A PRIVATEER.

———

By E. H. BURRAGE.

———

SPLENDIDLY ILLUSTRATED.

Everybody should Buy and Read the

BIGGEST
BRIGHTEST
BEST
BOY'S
BOOK

EVER PUBLISHED

WHICH IS

THE BEST FOR

MERRY BOYS

"CHING CHING'S OWN."

3 SENSATIONAL SERIAL STORIES

AND

A COMPLETE TALE
(WITH COLOURED PICTURE)

IN EVERY NUMBER.

ONE PENNY WEEKLY.

The Most Original Journal for Boys ever issued.
FULL OF COMIC ILLUSTRATIONS.

DONALD DREW;

OR,

PRESSED FOR A PRIVATEER.

———————⟨∞∞∞∞∞∞∞∞⟩———————

CHAPTER I.

NOTHING TO DO—A FOGGY DAY IN THE EAST—THE INN BY THE RIVER—CAPTAIN CARKER.

IT was a dark November day—one of the darkest of that dreary month—for a dense fog hung over the great City of London. Eastward and down by the river it was especially thick—so dense, indeed, that the lighted shops were of little service, doing little more than making the murky air a bit luminous for a few feet, and by contrast increasing the density of the gloom.

Pedestrians walked warily ; drivers ceased to drive, and led their horses ; the air echoed with muffled voices ; strangers floundered against each other, and with muttered apologies passed on.

The ragged and the thinly-clad shivered as they crawled along ; the busy cursed the gloom as a hindrance to business ; the man out of work felt as if the chill garment of Despair had been wrapped around him.

Among the many wayfarers wandering helplessly about the narrow streets of Wapping was a tall, well-built young fellow of eighteen or so.

His clothing was that of a mercantile clerk, a bit worn, but well brushed.

By name Donald Drew, and by occupation an accountant, he was there seeking work.

He came early in the morning, before the fog settled down, which it did suddenly, and being a stranger in the district he soon lost his way.

But what sort of work was Donald seeking?

For three months he had been out of employment, and as a last resource, as something to keep body and bones together, he had come down to try the docks.

Donald was proud and high-spirited.

He was an orphan, but he had friends—rich friends in the north—of whom he might have asked help.

But that he would not do;

The bare possibility of being refused, or having a small sum with a homily on perseverance doled out in reply, appalled him.

Perseverance !

Had he not persevered, as many have done, and found it did not help him?

The head of the firm in which he had been engaged died, and his heirs disposed of the business.

The purchaser brought in a staff of his own, and Donald was turned adrift.

Clerks are at a discount, thanks, in a measure, to the Germans, who know so much and will work for so little ; and Donald went here and there, advertised, answered advertisements, made enquiries, tried his best, and failed.

"I'll do anything rather than starve or beg," he thought.

So he went down to the docks, and found he had as much chance of getting work there as he had of becoming premier of England.

The tougher characters—men used to the place—chaffed and elbowed him! They asked him who his mother was, and why she did not take care of him at home. His blood boiled, and but for a prudent resolve not to mix himself up in a quarrel, he would have got into trouble.

What chance would he have stood among the body of rough men round the dock gates?

Their lot was hard enough without having black-coated dandies coming in to chip the corners off their bread.

"Get away," said one; "harf an hour of our work

uld break you up."

"I am as strong as many here," he replied.

At this they laughed, for he looked a "whipper-snapper;" but for all that there was a good right arm, with muscles of steel, under his black coat, and he could and would have worked.

However, there was nothing for him to do then, and he turned away—to be enveloped, lost in a fog.

As he moved cautiously along the street, he jingled in his pocket the last few coins he had in the world.

A solitary shilling and a few coppers.

And he was hungry, too.

The walk from his lodgings in Islington, and the wait at the dock gates, had roused his naturally healthy appetite.

He felt as if he could have eaten a leg of mutton, and for two days he had tasted no meat.

"I MUST have something to eat," he muttered, as he stopped under the glare of a gas-lamp.

On his left he could distinguish the outlines of an open door, beyond which was a faint illumination.

From the interior of the house came the clinking of glasses and the murmur of voices.

"It's a public-house of some sort," he muttered.

And then there cropped up in his mind stories he had heard of water-side inns of evil repute; and he was passing on when a voice within cried out—

"Close that door, will you? We don't want all the fog in the house."

It seemed to him as if it would be the closing of a friendly door.

There were light and warmth within, if nothing else; and surely he could venture to spend a little of his small store of money for some beer and bread and cheese?

He wanted some form of nourishment, and, with a feeling something akin to desperate rashness, he dashed into the house just as a man was closing the door.

Inside the fog was not by any means so thick, and, the murky day being shut out, he could see tolerably clearly about him.

There was a bar, with a roughish-looking man behind

it, and several men in front of it rougher still.

It was one of the latter that had closed the door.

He was a grizzle-headed, hard-looking man of fifty, with a sea-faring look about him.

A pea-jacket, wide blue cloth trousers, loose black necktie, check shirt, and a cap of foreign make constituted his attire.

" Hullo ! youngster," he cried. " What do you want ?"

" A little refreshment, that's all," replied Donald. " I've been walking about a great deal and feel rather hungry."

" But what brought you walking about here ?" asked the man.

" Really," said Donald. " I cannot see that that is any affair of yours."

" Perky," said the man ; " but that's common to young 'uns, and I don't like to see it."

" Have you a room where I can sit down ?" asked Donald, turning to the landlord.

" There's the tap and coffee rooms," was the reply. " Make your choice ; both doors are near you."

" But stop a moment, youngster," said the grizzly man. " I don't quite like the way you spoke to me just now. Young fellows of your age ought to be civil to men of my years."

" You asked me an impertinent question," said Donald, " and I gave you a fitting answer."

" Oh ! no you didn't. I—"

" Let him alone, Mike," said the landlord.

" I am a-letting him alone," said Mike. " Leastways, I will do so in a minute ; but, as I'm mate of the Water Fiend, I'll know what the like of him means by trotting round here."

" I shall certainly not tell you," replied Donald.

" Then I must make you," was the answer ; " and when Mike Barlow talks of making anyone over or under him DO a thing he means business."

" Let him alone," said the landlord again. " What do you mean by worrying the youngster ?"

" I'm not a-worrying," said Mike Barlow, mate of the

Water Fiend, suavely. "All he's got to do is to give me a civil answer to an ornary question, and I'll let him go in and enjoy himself."

"I'm going in without answering you," replied Donald, quietly.

"Oh! no you ain't."

"But I say I am."

Donald's voice was raised just the fraction of a tone. His blood was getting up.

As he spoke he endeavoured to cross over to the coffee-room, but Mike Barlow barred the way.

"Your answer?" he said.

"This!" replied Donald.

And, without any more nonsense, he knocked him down.

Mike Barlow, mate of the Water Fiend, went down upon the flat of his back so suddenly that his friends were both astonished and staggered, and he on his part was staggered and astonished still more.

He felt, as he subsequently declared, as if he had been knocked down by a small cannon-ball.

And, being down, he was really and truly at first unable to get up again.

He made an effort or two, and then fell back, exclaiming—

"May I be frizzled if he can't hit."

To this remark there was a chorus of laughter from his friends.

Donald stepped over his prostrate form and passed into the coffee-room, followed by the applause from the spectators, the landlord rattling a pewter pot on the metal top of the bar.

There was nobody in the coffee-room. It was not a very inviting place; but a fire was burning in the grate, and that, on such a raw, chilly day, was inviting.

Donald, outwardly unruffled by his encounter with Mike Barlow, mate of the Water Fiend, drew a chair up to the fire, rang the bell, and sat down.

The landlord responded.

He came in, and, after a glance backward, closed the door.

"Brayvo, young gentleman," he said. "That 'ere floorer will do Mike Barlow good."

"Why did the ruffian interfere with me?" asked Donald.

"Oh! that's his way," returned the landlord, slily.

"And now he knows my way," said Donald. "Please bring me a pint of mild ale and some bread and cheese."

His order was soon attended to, and, as he was paying for the refreshment, the landlord stooped over the table and whispered—

"It's settled Mike for the time : *but he'll remember it.*"

"I hope he will," said Donald, calmly.

The landlord turned towards the door, as if to go.

Half-way there he stopped, and turned to Donald again.

"May *I* ask what you are doing down here?" he said. "I don't mean to be rude."

"I came to look for work."

"For work? Where?"

"In the docks. I have been out of work a long time, and am jolly hard-up."

"Whew!" whistled the landlord. "Who'd have thought it?"

"People can be hard-up," said Donald, "without being in rags."

"Oh! just so." responded the landlord, as he retired ; "just as some people are dirty and ragged, without being particularly hard up."

Donald smiled.

He knew enough of life to see the point of the landlord's remark.

Left to himself, he fell upon the bread and cheese with the quiet eagerness of a well-bred, hungry man, and quickly succeeded in reducing his appetite so that it no longer troubled him.

With half his ale to consume, he turned to the fire, and fell a-thinking.

His stock of money was now reduced to tenpence.

That was all he had between starvation or the pawnshop.

He did not like the idea of either. The latter was repugnant to him mainly because he had had no experience of it.

A pawnshop is not, in itself, an objectionable place. It has often been the means of saving a man or woman from the pangs of want, or even suicide.

Many a time of trouble has been tided over by its aid.

It was the idea of parting with his clothes that was so repugnant to Donald.

"If I must I must," he said ; "but it goes against the grain."

The party in the bar were talking loudly, and high above all was heard the voice of Mike Barlow.

Donald expected he would come in to renew the disagreeable encounter ; but he did not, which was rather surprising.

Suddenly all the voices were hushed.

Then, after a moment's silence, a clear, rich-toned voice was heard asking—

"What the deuce are you idling here for, Mike ?"

"I'm not idling, sir," Mike replied. "The fog is so thick that I can't get aboard."

"Oh ! hang the fog," was the rejoinder. "Go and see what you can do. What's the matter with your eyes ?"

The answer Mike gave in a low tone.

It was rather a lengthy one, but Donald was not curious.

It did not trouble him much what it was.

Mike Barlow, mate of the Water Fiend, was at liberty to make the best of his well-merited chastisement.

"Oh ! that's it, is it ?" said the clear-voiced speaker. "Well, it served you right. Where is this fiery youngster ?"

"In the coffee-room, sir," replied the landlord.

A quick footstep was heard, the door opened, and the clear-voiced speaker sauntered into the room.

He just glanced at Donald before he crossed over to the fireplace, and rang the bell, but he did not seem to take much notice of him.

Donald inspected him narrowly.

He was a tall, dark, handsome man, with a determined and not altogether agreeable expression of face.

His attire was that of yacht captain and owner.

"Landlord," he said, "bring me a bottle of port. Confound this fog ! I want something to take the chill out of my bones."

CHAPTER II.

DONALD MAKES A NEW ACQUAINTANCE—LIFE IN ANOTHER LAND—THE OFFER TO DONALD.

A FEW minutes' silence ensued, and then the stranger spoke half to himself and half to Donald as it seemed—

"What a fog ! The densest I have ever known."

"Has it become thicker ?" asked Donald.

"It is like a night in Hades outside," said the stranger ; "and this is not a nice neighbourhood to be in at such a time."

"You know it," said Donald.

"I do and I do not," was the reply. "I bring my ship, a mere yacht, into the river every now and then. I lie off here when I am short of men. I am short now."

He poured out a glass of wine, drank it, and took out his cigar-case.

"You smoke, I suppose ?" he said.

"Very rarely," replied Donald.

"Try a cigar now ? These are mild, and the real thing."

Donald did not like to refuse, the stranger was so courteous.

But for the strange, indefinable, repellent look on his face he would have been the most agreeable company.

"Yes," he said, musingly, as he struck a match and passed it to Donald, "I am short of men, the right sort of men. Of course I could pick up any amount of loafers —weeds and scum of society—but they won't do."

"You want thorough seamen, I presume ?" said Donald.

"Give me the right man," said the stranger, "and I will soon make a thorough seaman of him. My name is

Carker, and I'm captain of the Water Fiend—she is, in fact, my own vessel."

"I thought as much," said Donald.

"What made you think so?" asked Captain Carker, with a keen glance at him.

"I heard you talking to a man who calls himself Mike Barlow. He said he was mate of the Water Fiend."

Captain Carker cast a backward glance at the door, which he saw was warped. There was a wide opening at the top to let through sounds from the bar.

"It is like being in the same room," he said, with a short laugh. "Mike is rough, but he is a good fellow, and trustworthy."

"He seems to like riding over those younger than himself," said Donald.

"Apparently he did not ride over you," returned Carker.

Donald smiled. He was only mortal, and the compliment was just a little bit pleasing.

"What are you doing here?" asked Carker, after a pause. "Have you a craft of any sort in dock?"

"Neither in nor out of dock," replied Donald, a little sadly. "I am only a young fellow out of work."

"Out of work? What sort of work?" asked Carker.

"I was an accountant's clerk."

"Pah! was that *your* style?"

"Hardly," said Donald, flushing a little; "sometimes I used to feel it irksome, but *any* honest work is better than starving or begging."

"Well, why don't you go to sea?"

"I never thought of that—and yet, I have sometimes longed to see foreign countries."

"Go and see them."

"How? I am not a sailor."

"Join my craft, and I will make you one—a free-and-easy *money-making* sailor."

He bent over towards Donald as he spoke, and looked at him with eyes that pierced the young fellow through and through.

"Is there much money to be made at sea?" asked Donald.

"Come to sea and see," replied Captain Carker, with a light laugh.

"Will you have a little wine?" he asked, a moment later. "Ring the bell for a glass."

"Thank you—no," said Donald; "I have just had some beer, and the mixture would not do for so poor a toper as I am."

"By-and-bye, then," said Carker, "for of course you will stop here until the fog lifts?"

"I fear I must," returned Donald, ruefully.

"Then make up your mind to be my guest," said the captain of the Water Fiend; "don't be squeamish about such a matter. We sailors are naturally hospitable—the more so, I expect, because we have so few opportunities for giving our impulses vent."

"I can hardly do that," said Donald, a little stiffly.

"Why not?"

"Hospitality should be reciprocated, and I cannot return it."

"Hang all that!" said Captain Carker. "Put away that nonsense. You are going to join me in the Water Fiend."

"What is she—a trader?"

"Trader be hanged! No, a pleasure-yacht. I am just wandering about the wide waters with it, and I want lads of spirit to join me. There is lots of money to be had for the seeking; on some shores the gold lies like sands, and jewels as pebbles. I can see that you intend to join me."

"I am not so sure of that," said Donald.

For all the genial air of this stranger, Donald did not like the man.

He was not afraid of going to sea—indeed, the idea was rather pleasing to him; but if he went at all he wanted to know exactly who he was to serve under.

The memory of Mike Barlow acted as a deterrent.

Donald had not the least doubt that he was an unmitigated ruffian, and to be in his power on board ship would be a terrible fate.

Donald had read of cruelties perpetrated by officers that had driven the men to mutiny, the end being the gallows

"Hurry up!" cried Captain ... "He's coming round."

for some of them.

Naturally, he did not desire to figure in either capacity —as oppressed seaman or murderous mutineer.

"I could not give you an answer now," he said, after a ong silence.

"Take half an hour to think it over then," replied Captain Carker.

"I should want more.'

"Take an hour then."

"I should want more than that. I could not give you an answer until to-morrow. I should like to sleep upon your offer."

"Very well," said Captain Carker, cheerily. "Sleep on it, and you will then see the wisdom of joining me. Good pay, a roving life, freedom, money, *adventure !* Oh ! it's just the sort of thing for a lad like you."

"Well, we shall see," said Donald. "To-morrow !"

"And to-day, while the fog lasts," said Captain Carker, "you are my guest. How is that cigar ?"

"Very good," replied Donald. "I have never smoked one like it before."

"You cannot buy such cigars here," said Captain Carker. "They are the pick of the Havannah crop. As with cigars, so with everything else, we sailors get the cream. I'll just go out and see if the fog is rising."

He left the room, and was absent three or four minutes. When he came back he threw himself into his chair with an air of vexation.

"Thicker and thicker," he said. "You are boxed up here all day, and perhaps all night. Now, don't be squeamish about accepting hospitality under such circumstances. Only a fool would hesitate for a moment."

"As a fact," said Donald, "I may say I have no money worth speaking of, and I could not pay for a day's living here."

"Then I will do it for you," said Captain Carker, "and if you don't like to join me you can pay the debt at some future time. Have another cigar. Good tobacco never hurts anyone."

CHAPTER III.

A LONG AND WEARY DAY—THE GLASS OF WINE— PRESSED FOR A PRIVATEER.

THERE was no doubt about it—the fog was getting thicker and thicker. Day had been turned into night.

At the lower end of the room in which Donald sat there was a window, grimy with dirt; but neglect to clean it was not sufficient to account for the dense darkness outside.

Donald was fairly a prisoner for the time in that water-side inn.

A little later on Mike Barlow knocked at the door, and at the bidding of the captain, came in.

He was altogether a different person to the bully in the inn. His manner was very respectful, he spoke quietly, and, in a general way, he had been brushed up and improved.

"There's no getting on board the Water Fiend, sir," he said.

"I am sorry for that," replied Captain Carker. "It was my intention to have taken this young gentleman on board, and letting him see her."

"Once on board, sir," said Mike Barlow "he might like to stay. It's a pity we can't get some provisions stored away."

"What is there to go on board?"

"The preserved meat and fruits, sir, for the crew."

"Well, they can be got on board to-morrow," said Captain Carker, carelessly. "There is no hurry. Pleasure crafts are not tied to time like traders."

The morning wore away, and there was no change for the better in the weather.

It would have been madness for Donald to have gone forth with the hope of finding his way out of the mazy neighbourhood.

Inevitably he would have failed.

About two o'clock the landlord served dinner for two —a thick, juicy rump-steak, with a few onions delicately fried, and floury potatoes.

The cooking was very superior to what Donald would have looked for in such a place.

Whatever doubts he might have had about accepting the hospitality of a stranger were dispelled by the arrival of the dinner.

It was such a meal as he had not sat down to for weeks.

He took his seat at the table and ate heartily.

When it was over the two strangers thrown together drew once more up to the fire, and the captain of the Water Fiend brought out his cigar-case again.

He made no further reference to his proposal for Donald to join his ship, but Donald was thinking it over, and despite a newly developed desire to go abroad, he felt he would rather have gone with any other captain than the man before him.

But what was the objection to him?

He could not definitely say.

There was a forbidding look about this handsome man that warned him to let this acquaintance begin and end that day.

Donald now felt that he could cheerfully have given a year of his life to have been able to repay him for his hospitality.

He did not want to be in this man's debt, and as the afternoon passed on, he was more than once on the point of leaving him, and going away from the place.

But that fog!

"It is the densest I have ever known," the landlord said, when he brought in some coals for the fire, "and no end of accidents are happening in the streets."

"I've got to stay, whether I like it or not," thought Donald.

So he stayed, and the night came on.

With darkness—which scarcely added to the gloom of the fog-burdened day—the dangers of the street increased, and Donald was bound to the house for the night.

It was weary work waiting there.

He was sick of it, and his yearning was to leave the place and never return.

"I have got among a bad lot," was the conviction of his mind.

Nobody but the landlord came into the room that day, and if Captain Carker left it he was absent only for a few minutes.

It seemed as if he was determined not to lose sight of Donald, but the young fellow tried to pooh-pooh the idea.

"Who am I," he thought, "that this man of money with his pleasure-yacht should want me? It is sheer nervousness."

Neverthless, he was bent on getting away as soon as possible. He did not wish to appear churlish, and chatted as pleasantly as he could with his host.

So the evening passed, and a little clock on a bracket in the room struck the hour of eight.

"Supper-time," said Captain Carker.

"I do not want any, thanks," replied Donald.

"Oh! but you must have some."

"I never do eat suppers."

"A glass of wine and a biscuit, then? I insist upon it!"

Donald yielded, and the bell having been rung, the wine was ordered.

The landlord brought in a cobwebbed bottle, two glasses, and a plate of biscuits on a tray.

"It is nearly the last of 'em, captain," he said.

"Oh! it is good, rare wine," replied Carker, as he filled the glasses. "It warms the blood without poisoning it. Drew, my dear boy—your very good health."

Donald tossed off his wine, eager to get away to bed.

He was beginning to feel horribly wearied of the place and the society he had been in all day.

Captain Carker did not drink his.

He stood still, holding his glass up to the light.

"There is not so much beeswing in it as I thought," he said.

Over Donald a strange sensation was creeping.

It was not the glow created by good wine, but a numbing feeling.

A horrible thought flashed upon him.

Had he been drugged?

"Drink your wine," he said.

"All in good time," said Captain Carker, deliberately setting down his glass. "Sit down a minute. It is too strong for you."

Donald made an effort to reply, but found all things around him becoming chaotic. A cry burst from his lips.

"Catch hold of him," cried Carker.

The landlord sprang to Donald's side, and caught him as he fell insensible.

"Got him!" said Captain Carker. "Now, all we have to do is to get him on board as soon as we can."

"And that won't be till the fog lifts," replied the landlord. "What a fine lad it is! Just feel his muscles."

"I will find a use for them by-and-bye," said Carker, grimly. "Seat him in his chair, and get in a rug or two. He will sleep on the floor until we can shift him on board. I can manage with three or four like him. Indeed, I want them."

.   .   .   .

The fog did not lift that night, but as the dawn drew near it began to disperse.

Down by the river all was still, and the coming of the cold grey light showed but little activity on the water.

Moored by a landing-stage was a boat, in which sat a ruffianly looking fellow, eagerly, and half-angrily, watching a narrow lane on shore.

"Why don't they come along?" he muttered. "We shall soon have the police about."

As he spoke a strange cortège was seen coming down that lane—two men bearing an apparently lifeless body, with a sack drawn over it.

Being a short sack, it had rucked up so as to show the feet.

In the rear came Captain Carker, directing their movements.

"Hurry up," he said, as they reached the landing-stage; "he's coming round. Never mind his feet showing. He can shout in the sack, and won't be heard far away. Steady with that boat!—now lower him. You need not break his bones—I don't want cripples on board the Water Fiend. Give way, there!"

The boat pushed off, and two of the men pulled

steadily towards a long, rakish-looking vessel anchored a short way down the river.

CHAPTER IV.

MISSING—BENNETT THE PHILANTHROPIST—JACK JOHNSON SEES SOMETHING IN THE RIVER.

ONE more scene by the side of the river, and then we will away to sea. Let us describe it as briefly as possible.

Two hours after Donald Drew had been borne away to the vessel Captain Carker returned to the shore.

But he did not go to the same landing-stage; the boat of the Water Fiend, manned by three men, carried him higher up. It was just daylight then, and the usual business of the day had begun.

Wharfs, warehouses, and other places were in full activity, for there was not only the work of the day to be done, but much of that of the day before, which, thanks to the fog, had perforce been neglected.

Captain Carker, on reaching the landing-stage, walked up a narrow street to a broader thoroughfare. On the opposite side of the way was a large warehouse; over the door ran a long board, on which was painted "Basil Bennett and Co., Shippers and Foreign Importers."

On the right-hand side of this door was pasted a bill, part of which had been torn away.

It was a bill that would have attracted any ordinary person's attention. Although torn, the part remaining was full of terrible significance.

It ran thus :—

MISSING FROM HOME.

"*A young lady, aged eighteen years, fair, with blue eyes, slight figure, and general pleasing appearance. When last seen was wearing a dark silk dress and sealskin jacket trimmed with otter.*

£1,000 REWARD.

Will be paid to any person who will bring information to. . . ."

The rest had been torn away. Judging by the look of the bill, it had been pasted up fully a week, perhaps more.

Just glancing at it as he would at anything familiar, Captain Carker entered the passage, and, passing by a door on which was inscribed " Clerks' Office," he opened one higher up marked " Private."

" Are you there ?" he asked, peering in.

" Yes," was the reply from behind a screen.

Captain Carker passed round that screen and confronted an elderly man seated at a writing-table, which had been drawn up near the fire.

This was Mr. Basil Bennett, a merchant of benevolent reputation and decidedly benevolent appearance.

Looking at the man it was impossible to think ill of him, so mild in expression was the well-fed rosy face.

Black clothes and a white tie added to his philanthropic appearance.

Carker drew up a chair to the fire and sat down.

" No news of her, I suppose ?" he said.

" None," replied Basil Bennett ; " not a word, not a sign, although the private detectives have been set to work."

" Where CAN she have got to ?"

" I don't know. But she has to be found dead or alive."

" If dead, how then ?" asked Carker.

A shade passed over the serene face of the merchant. It was like a rapidly-flying cloud passing over the face of the sun.

" If dead," he said, slowly, " *nobody but ourselves ought to know a word about it.*"

" The danger of her being alive," said Carker, " is that she may be in the hands of those who are holding her back to play her against us at any moment. It's the uncertainty of the thing that goes against the grain."

" The uncertainty," said Basil Bennett, " is to me almost unendurable. Ah ! Carker, I should like to change places with you. You can look what you are."

" Not quite."

" Well, nearly so, and you can speak out—to an extent, while I have to play the part of a smug-faced citizen, and

I have done so long enough. Am I to go down to the grave without being able to be natural and *free ?*"

"I don't know," said Carker, carelessly ; "but it looks like it. You are getting up in years.'

"I am not so old as I look by ten years," said the merchant, eagerly. "It is the strain of the last few years that has blanched my hair. I can't hold out much longer. The whole thing is hollow, and when the crash comes—"

"Will you wait for it ?"

"I must. I can't get away without raising suspicions that would be my ruin."

He bent his head down and shivered like one with the ague. Carker watched his emotion with amused contempt.

A knock at the door aroused the merchant.

He started up, composed his face with wonderful quickness, and, in a deep-toned voice, cried—

"Come in."

A spare-built old man, looking like what he was, a head clerk, entered the room.

He bowed to Captain Carker with cringing deference.

"I have just heard something," he said.

"Anything important ?" asked the merchant.

"Yes, sir. I suppose I may say what it is ?"

"Yes ; go on, Jacobs. I have no secrets from Captain Carker."

"I would not trust you for that," said Carker, grimly.

"It's about Miss Isabel," said Jacobs. "She—is—dead ; at least, I think so."

This announcement came upon the two listeners with such startling effect that for a few seconds neither uttered a word.

"Dead !" exclaimed the merchant at last

"Yes, sir ; drowned."

"Is she found ?" asked Carker.

"Not exactly, sir ; but the river men are after her. Young Johnson has seen her, or, rather, to be strictly correct, he has seen her hand."

"Jacobs," said Basil Bennett, in a suppressed way, "speak out. Let us have the whole of your story."

"Half an hour ago I sent young Johnson down to the

river-side to see if any of the Tilbury barges were in sight. While standing there he saw two of the river men in a boat. One was in the bows eagerly watching the water. You know what that means, sir?"

"Yes; somebody drowned, and the brutes after the body like carrion crows."

"Just so, sir. Johnson knew what it meant, too, and he watched their proceedings. Before long he saw the body, or part of it; he saw a hand and part of the arm. It rose in the most extraordinary manner out of the water, and it was so near the stage that he knelt down and put out his stick to help the drowned person; but the body was only turning, as I judge, over and over in the rapid eddies, and it passed away."

"And that is all he saw?" asked Carker, gruffly.

"All," replied Jacobs, slowly, "except that on the third finger of the left hand there was a ring—*a gold hoop with a star of diamonds*."

"Ah!" exclaimed the merchant and Carker together.

Then there was another silence.

Jacobs stood still, with his head bent forward, furtively watching the other two. Presently Basil Bennett looked at Carker.

"What do you think of that?" he asked.

"It's all right," was the reply. "She is dead."

"And what next?"

"Let them find her, and make the best of her. If she has jewellery about her the river carrion-birds will probably strip her of her valuables and turn her adrift again. It is their safest game."

"But others may find her?"

"Not until she is battered out of all recognition."

"But there is Johnson," said the merchant, slowly; "he will talk."

"Has he talked yet?" asked Carker.

"No, sir," replied Jacobs. "He came to me like a good boy and told me about it first. I have left him in my room—locked him in quietly, in fact, until I could place the facts before you."

"Who is Johnson?" asked Carker.

"Well, really, I don't quite know," said Jacobs. "He comes from the country somewhere. He is one of the ordinary lads who come up to London to make their fortunes."

"Where does he live?"

"He lodges with me."

"Does he get many letters?"

"Only one now and then—from his mother, I believe."

"What is his build?"

"Stoutish; a strong lad of seventeen, with plenty of life. He is the little jester of the office, although this affair had taken the fun out of him."

"Good!" said Captain Carker. "I will see that Johnson is of no further trouble to you. Keep him in your room for a time, and then send him on board the Water Fiend with a message to me. Write a note of some sort. We raise anchor with the turn of the tide, and you may rest assured that you will never see young Johnson again."

"Carker," said Basil Bennett, as Jacobs retired, "I wish I had half your dash and go!"

"If you had," was the reply, "you would not be the smooth-faced humbug you are."

"Plain-spoken, at all events."

"It is my way—with friends. Now I must on board. You will hear from me somewhere when I get down south. Good-bye!"

Basil Bennett held out his hand, and as Carker grasped it he said—

"I long to get away to that same south, and enjoy the life of ease which wealth can give there. I think it is all right now, but I will just look about me and make *sure*!"

"All right!" said Carker; "nothing like it. Good-bye! You may advertise for another clerk in the place of Johnson."

Carker lit a cigar by he fire and strolled out, leaving a pleasant aroma behind him which penetrated the clerks' office, and made them envious of the man who could smoke such good tobacco.

Half an hour later Jack Johnson, the jester of the office, joyously left the place.

As with many other young quill-drivers, the desk was irksome to him, and anything in the way of an outing during business hours was especially pleasing.

By the riverside he engaged a boat and was rowed to the Water Fiend, near which a tug was lying to take her clear of the busiest part of the river.

Mike Barlow was on the look out for him, and politely lowered a ladder for him to ascend by.

Jack was soon on deck, looking about him with a bright, cheery gaze of enquiry.

" Is Captain Carker on board ?" he enquired.

" He will be in a minute, sir," replied Mike, politely. " Step down into his cabin and wait."

" I would rather remain on deck, thank you."

" But it's the captain's orders that all visitors are to be shown into his cabin, and it's as much as my berth of mate is worth to go agin his orders."

" Then I will go down," said Jack.

" This way," said Mike, as he beckoned him to the companion.

They went down together, and after a few minutes had elapsed Mike Barlow returned to the deck again.

Sauntering to the vessel's side he looked over and addressed the waterman in waiting.

" The young gentleman isn't going back," he said. " He wishes to run down to Gravesend with us."

" All right," growled the waterman. " All I want is my fare paid."

" How much ?" asked Mike.

" Two bob."

" You mean one. Here it is—catch hold !"

" A man can't get bread and cheese out of fares like this," snarled the waterman.

" Then you must get the bread without the cheese," replied Mike ; " it's as much as most people can do nowadays."

Mike walked away chuckling, and the waterman rowed away growling.

The tide was on the turn, and shortly after a signal was given to the tug, the anchor of the Water Fiend was hoisted, and slowly, with her crew and the two pressed men, she threaded her way through the boats and shipping of the river.

———

CHAPTER V.

ON BOARD THE WATER FIEND—THE TWO NEW FRIENDS —DEFIANCE—CAPTAIN CARKER'S ULTIMATUM—IN IRONS.

FROM out of chaotic dreams, like one who has suffered from fever, Donald Drew returned to consciousness.

He found himself lying in a bunk in a cabin lighted by a small, round porthole, through which came the *swish-swish* of the waves and other sounds as the vessel was tugged down the river.

A languor, or rather sense of utter exhaustion, was upon him, and he felt at once indisposed and unable to stir. He only moved his head to take a look around him.

To his surprise he saw he was not the only occupant of the cabin.

On his left sat a youth a year, or perhaps two, younger than himself—Jack Johnson to wit—whose eyes were fixed upon the porthole opposite as a bird would look at half an outlet from its cage.

" Where am I ?" asked Donald.

It cost him an effort to speak, and he was astonished at the tone of his voice. It was several tones higher than usual, almost the voice of an old man.

Jack Johnson started from his day-dream and looked round, at first with no particular favour.

There was something in Donald he did not seem to like.

" You ought to know where you are," he replied.

" But I do not," said Donald.

" It's your old ship," returned Jack, gloomily.

" My old ship?" said Donald. " I have no ship !"

" It's a pity you drink," said Jack. " To look at you one would reckon you to be the last to give way to that sort of thing."

" I drink !" exclaimed Donald. " Who told you so ?"

" The fellow who brought me here and locked me in."

said Jack. "'Go and keep the boozer company,' he said. 'It's one of our crew who came aboard drunk.'"

"He lied!" said Donald. "I do not drink to excess, never did in my life; and I was brought here—drugged, as I feel certain—against my will."

"Never!" exclaimed Jack.

"It is true. How is it you are here?"

"I came on board with a message to the captain, but he doesn't show up, and I am locked in."

"Where are we?" asked Donald.

"Off Tilbury," said Jack; "the tug has just left us. I wonder what the game is? If it is a joke I'll have my revenge for it."

"Is this the Water Fiend?"

"Yes."

"Then," said Donald, "it is no joke. We are both pressed for service!"

"I won't serve," said Jack, between his teeth.

"Nor I," responded Donald. "I am terribly pulled down, but I am not broken. I say, old fellow, what is your name?"

"Jack Johnson."

"Thanks. Mine is Donald Drew. Now, Jack, what we have to do is to stand together and refuse to do anything. They will soon be glad to put us ashore."

"Or into the sea," replied Jack, with a forced laugh. "That Carker is the very devil!"

"You know him?"

"Of course I do. He's a chum of my old governor, Basil Bennett. Do you know him?"

"No; I never heard of him."

"He's one of the right sort," said Jack, in all faith— "so kind, so good! I daresay Carker has smuggled me away in revenge for something Bennett has done. But the good old man won't stand it. He'll be advertising for me all over the place, as he did for his ward."

"What is that bottle over there?" asked Donald.

He pointed to a bracket on the wall opposite. On it was a small bottle, with a label attached.

Jack Johnson crossed over and looked at it.

"It is for you, I think," he said.   "It is labelled 'To be taken as soon as the sleeping draught works off.'"

"Let me see it," said Donald.

Jack brought it to him.   Donald pulled out the cork and put his tongue to it.

"It tastes all right," he said ; "perhaps it is a genuine pick-me-up.   I feel as if I wanted it.   Here goes, on the off-chance of its being the right thing !"

He drank the draught, and lay back to see what the result would be.

It was a genuine draught, and, without a doubt, prepared for him.

The effects of the sleeping draught were dispersed, his languor disappeared, and in a few moments he sat up.

"I feel quite my old self again," he said.   "Jack, where's my clothes ?"

Whoever had put him into the bunk had undressed him first and taken his clothes away.   On the chair they had put an ordinary sailor's attire.

"Those are yours, of course ?" said Jack, pointing to them.

"They are not !" said Donald; "but as there is nothing else I suppose I had better get into them.   One cannot play the defiant rebel in a shirt."

He was soon attired, and, as Jack declared, this rig-out became him admirably.

"You look LIKE a sailor," he said, "whether you are or not."

"On my word," laughed Donald, "I hardly know the bow from the stern of a vessel."

"Oh ! come."

"Well, in a manner of speaking."

Footsteps were heard outside, the bolt was turned, and the door opened.   Enter Mike Barlow, with a rope's-end in his hand.   Behind him stood two men.

"Now, young Drew," he said, "you have skulked long enough.   Come on deck and learn your work."

"I am not coming," Donald replied.

"Halloa !" said Mike ; "what's this—mutiny ?"

He advanced a pace or two, flourishing his knotted rope.

Donald looked at him steadily.

"I give you my word," he said, "that if you touch me with that rope, I will do my best to KILL you !"

"Oh ! indeed," said Mike. "I suppose you know what mutiny leads to ?"

"I am here against my will," said Donald, "and I cannot be guilty of mutiny."

"Here, give me the t'other chap's clothes," said Mike, addressing the men.

One of them picked up a bundle from the floor outside, and tossed it to Mike.

He, in turn, threw it at the feet of Jack Johnson.

"There's your rig," he said ; "get into it and come on deck."

"Thank you," replied Jack, suavely, "but I would rather not."

"But you've got to do it."

"Somebody's got to do it, for I won't."

"Now, look here," said Mike, "I don't want any more nonsense than I can help on board here. I give you half an hour to come to your senses. If you don't do it by that time I must make you."

He was making off, when Donald stopped him with an enquiry—

"Is Captain Carker on board ?"

"In course he is," Mike replied. "Where should he be if not aboard his own little craft ?"

"Ask him," said Donald, "to come and see me."

Mike smote his thigh with his rope's-end, and burst into a roar of laughter.

"I like the cheek o' that," he said.

"Well, if he objects to do so," said Donald, with an angry flush on his face, "ask if I may come to see him."

Again Mike laughed and bent down so as to be almost double.

"Oh ! bother your grinning," cried Donald, angrily. "Get out."

As he spoke he made use of his foot in such an effective manner that Mike Barlow was shot out of the room and spread-eagled on the floor outside.

His two men, who had neatly stepped out of the way, now took their turn at laughing, and Jack Johnson joined in.

Donald was too angry to laugh, and with a second movement of his foot he closed the door.

"It has to come to a struggle, I can see," he said, "and the sooner it gets to an end one way or the other the better."

The door opened, and Mike thrust his head in.

"It's *death* to strike an officer on board the Water Fiend," he said.

And, with an angry jerk, he closed the door again.

"I say," said Johnson, "he can't be serious. Death for striking that fellow ! He is surely joking !"

"I don't know," replied Drew. "I fear we have got among a desperate lot. The old days of pressing for sea are over, and I cannot understand any law-abiding men smuggling us on board."

"What good am I ?" asked Jack. "Do I look like a sailor ?"

"Not at present," replied Donald, with a smile. "We shall see more of that by-and-bye."

"I'll put on the clothes," said Jack, "just to see what I look like ; but I vow I won't work under compulsion."

The fact was, Jack Johnson, like Donald, was not averse to the idea of being at sea. His objection to it was that he had been brought there under compulsion.

The clothes in the bundle were like those of Donald.

A simple sailor's suit, but of the best material—quite unlike the clothes worn by ordinary seamen.

Inexperienced as they were, they both recognised the fact.

"It is clear to me," said Donald, "that we are not aboard any ordinary vessel, but on one that does not pursue a lawful calling.

"A smuggler ?" said Jack.

"If it is no worse than that," replied Donald, "we have not much to fear."

He was interrupted by the door opening again to admit Captain Carker.

He came quietly in alone, and, closing the door, stood

with his back against it.

"Now, you two lads," he said, "just listen to me. It will not do for you to rebel against authority. You are here, and you have to stay."

"By what right are we here?" asked Donald.

"The right that rules the world—force," replied Carker.

"I, for one, will not yield to it," said Donald.

"You MUST yield to it," returned Carker. "Come, don't be a fool. Here you are on board a ship where everything is of the best, the work light, and the prospect of wealth for all pretty clear."

"How is it to be obtained?" asked Donald.

"You will see when we get further south," said Captain Carker.

"I would rather see now; and until I do I will not join you."

"If you continue to refuse you will be put in irons."

"Very well."

"And what say you?" said Captain Carker, turning to Jack Johnson.

"The same as Drew," replied Jack.

"Now understand me," said Captain Carker, with an evil glint in his eyes; "if you are not tractable I will make you—if you are obstinate I will break you. I am absolutely *master* here. My men do as I tell them, and *ask no questions.* If I have you thrown overboard as food for the fishes, who is to know anything about it? I can easily report you as lost at sea, if I have to report at all."

Jack Johnson grew pale as he thought of his grey-headed mother, who would soon miss him anyhow, and to whom his complete loss would be very terrible.

"My employer knows I am on board," said Jack.

"Yes," replied Carker, "and he will keep all he knows to himself. He and Jacobs alone are aware of it. As for for you, Drew, nobody knows that you are here."

"Captain Carker," said Donald, "you are a scoundrel,"

Carker started as if he had been stung with a blow from a whip, and something hot and bitter rose to his lips, but he did not utter it.

After a moment he said, quietly enough—

"I see that I must break you, as I have done others. Many a good man on board this craft has been as bold as you, but now they are tractable enough. I shall waste no more words on you."

He walked to the cabin door, opened it, and left them without another word.

He did not close the door, and Donald was wondering what that meant, when a rush of footsteps was heard, and a dozen or so of the crew dashed into the room.

Mike Barlow was with them, but he did not put himself —as far as his precious body was concerned—prominently forward as a leader.

"Secure them, lads !" he yelled.

"Hit out, Jack," cried Donald.

"I'm there," answered Jack.

Both the lads had a fight for liberty, but the odds were too heavy, and they were overpowered.

Irons were put upon their limbs, and they were carried out of the comparatively light and airy cabin to a hole of a place, apparently in the bow of the vessel.

There they were thrown down like some worthless bundles of rubbish and left to darkness and their own reflections.

"We have brought our pigs to a nice market," said Jack.

"My dear boy," replied Donald, "we did not bring them—they were brought for us. But whatever market it may be it won't be me that is sold."

"Nor me."

"We stand by each other, Jack ?"

"To the death."

"One day," said Donald, after a short silence, "I will have my revenge for this. Nay, it will not be revenge, but common justice to bring this Carker to book."

"I only hope you will have the chance," said Jack ; "but suppose he took it into his head to put an end to us ?"

"Well, let him do it," said Donald, in a steady, determined way. "We may not be able to avenge ourselves, but the sword will one day fall upon him. I will not be the tool of this man, whatever he may be."

"Nor I," said Jack. "And now, if you will allow me, I should like to do something to keep my spirits up. Can you sing?"

"Not much."

"Nor I," said Jack; "but I can whistle a bit. Hear this."

And then Jack favoured Donald with a specimen of whistling, the like of which he had never heard before.

It was loud, clear, and of wonderful tone.

He went right through the "Huntsmen's Chorus" with variations.

"I call that marvellous," said Donald, when Jack had finished off with a flourish.

"I took to whistling when quite a little boy," replied Jack. "More than once I have been advised to try what I could do with it in public; but I'm shy."

"Very," said Donald.

"Well, modest," said Jack. "I am not one of those fools who think they can do everything better than everybody else. But I mean to whistle to the last; I always feel better after it."

Then he whistled again and whistled his hardest—louder than he was to whistle again for many days to come.

CHAPTER VI.

THE OFFICER OF THE WATCH—NOT BROKEN YET—A SAIL—AN ATROCIOUS PROCEEDING.

"MIKE, what of our dogged boys?"

"They still hold out, and it's all the doing of that Drew. He's the mainstay of the other."

"I don't dislike him for it," said Captain Carker. "What pluck—what grit! With a hundred like him I could knock a hole in the bottom of some big ship."

"You don't pick them up every day," said a tall, dandified-looking man standing close by.

The two men were on the deck of the Water Fiend, aft by the wheel.

Above them was a clear blue sky—around them an opal sea.

No land was in sight.

"Ah! Danby," said Carker, "I do not often land a fish like you."

"I suppose not," said Danby (he was first mate of the Water Fiend); "and, perhaps, if I had my time over again you would not land me at all."

"What, *you* getting squeamish?"

Carker looked at him in surprise, and Mike Barlow chuckled.

"I am here," said Danby, "and I shall go on. Let that suffice. Anyway, you ought to know there is no going back for me. To what honest man could I offer these hands of mine," he spread them out as he spoke with a gesture of contempt. "They were white once; now they are red and black. Bah! enough of such talk."

He walked away as he spoke, leaving the captain and first mate together.

"He's getting soft," said Mike Barlow.

"He never was very hard," replied Carker; "when he joined us something was wrong somewhere. He did it out of sheer defiant devilry."

"About these two young 'uns," said Mike; "they hold out. What's to be done with 'em?"

"You have done all you can," said Carker—"irons, starvation, short allowance of water, blows, torture—and still they defy you. What else can you do?"

"Tie 'em together and chuck 'em overboard," growled Mike.

"Danby is against it. He says it's not to be done."

"Danby be hanged!"

"Danby will hang you if he hears you say that. It's no good, Barlow. Danby is a better man than you are to me; I can't get along without him—at least, not for the present, so you've got to keep your rebels alive."

"They might die," said Mike, in an undertone.

"None of your fool's tricks," returned Carker, roughly. "Danby, when he says a thing, means it. You may do ANYTHING but kill or maim them for life."

"I'll try the suspendin'," said Mike.

"If that fails," said Carker, "you must give them up. We must land them somewhere where they are not likely to trouble us again."

"Or anybody else, sir."

"Just so."

"Sail ho !"

The cry came from the man on the look-out, and immediately all on deck were alive.

"Where away ?" sang out Mike Barlow.

"On the starboard bow !"

"Crowd on all sail !" cried Carker.

He took out a field-glass from his pocket, and took a long and steady look at the horizon.

A sail was just peeping above the line of water.

"Looks like a trader," he muttered.

Turning to the man at the wheel he gave him some directions how to steer, and then joined Danby, who was amidships, standing with his hands in his pockets, gazing seaward.

How different the Water Fiend was to the peaceful looking yacht that had crept out of the Thames a few weeks before.

She was no longer a fine pleasure ship, but a cruiser armed to the teeth.

Carker called her a privateer, but some would have stamped her "pirate," and not been far wide of the mark.

At the main masthead floated the Chilian flag. Chili was then at war with Peru, and Captain Carker had papers on board either signed by the former government or forged.

What mattered ?

To the strong he was simply at war with Peruvian vessels ; to the weak he was a remorseless foe, and all weak vessels he called Peruvians.

The Water Fiend was two days round Cape Horn at the time we write of, having had a favourable voyage from England.

What our young heroes had suffered during that voyage may be inferred from the foregoing conversation.

Resolutely they had stood out against all inducements to be enrolled among the crew.

"Death rather !" was their motto.

They had suffered like Spartans, and not budged an

inch from their original resolve.

Donald bore his sufferings in grim silence ; Jack whistled when they were over.

But, alas! the old strong music was gone, and as a professional he would have been a rank failure.

In a short time we shall see more of them in their captivity ; for the present we must keep on deck, and see how the stranger fared.

Higher rose the sail above the horizon ; the hull became visible.

There was now no doubt about her class. She was a trader.

A flag floated, and in a little while Carker made out that it was the Union Jack.

Danby—known to the men as Daring Danby—did not take the trouble to make out what it was at all.

He stood quietly behind Carker, while he duly scanned her, showing no interest in the matter.

" Have a look at her" said Carker, handing him the glass.

" No, thanks," was the calm reply.   " I will take your word for what she is."

" Danby, man, what has come to you ?"

" Nothing."

" Nothing be hanged !   You seem to have lost all interest in the work."

" I don't think I can take much interest in it or in anything else.   May I ask what has come to you ?"

" To me ?"

" Yes ; that you should allow that cur Barlow to torture those poor lads.   Carker, it's a blackguard business ; worse than anything you have gone into yet."

" I wanted one to join us, and the other was thrust upon me," Carker replied, biting his lip ; " and I was not prepared for their obstinate resistance.   If any man in the crew dared say or do half as much as they have said or done I would have pitched them into the sea."

" The right place for any or all of them," said Danby ; " and for you or me too.   Carker, I joined you with my eyes open, and as long as you act in any way like a man I'll not turn against you ; but, by Heaven ! if you don't stop Barlow at his game with those boys, I—"

He stopped short, and was turning away when Carker stepped up to his side, and said—

"Well—what?"

"I will rebel too," said Danby, deliberately, "and then you may toss us overboard together."

CHAPTER VII.

THE FIGHT—DANBY TO THE RESCUE—THE YOUNG PRESSED MEN—A FRIEND IN NEED.

"Go and stop Barlow," said Carker, between his teeth.

"Stop him yourself," returned Danby, as he walked away.

Carker's eyes had never looked more evil than they did at that moment, but he made no rejoinder.

Glaring round he saw that Barlow was just going below, and he called to him to stop. Barlow came slowly up to him. He anticipated what was coming.

"Let the lads alone for the present," said Carker.

"It seems to me," grumbled Barlow, "that you are not master of your own ship."

"Say that again," hissed Carker, "and I will prove to you that I am. Just see that the men are ready. Load two of the starboard guns—one with powder and the other with shot cartridge. We may want both."

Again he turned his attention to the approaching vessel.

"English all round," he said; "but what of that. Sunken ships and dead men tell no tales."

Steadily the two vessels approached each other.

At first the English craft showed an inclination to sheer off, but after a short time it continued its course. Probably its captain had made out the Chilian flag, and feared no harm.

They were soon within easy distance of each other, and then the Water Fiend was brought half-round across the bows of the other vessel and the blank cartridge fired.

In response the Union Jack of the stranger on the mainmast was lowered a little and raised again.

Then she bore away a little and continued on her course until she was broadside on.

"Give her the shot," cried out Carker; "that's MY signal for heaving to."

A number of men were looking over the side of the trader, not dreaming of evil.

They considered that the display of their flag was sufficient.

Boom !

The shotted gun, with too good an aim, was fired.

A shower of splinters from the trader's bulwarks flew up in the air like smoke, and half the watchers disappeared as they fell wounded or dead upon the deck.

The rest, uttering loud cries, were seen to disperse about in search of weapons wherewith to defend themselves.

A man, who looked like captain, sprang into the ratlines and waved his white handkerchief as a flag of truce.

"Too late !" cried Carker. "Give her a charge of grape. Cut her rigging up. Now, smart there. Bring her round. Port your helm. We have her now. There are not twenty men aboard, nor a handful of powder among them."

Carker smiled sardonically at the commotion on board the strange vessel, for he knew that all their efforts to defend themselves would end in one way—in his favour.

He liked a little resistance from victims, as it gave him an excuse for the exercise of violence and the perpetration of atrocities.

He wore his ship round, and ordered the helmsman to steer in close.

When that was done he gave the really helpless craft the contents of two guns, under which she reeled.

The Water Fiend then ran in quite close, and her experienced crew fixed their grappling-irons and swarmed over to the attack.

About twenty men and officers, for the most part imperfectly armed or not armed at all, opposed them.

The captain, who was foremost, fell first.

It was Carker who shot him down. The other officers and several men met a like fate, and then the rest yielded.

What else could they do ?

The pirates—we will give them their right name now—had not come off scathless in the brief encounter. Two were killed and three severely wounded. Carker had received a slight cut on his sword arm.

The men of the trader—for that was the class of vessel just taken—would have received little mercy but for Daring Danby.

He had taken no part in the attack, and did not board the vessel until the fight was over.

Then when the defeated crew retreated and gathered together like frightened sheep, he stepped on board and put himself between them and the pirates, whose blood-thirsty instincts had been aroused.

With a revolver in one hand and a sword in the other, he cried—

"Stop!"

The resolute man was too well known to be disobeyed. Half-mad as they were, they yielded to his superior moral force.

Carker broke through his men and faced him.

"Danby," he said, "you are going too far!"

"You mean you were going too far," replied Danby. "Carker, you know I have never shared in the slaughter of helpless men!"

"But you have never interfered."

"Heaven forgive me!—no. But I interfere now, and, if need be, I will defend them with my life."

"You are mad, I say!"

"No, I am sane enough, Carker. Why should I stand and witness the slaughter of these helpless creatures?"

"But what is to be done with them?"

"There are a thousand places where they could be landed with a chance of their lives being spared, and yet never trouble you again."

Carker did not immediately answer him.

For a moment it seemed as if he were about to attack Danby and settle the question by combat, but his wound, though in a sense slight, was a bar to the use of the sword. With a bitter expression of face he said—

"I give way to you, Danby, but it is for the last

time."

"It shall be for the last time," replied Danby, quietly. "I will not interfere with you again."

"The men may be confined, I suppose?"

"Oh! certainly."

The men. who were, as many crews of our traders are, of a mixed nationality, had listened to the foregoing colloquy with absorbed interest.

On the issue of it their lives depended.

Who Danby was they did not know, nor could they understand how one man should be able to defend them from a cruel foe.

But he had done it, and their hearts warmed with gratitude towards him.

They were spared, for a time at least, and that was something to be thankful for.

Carker ordered them all to be driven forward into the cuddy and a watch set over them.

Then he proceeded to examine the vessel, to see the worth of his prize.

But here he had a bitter disappointment.

She was in ballast, and beyond the ordinary fittings and stores, and the officers' chests, there was nothing of service to him.

In his fury he would have fired her there and then, and have roasted her crew in her, but for the fear he had of Danby.

It was not the physical fear of a man in the presence of a strange foe, but a curious, inexplicable weakness.

It was Danby's spirit that awed him.

Among the crew it was said that the first officer of the Water Fiend bore a charmed life.

They had witnessed half-a-score hairbreath escapes of his.

Once he fell from a cliff a hundred feet high and received no hurt.

He touched on his way down a jutting mass of soft earth, which he broke away and carried with him.

It actually made a soft bed for him to fall upon.

On another occasion he had been fired at point-blank by two Mexican ranchmen and not received so much as a scratch.

Then he shot them down in quick succession, and walked quietly out of the drinking-saloon where the quarrel took place.

Half-a-dozen of the fallen men's comrades tried to bring him down with their six-shooters and rifles as he strolled away, but he escaped unhurt.

He did not hurry up, or so much as look back, but with a coolness that dazed the men of the Water Fiend who witnessed it, stopped on his way to light a cigar.

Having lit it, he strolled on down the town and returned to the ship.

Nor did he ever afterwards so much as allude to this affair.

The men with this belief were not likely to attack him, even at the bidding of Carker; and Carker knew it.

It was a question as to the possibility of an attack by himself, and at present he did not feel it safe to attempt it.

Danby returned to the deck of the Water Fiend, and while Carker and Mike Barlow were overhauling their prize, the Morning Star, he went below and tried the door of the fore-cabin in which Donald Drew and Jack Johnson were confined.

It was fast, and the key not in the lock.

Serenely, as if engaged in an ordinary task, Danby fetched an axe and smashed the door in.

Stepping over the *débris*, he looked about the gloomy prison-house, and saw the two young fellows lying on the floor bound hand and foot.

They were looking at him, wondering what his entrance might mean; but neither spoke.

Danby was quite a stranger to them.

During their long and painful confinement he had not been near them to their knowledge.

But for all that he had seen them more than once as they slept.

What troubled thoughts he had known as he looked on the calm, handsome faces he kept to himself; and even, too, when he had come with the full determination of releasing them from their captivity, he made no demonstration.

He went up to them in a leisurely manner and stood still, regarding them with an unmoved face.

"Well, young men," he said, "you seem to be in trouble."

"May I ask who you are?" said Donald.

"Oh! that is no great matter," replied Danby. "Here, what are these—cords? A little too tight? Suppose we loosen them a bit."

He drew a small, keen-bladed knife from his pocket and coolly began to cut their bonds asunder.

Jack Johnson hitherto had not said a word.

He thought there was another trial in store for him.

But when the cords that held his hands were cut, he said—

"Thank you!" and then began to whistle.

Both the words and the whistle were of the feeblest.

Poor Jack! he had been brought down to a shadow of his former self.

But it was not so with Donald.

He was a little thinner about the face and terribly pale; but the muscular frame showed no signs of suffering.

When released he got up—a bit stiffly, but without exhibiting any weakness.

It was not so with Jack.

He was pretty well done up, and had to be assisted to his feet.

"I won't ask what they have done to you, lads," said Danby; "but now listen to me. *You shall one day avenge it all,* if you will be guided by me."

"I will," said Donald. "And if you will not tell me who you are—"

"Another time," answered Danby. "Let it suffice or the time that I have set you free. But your freedom will not last. In a little while you will be removed to another vessel and confined again."

"Is there any fresh torture in store for us?" asked Donald. "If so, why are we not killed at once? We will never serve on board this vessel."

"Certainly not," said Jack.

"You will not be asked to do so," said Danby. "Make

Donald seized him by the *** as he pulled the trigger.

no further resistance, but trust in me."

"We will," they replied.

"First, then, remain here until I get you some food," said Danby.

They promised to do so, and he went away for a time. When he returned he had both good food and wine—such food as they had not known for weeks, and such wine as they had never tasted before.

"Be careful of it," he said, as he poured out some into a tumbler. "It is rather strong."

They both drank sparingly, and, having refused more, Danby said—

"Now, my lads, wait here until I come or send for you."

CHAPTER VIII.

THE PRIZE—DANBY MAKES AN ARRANGEMENT WITH CARKER—UNLOOKED-FOR PRECAUTIONS.

CAPTAIN CARKER had returned to the deck of the Water Fiend, and was talking with Mike Barlow as Danby stepped up.

"Oh! here he is," said Carker, in an undertone. "Not a word more."

"Carker," said Danby, strolling up with his hands in his pockets, "what are you going to do with your prize?"

"I don't know," was the somewhat short reply.

"Why not send her to Needle Island," said Danby, "with the captain, crew, and those two young fellows below on board?"

"Who will take her there?"

"I will."

"But I cannot spare any men."

"I do not want any. I will make those fellows obey me."

Carker seemed to hesitate, but in reality he rather liked the proposition.

Not that he intended that the Morning Star should get clear away.

No! Immediately Danby spoke a plan of ridding himself of Danby, Donald Drew, and the ship and crew flashed upon him.

"Well, Danby, if you think you can do it," he said, "let it be so, but I should not like there to be any slip in the matter."

"There will be no slip," said Danby. "Mike !"

"Well, what is it ?" asked Mike, sullenly.

He had been standing a little aside, sullen and bitter. To him it was incomprehensible that Carker should so much as discuss any question with the rebellious Danby.

"Go below and bring up your young friends," said Danby.

"I don't think I can do that," replied Mike. "Why, it is like eating dirt."

"Then I must go."

He returned to the cabin, and after a short interval Donald Drew came bounding upon deck.

It required all his energies to put on an air of lightness, but he succeeded, and his eyes as they fell on Mike Barlow expressed unutterable contempt for the bully.

Mike was exasperated.

He was beginning to think that he should be foiled in his thirst for cruelty.

He hated Donald from the first, and day by day his hatred had increased.

The defiant spirit of the youth made him feel small and mean.

And he had never felt more so than he did at that moment.

His reason seemed fairly to desert him.

"What are you doing here ?" he hissed. "Get below again."

Donald took no notice of him whatever, and was rambling on when Mike with a curse drew out a revolver, and cocked it.

Donald saw the movement, and seized him by the wrist just as he pulled the trigger.

Luckily his arm was upturned, and the bullet flew harmlessly into the air.

By a quick action, Donald had succeeded in saving his life ; but he was, in his present condition, hardly a match for the burly ruffian.

Mike endeavoured to wrench his hand away, and in the effort accidentally fired off two more chambers, one of the bullets striking the mainmast.

Captain Carker looked coolly on, so did the crew, who were accustomed to scenes of violence.

"I'll have your life," hissed Mike.

As he spoke, Donald yielded to the efforts of unwonted exertion, and, slipping, fell upon the deck.

Mike, with a cry of joy, threw himself upon him.

"I've got you now," he said.

"Steady there!" cried out Captain Carker; "that will do, Barlow."

"It will do when I have done for him," hissed Barlow.

Two hands seized his arms, pinioned them to his side, and dragged him off Donald.

Kicking and breathing vengeance, he turned his head, and saw Danby was the man who had pinioned him.

"You again!" he yelled—"always interfering. Let go of me, will you?"

Danby dragged him to the companion, and cast him headlong down.

"Come up again whilst I am here," he said, "and 1 will pitch you into the sea."

"You ought to have stopped him, Carker," he added.

"I might have nothing else to do if I interfered with every quarrel," Carker replied.

Jack Johnson had been assisted on deck, but he was scarcely able to stand. Nevertheless, he tried to be jaunty, and returned Captain Carker's enquiring gaze with one of defiance.

He also screwed up his mouth, and tried to whistle.

But, alas! with suffering and recent excitement, there was not a whistle left in him.

All he could do was to BLOW a tune.

"Assist your friend on board," said Danby to Donald. "That is our craft."

Donald looked as he felt—puzzled.

He could not understand matters at all.

But that was not a favourable opportunity to make enquiries.

"May I ask you a few words below?" said Danby, addressing Carker.

A distant bow was the reply, and they descended together.

At the foot of the stairs they found Mike rubbing his knees and elbows, and looking as black as night.

"You are not to go on deck," said Danby.

He and Carker entered the chief cabin, and closed the door.

The private interview occupied at least a quarter of an hour, and Mike, hanging around, tried his best to get at what passed between them.

But he could only catch a hum of two voices, loud enough for him to distinguish which was which.

He could, however, discern the fact that Daring Danby took the more decided tone, and Carker appeared to be expostulating rather than commending him.

Mike shrank away as footsteps approached the door and Danby ascended the companion alone, leaving Carker n his cabin.

Then Mike heard commands given on deck for certain things to be done on board the Morning Star, and he ventured to creep up and take a peep at what was going on.

Danby was having all sail set, and as soon as this was done he ordered out the men of the Water Fiend to return to their vessel.

This they did, and the grappling-irons being cast off, the two vessels separated.

Free on the deck were the rescued crew and the two young fellows who had so boldly withstood all persuasion to join the pirate crew.

The men of the Morning Star were obeying Danby's orders with alacrity.

"Gone away," muttered Mike; "what is the captain thinking of?"

"What should I be thinking of?" asked the captain, who had emerged from his cabin and come up quietly behind him.

"I call it madness to let him go," growled Mike; "but I suppose he has been giving you all sort of lying promises ?"

"He has really promised nothing. I did not need it."

"Then you trust him?"

"No."

"Not trust him?" said Mike, "when you know that if it gets about what we really are that our lives wouldn't be worth a month's purchse!"

"Well!"

"It ain't well, captain—it's bad. See, he's heading back for the Cape, and will fall in with some cruiser off the Falklands and blow upon us."

"We will head for the Falklands, too. It is my intention to accompany him a little way."

"Save us, captain, but I think you are clean gone!"

"Danby will be ere the sun sets to-night. Mike, I am no fool. I am going to sink the Morning Star just as she is. The whole lot shall go down to the bottom of the sea together. Go on deck and bring the Water Fiend round, so as to keep a bit on her track. We can overhaul her when we please."

"As I'm a sinner, but you are a good 'un, captain," said Mike, striking his thigh with his palm.

"I thought it would be better than any bother on board," said Carker; "half the crew believe in Danby's life being invulnerable."

"And the other half too, captain."

"Well, we will sink the ship, and see if he will get out of that."

"But he's got boats. He may take to them."

"And we can run them down. Go and do as I tell you. Go steady for an hour or so, and then overhaul him. We will send him with the sun down into the sea."

Mike hurried up the stairs, and Carker returned to his cabin.

Then he took a bottle from a locker, and drawing the cork, filled a tumbler with rich, red wine.

"Here's my friend," he muttered, as he raised it to the light; "come and comfort me." He tossed off the wine. "What was it he said? Go and hide away in some quiet spot and give up a pirate's life? If we meet again he will treat me as a foe, and hang me! What has made him pulp-neaded? He who used to go into a fight as some men enter into a football fray. Let me see, though. That was when the Water Fiend was a privateer. Since I changed my colours he has never, that I can remember, struck a blow. Come in !"

A knock at the door aroused him from his soliloquy.

Enter Mike Barlow.

"All's well," he reported. "We are not many cable's length from him, and he cannot shake us off, although he is doing his best."

"Mike," said Carker, thoughtfuly, "I want to ask you a question. Since we took up with this more lively business, have you ever seen Danby strike a blow ?"

"He fought well when we sunk the Yukra Bat and the old Centurion."

"Yes, but they were vessels of a nation at war with our employers. What I mean is—have you ever seen him busy with his sword since we started on *our own account?*"

"Can't say I have," replied Mike ; "but he always had the look of one having nothing particular to do with the former, but just walking around to see how we were getting on."

"He joined me, knowing what I was going to do ; but I'm hanged if he ever done much more than look on."

But Mike was not sure of that nor Captain Carker either, and after discussing it outside with no entirely satisfactory result, they went on deck.

It was now late in the afternoon, and the sun going down.

A southern winter was approaching, and the days were short.

In another hour it would be dark.

The Morning Star was a slow craft, and however well handled she might be, she could not hope to shake off the Water Fiend.

It was almost a case of a race between the hare and the tortoise.

In the old story the hare went to sleep, but Carker was not going to be caught napping.

He kept close to the vessel he had doomed, and when the sun had about another quarter of an hour above the horizon, he ordered the men to load the two larboard guns.

The Water Fiend had eight in all.

Two on either side—one at the bow and the other at the stern.

These were muzzle loaders, and, therefore, old-fashioned, but they were well made, and could do a good deal of execution in a short time.

Both shot and shell were on board, and it was with the latter that Carker ordered the guns to be charged.

The two vessels were now sailing within fifty yards of each other, and on board the Morning Star they could see all that was being done by the men of the Water Fiend.

Daring Danby was standing aft in full view coolly smoking a cigar; he showed no signs of perturbation or did anything to meet the coming catastrophe.

Close by him stood Donald and Jack Johnson—the former also smoking and as unconcerned as Danby himself.

"Confound them !" muttered Carker, "are they blind. One would think that they would be looking to the boats, or getting out the life-buoys, or something else on a chance of safety. Perhaps they want to die."

"Only a few minutes more sunlight, sir," said Mike Barlow.

"All right. Blaze away into him," said Carker; "hit between wind and water. I don't want to kill any outright. Let them have a few moments to repent as they sink under the sea."

"All right, sir," said Mike."

He put his eye to the breech of the gun and was proceeding to take aim, when something caught his eye which gave him a bit of a shock.

He started up and ran his finger over the touch-hole.

"What's the matter ?" asked Carker.

"Matter !" replied Mike, "everything. This ere blamed gun is SPIKED."

"Spiked !" cried Carker.

He ran up to the gun and stared at it for a moment.

It was too true.

The gun had been neatly spiked, and with malice aforethought.

Like a madman he ran from gun to gun, and found them all the same.

They had been rendered utterly useless.

"I didn't know there was such things on board," gasped Mike.

"I did," replied Carker. "We used to carry them when out on the legitimate business. I had a bag full in my cabin, and that cunning devil, Danby, must have got at it."

A derisive cheer was heard from the deck of the Morning Star.

Not only Danby, but Donald, Jack, and the merchant crew were cheering and waving their hats.

The edge of the sun rested on the sea.

In ten minutes at the outside it would be gone.

But with the sun was going the wind.

"Set every stitch of canvas," cried Carker, hoarsely. "We'll run into him, and either board or sink him !"

"We might sink both crafts," suggested Mike.

"Do as you are told !" roared Carker. "Who commands here? Run him down ! Be smart aloft there ! Shake out all sails ! If he gets away the seas are not wide enough to hide us from the cursed cruisers !"

The men were alive to their work, and the topsails filled out with the remnant of the wind.

Another cheer from the Morning Star.

A few rapid commands were given to the helmsman by Carker, and the well-found craft bore down upon the merchant vessel.

But there was no liveliness in the movements of either vessel.

The sinking wind caused the loose sails to flap about in a feeble, half-hearted way.

And then, with a sudden dip, the sun went down.

But there was a twilight, and the Morning Star, though getting dim to the view, was still in sight, and would be so for an hour or more. Carker could keep the Morning Star in sight.

The fury that burned within his heart was an all-consuming fire.

He was ready to do anything for revenge, cost what it might, and he would have given all he possessed to have Daring Danby helpless and in his power.

That his late lieutenant was the author of the mischief to the guns he could have no doubt, and the sting of it lay in the fact that he had made the Water Fiend useless for the time, either as pirate or privateer.

A spiked gun has to be carefully cleared of the spike ere it can be of any service again, and on board there was neither the requisite machinery nor the practical men to do it.

But the hour for Carker to avenge the act was not quite come.

With twilight the wind rapidly fell, and it was soon a dead calm.

Both ships lay like logs upon the ocean, within hail of each other; therefore the running down could not be accomplished.

One thing remained.

There were boats and men enough to cut out the Morning Star, and Carker was resolved to attempt it.

He called his men together, and addressed them quietly.

"They have no arms to speak of," he said, "and will be as children opposed to us. If you do what I ask I will forego my share of the next prize, and share it among you."

As his share was half, this was a tempting offer, but the men held back and whispered among themselves.

Carker guessed at the cause of their hesitation

"You are afraid of one man," he said, "simply because he has been lucky in two or three scrimmages."

"He's got a charmed life," the men said.

"I hope to prove to the contrary," said Carker, "by killing or capturing him myself. I go with you—the foremost man to the attack. We are armed, they are nearly helpless. What is there to fear? Barlow, get us some of the good old brandy from the store. We will drink to our CERTAIN SUCCESS!"

The brandy brought up by Mike Barlow was coarse, fiery stuff that had a maddening effect upon the blood. A strong dose all round brought about the desired change in the spirit of the men.

They became like bloodhounds thirsting for their prey, and at the word of command eagerly ran to the boats and owered them.

"Steady, there !' cried Carker ; "the long boat and another will be sufficient."

The men, save three or four whom Mike Barlow bade keep back, had all dropped down into the four boats of the Water Fiend ; but instead of doing as Carker bade them, they all began to talk loudly, and utter exclamations of surprise.

"What is the matter there ?" cried Carker.

"The oars are gone," cried the men.

It was a fact. All the oars, usually kept in the boats ready for use, had disappeared, and there were no extra ones on board.

Another burst of derisive laughter was heard on board the Morning Star.

Carker in his impotent rury clutched the lower ratlines with his hands until the force he exercised drove nearly all the blood from his fingers.

His cheeks flushed, and the veins of his forehead swelled almost to bursting.

"Come back," he cried, after a pause. "Mike, set the men to work to fashion something that will answer as paddles or oars. He hasn't quite beaten us yet."

" I doubt if there's anything aboard that will do," replied Mike.

"Get it from somewhere," hissed Carker. "Rip up the floor of my cabin if you cannot get it from any other place. If that lot escape me I shall go mad. Smart there, the whole of you. If the calm keeps we may have him yet."

And now a sound was heard from the Morning Star that added to his fury.

Somebody was playing the fiddle, and the crew, lately almost hopeless prisoners, were dancing.

This was the very acme of derision and mockery, and

Carker paced the deck of his vessel like an angry caged tiger.

"I'll rend—I'll tear—I'll torture them!" he cried. "A curse upon that Danby! I've doubted him for a long while."

He might have added. "And feared him, too."

CHAPTER IX.

THE ATTACK IN THE FOG—TWO INVADERS ON BOARD.

DARING DANBY had not taken any precautions to prevent the "making of oars."

He simply could not have done so had it entered his head. But knowing how resourceful Carker was he kept a keen watch over his movements.

But at last even that could not be done, for a fog settled down so thickly that objects a yard away could not be seen. The fiddling and dancing ceased, and the crew of the Morning Star, by the command of Danby, maintained the strictest silence.

Donald and Jack were both on deck, the latter having recovered sufficiently to keep near his friend. With the kmowledge of freedom there was a return of elasticity of body as well in spirit—one, in fact, indubitably acts upon the other.

Danby, leaning over the stern, listened closely to every sound on board the Water Fiend.

They were moving about, and every now and then a muffled word of command would be heard.

"Still busy, and mean mischief," thought Danby.

Turning to the two friends he bade them go below.

"There is nothing to fear," he said, "and a good night's rest will help you both."

"And you?" asked Donald.

"Oh! I am on duty here till morning, then I shall turn in. We are a little at sixes and sevens on board here yet," he added, "but everything will be righted to-morrow."

"I am in no humour for sleep," Donald said.

And Jack said so too, but a yawn broke up his speech, and showed how it was with him.

Danby took him by the hand.

"Let me lead you to the companion," he said, "you can find your way down. First door at the bottom, open it, feel for a bunk, roll in, and go to sleep."

Jack wisely allowed himself to be persuaded, for he had great need of rest, and Danby, having put him on the right road, returned to Donald, who said, quietly—

"They are rowing towards us."

"Impossible," said Danby.

But when he had listened for a moment he could hear the splash of the rude substitutes for oars made by the pirates.

By the sounds he guessed what they were, and the full force of the impending peril fell upon him.

But he was not at all alarmed. Not even flurried for a moment, but said to Donald—

"Yes, they are coming ; but they may not find us if the men keep silent. You stay here, and if a boat touches the vessel near you, take up this bar of iron by your feet and dash it down point foremost. It will knock a hole in the bottom of the boat, and perhaps sink it."

All this was said in the softest of whispers, and Danby, quietly removing his shoes, disappeared.

Already he had prepared his men for attack, and they were ready with such arms as they possessed to defend themselves.

They were stationed round the vessel in twos, and, in addition to axes and heavy bars, their chief weapons, they had heavy weights to throw into the boats to stave the bottoms in.

These were crude means of defence, but it has often transpired in similar cases that the simplest things have been effectual.

Danby showed the spirit of resource by utilising such things as he had at his command.

When he came back to Donald again, which he did like a shadowing spirit coming out of the gloom, the sounds of the approaching foe were more distinct.

Every caution not to alarm was being exercised, but they could not quite conceal their approach.

There were two boats a short distance from each

other.

Suddenly the sounds of their advance ceased.

Whispering voices were heard, apparently in dispute.

The sounds of movement were renewed, but the two boats had divided.

One was bearing to the left, and the other came straight to the Morning Star.

It came upon the vessel with a suddenness that was startling, both to those on board and those in the boat—in fact, it fairly ran into it.

Donald Drew, who had retained possession of the heavy iron bar, dashed it down into the boat with a force that sent it crashing through the bottom.

The men in her yelled like demons.

A rope, with a grappling-iron at the end of it, was thrown up, and a man clambered over the side.

He was followed by another, and they were all who succeeded in getting on board.

The injury done to the boat led to her rapidly filling, and she speedily sank.

The screams of terror of the drowning men were horrible to hear ; and the fact of being enveloped in fog and darkness, unable to see anything, added to the horror of it.

Shouts were heard from the other boat, and a light was faintly seen to flash for a moment ; but they could do nothing for their sinking comrades.

Nor could assistance be rendered from the Morning Star.

All Danby and the rest could do was to remain where they were and await the issue.

As for the two men who had got on board, they had not so much as been seen by anyone, and once on board were too bewildered to know what to do or where to go.

It was Mike Barlow and another ruffian who had thus placed themselves in a perilous position.

They crouched down amidships, and listened to the cries of their drowning comrades with feelings that may well be imagined.

"It's like being caught in a trap," muttered Mike. 'Why don't Carker come on ?"

Carker was in the other boat, but for some reason or

other he did not seem to be in a hurry to approach.

It was possible he did not exactly comprehend what had happened.

However it may have been, he did not come to the rescue of his drowning men, and in a little while it was all over with them, save in the case of one strong swimmer.

They could hear him going round and round, calling for aid, and moving gradually away from the ship.

At last his cries ceased, and a dreadful stillness followed.

It was a very nightmare to Donald Drew, who through it all scarce uttered a sound. He was aroused from his stupor by the voice of Daring Danby, speaking low.

"I felt a breath of wind," he said, "and the fog seems to be lifting."

It was so. Donald felt the soft wind fan his cheek, and the movement of the vessel was like the pulse of returning life.

She was running again before the wind, slowly, but still going.

A few words of command from Danby, and there was quick life again on board the craft.

More wind, and the fog sensibly thinning.

Danby kept his eyes in the direction of the Water Fiend, but he could see nothing of her.

Up went the fog and dispersed, the stars came out, and the wind blew sweetly; and then he saw her lying far away like a dark blot upon the water.

She was not following them, and presently she faded away and was lost in the gloom.

"We shall get away now," Danby said to Donald. "Carker doesn't want any more of us at present."

"It was a strange experience," replied Donald ; "more like a dream than a reality."

Danby laughed.

"That we have got away, or nearly so, is real enough," he said.

Brighter grew the night, fresher blew the breeze, and if the Morning Star was not exactly a smart vessel, she was not, as traders go, a bad sailor, and she made a lot

Donald was lying at the mercy of the two ruffians.

of headway.

Donald kept on deck with Danby, and á long and earnest talk they had together, but Danby said nothing of his past.

All his talk was of the future.

He proposed to take the Morning Star and her crew to the Falkland Isles, and there give them up to the charge of the authorities, and he and his two young friends, Donald and Jack, would go on to the mainland and find some plan to settle down a bit.

Donald wondered to hear him talk this way, as he had hitherto considered him to be in command of the Morning Star.

The whole affair was bewildering, and it became more so as time went on.

"I thought this was your vessel?" he ventured to say.

"Oh! no," replied Danby; "I am merely in charge of her."

"But who put you in charge?"

"Donald, my boy, don't ask me any questions. Take things as you find them, and take me as I am."

And Donald said no more.

CHAPTER X.

TWO RATS IN THE SHIP—THE SENTENCE ON MIKE BARLOW—THE STORM.

MIKE BARLOW, of the Water Fiend, and his companion ruffian were in a pretty fix, skulking away in the almost empty storeroom of the Morning Star, and afraid to show their noses outside it.

Morning had come, and, squatted down in the darkest corner in the place, they reviewed their position.

"It seems to me, Bowley," said Mike, "that you and I were in too much of a hurry to come on board here."

"I followed you, Mister Barlow," replied Bowley. "You said come on, and I come."

They were both armed, one with a cutlass, and the other with an axe, and were prepared to sell their lives dearly.

Mike, indeed, had no hope of being spared.

He judged that Danby would deal as speedily with him as he would deal with Danby—if he had the chance.

"We might keep stowed away," he said, gloomily, "until they touch some port, and then slink ashore, but I'm doubtful on it. Here, draw near—somebody's coming."

It was Donald Drew who was on a voyage of discovery over the ship, amusing himself by wandering around, and getting an idea of the general arrangements.

He came quietly down the companion, not dreaming of the presence of a foe ; but Mike saw that he had a cutlass by his side, and looked the young sailor all over.

The sight of him was to Mike Barlow what a red rag is to a bull.

He lost all prudence, and instead of lying quiet began to mutter bitter curses on his head.

Donald heard the sounds, and, turning, saw the two men.

He did not recognise them in the gloom, and came forward to see who they were.

The pair sprang upon him, and bore him to the deck.

"You measly warmint !" hissed Mike ; " I've got you now, and I'll do for you, if I hang for it ten times over.

Donald, by the double surprise of the presence of strangers and their sudden attack, was unable to utter a word.

He did not think even to cry out, and he must have been slain there and then but for the opportune arrival of Jack Johnson.

Jack, freshened by a night's sleep, and feeling as fresh as a daisy, happened at that moment to be in search of Donald, and, coming down from deck, saw him lying at the mercy of the two ruffians.

Jack was armed with a cutlass, too, and if he were no expert in the use of it he knew what it was for.

Whipping it out, he dashed down, and with a cut to right and left laid open the skull of Bowley and the right arm of Mike Barlow.

Their shrieks of pain brought Danby and half-a-dozen

men to the spot, and the wounded ruffians were made prisoners.

Donald, beyond a shaking, had suffered no injury, and told his story of the discovery of the men and the attack made on him.

Danby immediately had the whole vessel searched, to see if any more were skulking about, but, of course, found none.

Meanwhile, the wounds of the crestfallen prisoners had been roughly dressed, and a watch was set over them, pending Danby's decision as to what should be done to them.

If the matter had been left to the crew they would speedily have settled the matter with a few feet of rope.

But Danby had some compunction about taking their lives, and he gave them the choice of being hanged or turned adrift on the first land they came to.

They chose the latter, naturally, and the next day were put ashore on the terribly desolate coast that lies at the mouth of the Straits of Magellan.

Biscuit for three days was given them, and with it slung about their necks they started inland, without one look back or word of thanks for their lives.

"And I don't know why they should be thankful," said Danby; "their chance of living is small. For days they may march and find neither tree, nor verdure, nor living thing. It is the land of death."

The Morning Star then resumed her way, but at evening a great storm arose, and drove her, in spite of the exertions of her gallant commander and crew, back upon the coast.

It was Donald and Jack's first experience of a great storm at sea, and in no part of the world are storms so fierce as round about the region of the "terrible Cape."

The lightning was blinding and incessant, the thunder appalling.

And as the ship was forced back to the land, hills, unseen at first in the darkness, began to belch out fire, and enormous jets of water were thrown up from the sea by volcanic commotions beneath its surface.

It was like nothing the young fellows had ever heard of

or seen.

It was as if the world were being wrecked.

About midnight the Morning Star struck heavily on a rock, and immediately the top-masts came tumbling down with a mass of wrecked canvas and cordage.

No word of command could be heard, no order maintained.

There were two boats still in good condition, but it would have been folly to launch them.

No boat could live in such a sea.

The glare of the lightning showed the seething, tossing, leaping waves; the fires from the hill-tops tinged them blood-red.

It was a scene of commotion and horror, and the break-up must soon come.

The ship lay almost on her beam-ends, and must early go to pieces.

They could not hear her timbers creak, but they could feel the strain that was upon her.

All the seamen had kicked off their shoes and lightened themselves of their upper clothing for the last struggle.

Danby stood between Donald and Jack, with a hand on the shoulder of each.

They could feel the tender, sympathetic pressure, and could almost tell what words were in his heart.

"My dear boys, I am sorry for you—for you are young, and your lives are worth the living. But for me it is another thing. I don't know that I feel sorry the end is here. I have been a worthless dog, and it is only just that I should meet with such an end."

That was what he was quietly saying to himself; and his eyes were heavy and sad as he looked at the furious sea, beating madly on the forbidding shore.

He knew that in few minutes at the latest the break up would come, and then brief would be the battle of life.

It did not seem possible for any to reach the shore alive.

And at last it came.

Suddenly, as if the strong timber ship had been but a house of cards, it went to pieces, and they went down as into a gulf.

Donald felt himself torn from his friends, and he shrieked out a loud "Good-bye," but it was not heard, and would not have been heard in the roar of the storm.

Donald was a fair swimmer, but the best and worst in the world would then have been as good and no better than he.

The twisting, leaping waves caught him up and bore him shoreward with a rush that was like the tearing along of terror-stricken wild horses.

He felt himself dashed upon the hard rocks with a force that took away his breath, and started a hundred fires blazing before his eyes.

Then he felt himself drawn down into the depths of retreating water, to be caught up by another in-going wave and borne along again with shrieks of laughter to the solid rocks.

Once more dragged backward by the undertow, he was cast up again with dimming senses and a conviction that the end had come.

A longing to once more see home and friends, a desire to touch Jack Johnson by the hand, to say Good-bye to Danby, and then the sound of bells ringing somewhere afar off.

After that—silence.

CHAPTER XI.

A PARADISE ON EARTH—INA FRISBY—THE NEW HOME—ARRIVAL OF AN OLD FOE.

On the eastern coast of South America, on the borders of the Argentine Republic, stands the small town of Carita.

Perhaps it is hardly worthy of the name of town, for it consists of about fifty houses only, at the lower end of a miniature bay, away from the traffic of the busy world.

Not many had visited this peaceful spot, few have even so much as heard of it.

And yet here is a veritable Paradise for weary man to rest in.

First, the lovely bay, with its fringe of golden sand.

then the quaint houses dotted about a rising hill, and above a wooded country, on which Nature had lavished her gifts for the artist, the sportsman, and the student.

On this high land stood one house only, a spacious building of one floor, and a tower at the south end used as a look-out and a smoking room.

Around the house was a spacious garden, rich with a hundred horticultural beauties, the whole commanding a view of sea and land which would be difficult to match for varied and surpassing beauty.

The garden ran to the edge of the great hill, ending without fence or anything to keep off intruders.

There was, however, little likelihood of strangers coming there, and the people of Carita respected Captain Frisby too deeply to take liberties with him or anything that was his.

Captain Frosby was indeed, at the time we write of, the dominant man of the place, and the next ruler was his daughter Ina, a *petite*, high-spirited girl of seventeen.

They had half-a-dozen servants, half-castes, who were devoted to them, Ina's favourite attendant being Vampa, an old Mexican soldier.

Whenever she went abroad, to fish at sea or to hunt ashore—for the daughter of Captain Frosby was addicted to these sports—Vampa accompanied her.

Sometimes the fair girl would be left alone for weeks in the care of the attendants, while her father was at sea with his yacht.

Whither he went nobody knew, but it had been observed for years by the natives that he went away buoyant and hopeful, and returned desponding.

From which they agreed that he went in search of something he did not find.

One morning Ina stood upon the summit of the hill looking seaward. Her father had been away for five long weeks, and day after day she had looked in vain for his return.

Behind her stood Vampa, with a sad expression on his time-beaten face ; and he had drawn down his sombrero over his face, as if to hide it.

One hand grasped the barrel of his rifle, the other

rested on his hip, and in his short jacket, sash, and leggings, he was a picturesque figure.

Ina's dress was a silken cap, velvet jacket, and plain skirt reaching to the top of her boots. She, too, had a rifle, but it was lying at her feet where she had dropped it, so as to use a field glass in scanning the sea.

"There is a speck in the horizon, Vampa," she said; "but it may be a pointed cloud—anything."

"The saints send it be the Fairy," muttered Vampa. "It is a place of storms, that Cape."

"But the captain has rounded it a score of times," said Ina.

"The pitcher goes to the well, but is broken at last," muttered Vampa.

"You are getting a croaker," said Ina, smiling; "and the proof of it is that the speck has become a sail, and it can be no other than the Fairy."

"You are sure, senorita?" said Vampa.

"No, but what other vessel can it be?"

She dropped the field glass and walked to and fro awhile. Then she took another survey.

"It is the Fairy," she said, joyfully. "Go in, Vampa, and see that a good breakfast is prepared. The breeze blows landward, and in lesss than an hour she will be at anchor in the bay.

Vampa doffed his hat by way of salute, and strode with a lion-like gait through the garden to the house.

Ina began to descend the hill, leaving her rifle lying on the ground.

She lingered here and there to take another survey of the incoming craft, or rest a while.

As she passed some of the houses the people, mostly half-castes, came to the door to give her "good-day," or some salute equivalent to it.

She reached the sands at last, where half-a-dozen fishermen were seeing to their boats, drawn up high and dry, and stopped to talk with them, until the Fairy turned into the bay, and with majestic grace drew near and dropped her anchor a hundred yards from the shore.

Down tumbled her canvas, to be furled with great rapidity, and there was as graceful a craft as ever floated lying under bare poles, and her rigging like a cobweb against the sky.

A boat was lowered, and a tall, handsome man took his seat in the stern.

Four men tumbled into her and pulled ashore.

Captain Frosby was a man of fifty, with a grave, but not by any means sad face.

As he leapt out of the boat, and embraced his daughter, he was the beau ideal of a hearty Englishman.

"At last !" said Ina. "Dearest, you have been long away."

"We have had rough weather," he replied. "Familiar as I am with the storms of the Cape, I may say that this time they appalled me. But the Fairy rode gallantly through them all. Ah ! I see the question in your eyes. No, I have not found IT yet, but I have picked up something else. Ina, there are four hungry men who will breakfast with you this morning."

Ina opened her eyes.

It was the first time her father had ever brought home a guest.

"Shipwrecked strangers, and good fellows, Ina," he added. "Now see that something good is prepared for them."

Ina hastened homeward, with the pulses of her heart beating a little quicker than usual.

Such things as visitors to Carita were rare.

Vampa and three other men were busy preparing a table just without the house, over which they had stretched a striped awning. Vampa did not hear of the advent of visitors with any show of pleasure.

"They will bring no good with them, whoever they are," he said.

Nor did he like them the better when they came. Neither Donald Drew, Jack Johnson, nor Daring Danby, rescued from shipwreck, found favour in his eyes.

They and one man of the crew were the sole survivors, and when rescued by Captain Frosby they were living skeletons.

Seven days on that inhospitable shore had reduced them to the last extremity, and but for the need of the

Fairy to have fresh water, they would have perished.

The men sent ashore for it found the four survivors sitting on the ground, "waiting for the end," too far gone to struggle any more, too broken to fight against their impending fate.

Kindly care restored them, and there they were at breakfast with their kindly host and his charming daughter, surrounded by scenery of surpassing beauty — another dream.

Ina did not lack maidenly reserve, but she was not shy. The life she led endowed her with graceful ways and fearlessness. Her voice, her ways were charming, and Jack Johnson fell in love with her at once.

Vampa waited at table, standing for the most part behind Ina's chair when he had nothing to do.

On the strangers he cast nothing but looks of the strongest disfavour, and when the talk turned to their staying his brow grew black as night.

"What better life could you desire?" said Captain Frosby. "The land is free, and will grow anything at your bidding. Game abounds, and there is the sea. Now and then a trader comes this way, who will buy your skins and what not, and give you powder, shot, and clothes. What more do you need?"

It was the life that Danby wanted—far away from the world—and the ring of it had a fascinating sound in the ears of Donald and Jack.

They found they could write home, too, and so relieve the anxiety of their friends, and Jack had something to say to Mr. Basil Bennett about Carker which might make him "sit up" a bit, and look less benevolent than usual.

"When that is done," said Jack, "I shall be able to whistle again."

So they all said they would gladly stay, and that very afternoon Captain Frosby assisted them in choosing a spot for a home.

They preferred the high land, so a lovely spot about a quarter of a mile from their host's was chosen, and the ground marked out and certain timber selected for cutting.

"Help can be had in plenty," the captain said.

And so it was. At his bidding the fishermen left their

boats and gave a hand to the work.

Donald, Jack, and Danby did their share of cutting down trunks for more expert hands to cut into proper lengths.

Day after day the work went on, and Ina was often there, playing the part of a pretty, interested spectator to perfection.

And Vampa, with his gloomy brow, was there too, muttering prophecies of evil while others sang and laughed.

And the men of the yacht, smart, handy seaman, mostly half-castes, made the furniture—crude, but serviceable ; and Bob Bitters, the one seaman saved from the Morning Star, helped too.

He was a solid specimen of the English seaman, who said very little, but, as he used to say, "looked a bit,"

Bob was serious, taciturn, dry, and oracular.

When the house was furnished—and it was done within a week—Bob had a good look at it, and then gave his opinion—

"Purty ; but it won't last more'n a century."

Which meant that, in his opinion, the first gale would blow it down.

Bob had attached himself to Danby, and was as ready as a faithful dog to do his bidding ; and he had got to know that Danby did not wish to talk about himself.

Therefore, when Donald asked him, on one occasion, if he had known Danby for many years, he said—

"A long time, more or less."

And nothing more definite could be got out of him.

Thus was Danby's secret kept, and none around him knew or suspected that he had ever been an officer of a pirate craft.

Whatever dreams of retaliation on Carker he and the others might have entertained were for a time at rest, or in any case impossible of fulfilment.

They all looked forward to a life of freedom and enjoyment.

The instinctive love of sport was in their hearts, and their kindly friend the captain furnished them with excellent rifles and abundant ammunition.

"How the fellows at home would envy me if they only

knew," said Jack Johnson, as he and Donald sat by the door of their new home, examining their weapons.

On the morrow they were going out with the captain, Ina, and a party of men to beat the woods for game.

Danby was down in the town, but was expected back every minute.

The time went on and he did not return, and the sun set without his coming.

Donald and Jack sat and watched the moon rise from the sea, wondering what had become of Danby, but not troubled an his account.

Suddenly he stood before them.

He had come up so quietly that they had not noticed his approach.

"Boys," he said, "there's another craft in the bay, which may give us trouble. Guess its name."

They both instantly cried out—

"The Water Fiend !"

"Right," he said, quickly, "she came in an hour ago."

CHAPTER XII.

THE ARREST OF CAPTAIN FROSBY—ON THE WAY TO MONTE VIDEO—THE TWO STRANGERS IN THE CAPE.

"Yes," said Danby, "the Water Fiend came in about an hour ago, and she has dropped anchor close to the Fairy."

"And is that all she has done ?" asked Donald.

"All, save that she has run up the flag of the Argentine Republic ; and what Carker means by that I don't know."

"This is part of the Argentine country?" said Jack Johnson.

"Yes," said Danby ; "and that is where the mystery comes in. Carker is not given to putting his head into the lion's mouth, which, according to my notion, is what he has done."

"What does Captain Frosby think of it ?" asked Donald.

"I don't know," said Danby. "He and Ina are away. They went to make some arrangements for the morrow, but in what exact direction I don't know. '

That the arrival of the Water Fiend boded no good to anyone there was certain.

It is true that Carker might simply have put in for water or fruit, or some other form of supplies ; but as soon as he found out the weakness of Carita he would be sure to begin some of his old piratical tricks.

It was in the nature of the man to wantonly attack the weak and helpless.

"We had better go back to Frosby's place," said Danby, "and watch for his return."

"We ought to put him on his guard," said Donald.

"You can do that," returned Danby. "I don't know that I have anything to charge him with."

"You know he is a pirate," said Jack.

"Oh ! yes, I know that," was the dry reply. "So do you."

He set out as he spoke in the direction of Captain Frosby's house, and the others followed him.

He was silent until the lights of the house came in sight. All was quiet there.

"Carker hasn't landed," he said, "and I like the look of that none the better. He is not here by accident or for any casual purpose."

They could only associate his coming with themselves, and of course they felt disgusted.

"It does seem hard," Jack Johnson said, "that as soon as we are comfortable and everything aboard so jolly that this blackguard should crop up again."

They entered Frosby's garden and walked to the edge of the hill.

All below was quiet.

There were lights here and there among the houses and on board one of the vessels in the bay ; but which it was they could not be sure of.

Turning back to the house, they walked up to the windows that were lighted up and saw three servants engaged in laying the supper-table.

Captain Frosby and Ina were not there, and in all probability had not returned home.

"Boys," said Danby, "I don't see what good we can do by alarming these good people. We had better watch

Donald threw open the door and saw Captain Fingling with half-a-dozen soldiers.

over the place, and at the first sign of a movement from the Water Fiend give the alarm."

It was rather a dolorous suggestion, for after a night of watchfulness they could not hope to do much hunting on the morrow. An arrangement was made for them to take their turn at sentry duty, and Danby elected to begin.

As he insisted upon it, they had no resource but to obey, and retired to their new home, where they lay down just as they were, and speedily fell asleep.

Now, when young and healthy people sleep, they generally get through a great many hours, unless something happens to arouse them.

It was so with Donald and Jack.

Nobody came to awaken them, and they slept until dawn.

Donald and his friend had beds in the same back room on the ground-floor, and Donald, opening his eyes, stared at Jack in a dreamy, contented way, until the events of the previous night flashed upon him.

"Jack!" he cried, leaping up.

"Hallo! What's the time?" asked Jack, as he started into a sitting position.

"Where is Danby?" asked Donald; "he promised to come and wake us."

Jack's answer was to leap from his bed, put on his shoes, and give a few rapid touches to his toilet.

Mechanically Donald did the same, and the pair hurried into the front room, when the sounds of commotion outside fell upon their ears.

Donald threw open the door, and, to his astonishment, saw Captain Frosby struggling with half-a-dozen soldiers, who succeeded in throwing him to the ground.

"Jack," said Donald, "we can't stand that. Where's our cutlasses?"

"Come back, you hot-headed boys!" said a quiet voice behind them, and Donald was drawn back by Danby who closed the door.

"How did you come here?" asked Donald.

"Through the side window," replied Danby, curtly. "I came in to tell you to keep quiet."

"But what does it all mean?" asked Donald.

"That I don't know," replied Danby, " .... " I
watched all night, and saw nothing until this morning when
I caught sight of those soldier fellows toiling up the hill, and
thought they had come for you. Why, I did not know, but I
came to see fair play. Then as I drew near Frosby cropped
up from goodness knows where, and was pounced upon. It
is much a mystery to me as it is to you, my lads, but it
would have been madness to attempt a rescue at this
moment. Now, have you your rifles handy?"

They had them in their hands in a moment. Both
looked eager for action

"That is right," said Danby. "I have revolvers, and
now, boys, as these men have to make a circuit to their
boats, we can take a direct cut down the hill and quietly
ask what they mean by it. If their action is legal, boys,
we cannot interfere with it."

He threw open the door, and led the way across to the
slope.

Away on the right were soldiers slowly finding their way
down with Captain Frosby in their midst.

He walked with his head erect, and yielding with good
grace to the inevitable. Danby was not so particular as
the soldiers in his descent, nor his companions either, and
they reached the beach before the others were not more
than half way down.

The boat lay on the beach in charge of four sailors, all
of whom were strangers to Danby.

"Mystery on mystery," said Danby. "What does it
all mean? I'll swear that it is the Water Fiend and no
other."

The seamen took no notice of their appearance beyond
ust glancing at them, and then resuming their pipes and
whispered conversation.

Our friends waited at the base of the cliffs for the party
that presently came down.

The soldiers, though wearing a uniform that was
very European and had trimmed their moustaches in the
accepted way, were swarthy fellows, and spoke Spanish
when addressed by Danby.

Captain Frosby welcomed his friends with a quiet
smile.

"It is not exactly the beginning we arranged for the day," he said, "but do not blame me."

"What does it all mean?" asked Danby.

"Ask our friend here," said Frosby, with a motion of his head in the direction of the officer in command.

"The senor," he said, "is charged with dealing improperly with large sums belonging to the Republic. Our instructions were to arrest him as quietly as possible, and for that purpose, landed here so as to make a circuit to his house. But chancing to meet him on the hill we effected his arrest."

"I am to be taken to Monte Video," said Frosby. "Danby, do you and the others follow in my yacht and bring my daughter with you. Of my household, bring only Ina's servant, Vampa. Say that I have been obliged to leave on important business."

He tried to speak lightly, but his manner showed that he thought it very serious business.

That, however, was not the time for full explanations.

The strangest part of the whole thing was the non-appearance of Carker on the scene.

Danby had come prepared to use force to rescue. Truly, if Carker or any of his men were there; but here were all officials and strangers, and their good friend evidently in a fix he was not unprepared for.

They could only obey him, and turning away with hearts of lead, they walked along the beach towards Carita.

"It is the Water Fiend," Danby kept muttering, "but Carker is not on board. What does it mean? Have they caught and hanged the dog? If so, I can bear a few more hard knocks without murmuring."

They stopped a few moments to watch the boat as the strong seamen paddled it across the bay.

Captain Frosby sat in the stern between the soldiers, erect and immovable.

Carita was not yet awake, and when they had surmounted the hill the three sorrowful companions again ooked seaward.

They were just taking the boat on board, and Captain Frosby had disappeared. The canvas was already filling out before the light land breeze.

Close by lay the Fairy with all things still and silent on board ; no one there aware of the sudden blow which had fallen on its captain.

"On my word," said Donald, "I wish I had struck a blow for him."

"And so spoiled all," replied Danby. "I am sure the Water Fiend is no longer under the command of Carker, and came here armed with authority, but that Frosby has done anything petty, or mean, or criminal, I do not believe."

"I should just as soon believe it of you," said Jack Johnson, innocently.

It was a blow in its way, but Danby did not wince.

He smiled sadly, and, laying a hand on Jack's shoulder, said—

"The day may come when you will believe evil of me."

"Never !" said Jack, stoutly.

"What say you ?" asked Danby, turning to Donald.

"It would be very hard for me to believe it," was the reply.

"Oh ! cautious, far-seeing youth," said Danby. "You feel that you might believe it, and rightly, too. Well, we shall see what saucy tricks Old Time will play us. No more now. Here is Ina's watch dog."

The old Mexican had just come out of the house, and was leaning upon his rifle, his favourite attitude.

As they drew near he looked at them keenly from under his grizzled eyebrows.

"What's gone wrong, masters ?" he asked.

"Has Miss Ina risen yet ?" asked Danby, evading the question by asking another.

"She will soon be coming forth," said the old man, "and then you may give her your evil tidings. Is my master dead ?"

"No," said Donald, eagerly.

"Well, so far ; then he is only wounded ?"

"Nor wounded, either."

"Well, that is better. What is it that ails him, for on his head has the first blow fallen, as I can tell by your ways?"

"What we have to impart is to be told to Miss Ina," said Danby, impatiently.

"Ha! it is you say so, is it?" said the old Mexican, disdainfully. "You with the black mark HERE!" (He passed his finger across his forehead.) "You may frown, but I know it well."

"And may have it, had I the eyes to see," said Danby. "Now, old man, what say you to that?"

It was the Mexican's turn to be angry now, and a very forbidding snarl divided his lips.

Donald thought that he had never seen anything more striking than these two men as they stood in the morning sunlight.

There was something in the air of both which seemed to say to the other "You have a secret you want to keep, but it will come out some day."

They did nothing more than look, however, and not another word was exchanged between them.

The Mexican turned back into the house, and presently Ina appeared.

She did not go to Danby, but to Donald, and, looking up into his face, said—

"Tell me all, and tell me quickly."

"Your father," said Donald, "has been arrested on a charge of embezzlement of Republic monies."

"The poor, pitiful things!" said Ina; "and could they bring no heavier charge than that? Where have they taken him?"

"To Monte Video."

Then they told her of her father's wishes, and she expressed her assent.

"We shall be first there to welcome him," she said; "for the Fairy is the fastest thing upon the sea."

Then, looking at them in turn, she said, with a sad smile—

"We shall not go a-hunting to-day."

"Do not think of us, for Heaven's sake!" said Donald. "Our grief is that our coming has somehow brought misfortune upon you."

"Oh! that is but a tale," said Ina, "and I know

who told it you. Come into breakfast, while they prepare the Fairy for sea. It can be done in two hours."

Vampa had disappeared in the direction of the village, and did not attend at the breakfast-table.

But others were there, to whom Ina calmly gave them directions as to what was to be done to the house during her absence.

She also left in their charge the "strangers' home," as the building erected for our friends was called.

"You will need it when you return, you know," she said, with an arch look at Donald from under her eyelashes.

"As, of course, we shall return," said Danby, gaily. "It will be a fortnight's holiday—that's all."

"I hate Monte Video !" said Ina, vehemently. "It is a nest of scorpions and conspirators—of secret societies, and all that makes life hateful. I know why they have arrested my father ; but they have made a mistake. They have done it too soon, and he will get the laugh of them. Then we can return here."

Ina had not seen the Water Fiend, nor so much as heard of it, save from Donald and Jack, who, of course, had told the story of their captivity on board.

Why it should be sent to arrest her father she knew not, unless it were, as she said, with a bitter smile, "Any ship is good enough for the Republic, and any villain good enough to command it."

He returned home on the previous evening very late, and went quietly to rest.

No doubt he had risen early, and gone to wake his friends.

He always rose early, no matter what time he went to rest.

After breakfast, they went out to see what preparations had been made for departure.

The men of the Fairy were accustomed to be suddenly called upon to get ready for sea, and be away at a few hours' notice.

Already everything had been done, and even Ina's luggage was on board.

She did not, like a modern lady, travel with a dozen big packages each as big as a bedstead, but contented herself with two moderate-sized trunks.

The Fairy was an admirably fitted-up yacht. It was like many other pleasure boats of the sea, arranged with a thousand and one comforts not so much as dreamt of by our forefathers.

Ina had the cabin usually occupied by her father, which of course would, during her stay, be the sacred chamber of the vessel.

Danby occupied one adjoining, with Donald and Jack to share it with him.

Vampa needed no cabin. At night, like a watch-dog, he would sleep on a rug at his mistress' door.

Danby took command like one born to it.

Though armed by no better credentials than the word of himself and friends nobody demurred, but obeyed his orders with alacrity.

The whole of the population turned out to see the yacht sail, but there was no great public demonstration of any sort.

For the most part they were grave, quiet people, who thought more than they expressed.

A fair breeze from the south-west sent the Fairy bounding across the sea. As our friends stood on deck they felt something like a man who is a fearless rider and astride a good horse.

"By George," said Danby, "she is a grand little craft, and with a few TEETH would make short work of the Water Fiend. By the way, did either of you boys notice if she had guns on board?"

Neither had thought of doing so. It was a remarkable omission, considering that all had been guilty of it.

"She has two hours start of us," said Danby, "but if the wind keeps we ought to overhaul her ere sunset, or we may pass her in the night."

"How long will it take us to get to Monte Video?" asked Donald.

"If the wind keeps favourable, about five days," was the reply.

This sounded like a long time, but on board such a craft, with Ina for its mistress, the time might pass very agreeably.

And then there was his sea education to be thought of.

Danby was resolved to make a sailor of him and of Jack too, and both were willing enough to learn.

"You cannot tell when the knowledge may come in useful to you," Danby said.

Willing pupils are apt ones, and they got along famously, studying the names of ropes and spars and their uses, and all about winds and tides.

Jack Johnson studied geography as if he meant to lead victorious armies over the earth, and in the evening they studied that wondrous book aloft, in which all the letters are stars.

Of the Water Fiend they saw nothing.

Whether they were ahead of her or not they could only guess. Danby was of opinion that they had overhauled and passed her in the night.

The great water-basin of the Rio de la Plata was reached on the fifth day, and they crossed it, so as to be within sight of Monte Video by the following morning.

At noon they dropped anchor among the shipping of that seaport.

With a glass Danby scanned all the craft lying at anchor, and could not see anything like the Water Fiend there.

"We are here first," he said; "and now, boys, I think we may run ashore and see what information there is afloat about Frosby. If it is a big public matter, we are sure to hear something of it in the *cafés*.

Ina was consulted, and fell in with the idea. She would remain on board, and, after some hesitation, Donald offered to stay with her.

"One of us ought to be here," he said.

"You are kind to think of it," she said, "and I shall be glad if you will stay."

Jack made a wry face when he heard of it, but Danby approved.

"It is right that one of us should remain," he said. "You never can tell what will happen."

So he and Jack were put ashore on one of the landing places in the harbour, and passing through knots of busy men, and bales of goods and big bundles of hides, boxes of fruit, and other things, they made their way into the picturesque town.

In one of its best streets they found a *cafe*, into which they entered and sat down.

It was furnished with small marble-topped tables, by which sat a number of picturesque-looking fellows, smoking, drinking coffee, and in many instances playing dominoes.

At the next table, close by Danby, sat two swarthy half-castes—one a young man, and the other with a white moustache.

The latter stared hard at Danby as he sat down, and then whispered a few hurried words to his companion.

The elder man shifted so as to see Danby's reflection in a glass opposite.

He covered his face with his hands and stared at it for some time through his fingers.

"It is so," he said, in a low, hoarse whisper, and, rising, went out hurriedly.

Danby, unconscious of all this, ordered two cooling drinks for himself and companion, and asked if they had any good cigars.

CHAPTER XIII.

THE ARREST OF DARING DANBY—JACK JOHNSON'S GRIEF—RETURN TO THE FAIRY.

UNCONSCIOUS of impending evil, Danby and Jack sipped their drink, and the former smoked a cigar. They talked in an undertone, for Danby said the English tongue, though spoken freely in the town, was not popular.

"The mixed races of the Argentine Republic," said Danby, "are the veriest brutes on earth. Sneaks, and dishonest in all their dealings; cruel when they dare be, sneaking when they must be."

He was passing this true compliment on the combined races forming the republic when two men came swaggering in and sat down on the right of them.

They did not so much as look at Danby, but after ordering brandy and coffee plunged at once into conversation, speaking a patois—a mongrel mixture of Spanish and

English;

We give a translation of what they said, listened to with close attention by Danby, who understood every word.

"Is it not strange," said one," "that the don should take up with an accursed Britisher ?"

"He will make him useful and hang him by-and-bye," replied the other.

"And then there will be a bother with the British Government."

"Not so, for this Carker is a pirate, sailing under the Chilian flag without Chilian authority. When he came here and offered his services Venuezla accepted them. He also took his yacht."

Then they both laughed.

"And what is this Carker doing now ?" asked the first speaker.

"He is engaged in organising annoyances for the benefit of British residents. It is the don's plan to drive them out of the country.'

"Ah ! it is not easily done."

"No. By the saints ! these islanders—English, Irish, Scotch, or Welsh—are as leeches : where they fasten on they hold."

"But this Frosby—what is to be done with him ?"

"He is to be charged with robbing the exchequer."

"Which is already empty."

"So ! And he has never been near it, but simply lived quietly at Carita in luxury on money got from goodness knows where ; but Venuezla wants it."

"And so charges him with theft ?"

"So ! And to charge is to condemn. He will be simply asked to disgorge, say, two hundred thousand dollars, and if he does he will be allowed to go."

"And if he will not ?"

"Nothing more will be heard of him."

There was a cold-blooded infamy ring in the last sentence that made Danby's blood boil, but he kept an immovable countenance.

So did Jack Johnson, for happily he could not understand a word of what was being said.

It is doubtful if he had comprehended it if he would have kept calm or maintained silence.

After awhile the two speakers rose up and swaggered out, and then Danby told Jack what he had heard.

"But do you think that it is true?" said Jack, incredulously.

"I know it can be true—there is no doubt about it," replied Danby.

"But what villains they must be!" exclaimed Jack. "As bad as pirates!"

"Are you sure that all pirates are villains?" asked Danby.

"Why, of course they are," replied Jack. "What else can they be?"

Danby could not say anything in the defence of a pirate being, possibly, like a certain nameless personage, not quite so bad as he is painted, for the door was thrown open and the white-moustached senor, followed by half-a-dozen soldiers, entered.

"Arrest that man!" he said, pointing to Danby.

Danby had sprang to his feet and thrust his hand into his pocket; but on second thoughts he withdrew it again.

"I am ready to go with you," he said.

"But why? On what charge?" asked Jack, breathlessly.

He was completely taken aback by the suddenness of the whole thing.

"Is this man a friend of yours?" asked the senor.

"Yes," replied Jack.

"Do you usually consort with pirates?" asked the other.

Jack started violently, and an indignant flush overspread his face.

"He is no more a pirate than you are," he said.

"You are young and rash," said the senor, "so I pass by your rudeness; but let me tell you that this man was one of the officers of a ship that attacked one of my vessels on the high seas. It was plundered and sunk, and I was on board, doomed to drown, but I mercifully escaped."

"Did I do anything towards the destruction of your vessel ?" asked Danby.

"You were one of the pirate's officers," was the reply.

"Did I not endeavour to stop the foul work being done, and was it not already too late? The ship was scuttled."

"You were one of the pirates."

"Did I not cast overboard many things for you and the others to cling to?"

"You were one of the pirate's officers—I swear to it, was the dogged reply. "Away with him !"

Danby turned towards Jack, but he did not hold out his hand.

"Good-bye ! Jack," he said ; "it is all over with me. They will hang me like a dog, and I don't say I deserve a better fate. Ask Donald to think as kindly of me as he can. Perhaps when the list of my sins is totalled up it won't be quite so heavy as man makes it."

"But it CAN'T be true !" said Jack, with a broken sob. "YOU a pirate?"

"In the eyes of men, anyway," replied Danby, "and that is enough. I shall hang, and there will be the end of me. I am sorry it has happened now, for Frosby wants every friend he has in the world to save him from these sharks. Once more, good-bye. Don't bother about me. Think of Frosby, and do what you can to save him."

Jack sprang forward and grasped his hand.

"Whatever they may say of you," he said, I will never think ill of you ; nor will Donald or Ina. I don't know how you came into this dreadful position ; but I am sure it is not all your fault."

"There, Jack," said Danby, in a choking voice, "don't break down, or you will make a girl of ME, and that won't do before the grand senors, you know. Good-bye, old chap. I shall bear up now. I will comfort myself by thinking of you. Senors, I am ready."

He gently forced Jack back into his seat, and quietly placed himself in the midst of the soldiers.

Then out all but Jack went—prisoner, accuser, soldiers, and the idlers in the *café* who intended to have all the fun they could of seeing an Englishman taken to prison.

Jack would have followed too if he thought he could have done any good, but he knew it would be useless, and, overwhelmed with his new misfortune, he laid his head upon the table and moaned.

But only for a moment did he let his grief break him down.

Shaking off his emotion, he sat up and looked about him.

The only persons in the *café* beside himself were the attendants, who had gathered in a knot at the upper end of the place, and were whispering together.

As the little score had been paid, Jack had no need to trouble them.

Putting on an air of nonchalance which he certainly did not feel, he left the *café*.

The street in a picturesque sense was pleasing enough to the eye.

The houses were quaint in build, the Spanish and Moorish style predominating, and the attire of the passers-by was varied and picturesque.

There were impudent muleteers, half-caste ranchmen, swaggering bullies, holy friars, sisters of mercy, haughty dons, mules, horses and carriages, to make up a scene that at any other time would have entertained Jack.

But now he had no heart to enjoy anything.

The blow Danby's arrest had given him left a stunning effect behind him.

He could hardly believe it possible that the man he had learnt to admire and love had been arrested—not without some grounds as it appeared—for piratical acts upon the high seas.

What would Donald say to it?

What would Ina think?

And the reserved, surly Vampa, would he not rejoice?

"It is horrible—awful!" muttered Jack, as he glided through the throng of people.

He had a good idea of locality, and had no difficulty in making his way back to the harbour.

Nobody molested him in any way, although many a native face scowled upon him, for was he not of the dominant race—the accursed English ?

Was he not a son of those Isles that have sent forth more famous men than all the rest of the world put together ?

It matters little to the Argentine people which of the Isles they came from—Great Britain or Ireland, or from what part—they are lumped together under the generic term " Englese," and hated accordingly.

And yet it is British money, and not a little British energy, that has helped the Argentine ruffians to prosperity.

Jack knew very little of these matters then. All that troubled him was the sudden disasters which had fallen on what promised at Carita to be a very happy party.

First Captain Frosby under arrest, and now Danby. There were he and Donald left in charge of Ina and the yacht, and what were they to do with either ?

Jack was thinking this when he came in sight of the landing-stage, and his eye naturally roamed in the direction of the vessels at anchor, and one of the first he noticed was the Water Fiend.

There she was, just come in, anchor down, and the sails being rapidly furled. A boat was also being lowered, and Jack guessed what it was for.

He guessed aright.

Into that boat stepped Captain Frosby, an officer and half-a-dozen soldiers, and four sailors.

The latter pulled the boat ashore close to the very spot where the boat of the Fairy was lying awaiting the return of Jack and Danby.

Jack drew aside, and from behind a pile of fruit-boxes watched the landing of the prisoner.

No good could be done by making himself visible.

He was glad to see the captain bear himself bravely, stepping lightly on shore and walking through the gaping, grinning, jeering throng with head erect.

The haughty contempt of the captive was gall and wormwood to the gibbering fools, who shook their clenched hands at him as he passed on.

" He will go to the state prison," said one, " and the rats will devour him."

"What has he done?" asked another.

"I know not," was the reply. "He is Englese, and that is enough."

"And what are you?" thought Jack, as he came out of his hiding-place. "Neither Spanish, French, English, or anything else, simply dogs—curs."

In a state bordering on boiling indignation he walked to the boat and bade the men take him on board.

He gave no explanation of Danby's absence, and was not asked for one. The men, accustomed to obey, rowed back to the ship without a word.

CHAPTER XIV.

DONALD AND INA'S GRIEF—SOMETHING HAS TO BE DONE—PLANS FOR THE RESCUE OF CAPTAIN FROSBY AND DANBY.

"I CAN'T believe it of him."

"It is not true."

"And if it is he has been our friend."

"He is a noble-hearted man."

These were a few of the utterances that escaped the lips of Donald and Ina on hearing Jack Johnson's story.

That it had at first a startling and overwhelming effect cannot be denied; but they soon began to settle into a quiet and determined mood.

As Danby had fallen naturally into the place of leader a few days before, so Donald fell into it now.

"What we are going to do must be done promptly," he said, "for I can see that this place is a veritable nest of hornets. There is no knowing what they may do next. Say that they seized the Fairy—"

He stopped short, and looked at Ina, who said, quietly—

"Which they may do, and put us into prison, and then all we have to do is to bear everything BRAVELY."

"What a girl!" thought Jack; and he drew in a deep breath, preparatory to whistling his admiration; but Ina went on.

"Donald"—it was the first time she had ever called him by his Christian name, and she seemed to do it unconsciously—"I am a girl, and a poor hand at scheming. You and your friend must devise some plan for the rescue of my poor father and Mr. Danby. I can see that it won't do to trust to any merciful ruling of the judges, such as they are."

Everything on board Ina placed at Donald's command.

She did not exactly ignore Jack Johnson, but she placed him as naturally as possible under Donald, and Jack felt it to be his true position.

Donald did not dally at all with the work before him.

The first thing to find out was where the two prisoners were placed, and to do this they must go ashore disguised.

But disguised as what?

Here Jack Johnson came to his aid.

He called to mind certain cowled monks he had seen, and the dress was admirably adapted for concealing both features and such arms as they might carry with them.

But they had no such dresses on board, and they decided to go ashore in the evening. Ina said that Vampa should obtain them.

Vampa still hung aloof from our friends, in his hang-dog, sullen way, but Ina's word was law to him, and if he did not obey her injunctions with alacrity he did not exhibit any reprehensible hesitation.

He was sent ashore, and an hour given him to make the necessary purchases.

"There are a dozen shops where such things are sold for fancy balls," Ina said. "You can tell your own story to the dealer. Do not babble about our affairs and use all speed."

To which he simply answered—

"I do it for your sake, my mistress."

While he was gone Ina and Donald had a long talk together.

Both knew that there was a certain amount of peril in the undertaking of the two friends, and it was necessary certain precautions should be made.

"If we do not return by the morning," said Donald, "you must seek safety in flight."

"Can I command here !" asked Ina, with a sad smile.

"You have men who will know what to do," said Donald. "Perhaps you may fall in with some English cruiser, and if you will tell the captain your story—"

"He will make love to me and laugh," said Ina. "No; you go on your self-imposed duty, and I will pray for your safety. If you succeed in finding where our dear friends are, return at once; and if woman's wit and man's courage are of any account, they will soon be free. If you fail, leave me to dispose of myself as I will."

It was getting dark when Vampa returned.

He had with him a big bundle containing the chosen disguises, and he brought them to Ina as a dog would bring anything to his master.

Throughout all he steadily ignored Donald and Jack.

They lost no time in donning the garb of the sacred fathers, which, however, had plainly never been worn by a man in holy orders, but had been made to meet the requirments of frequenters at a fancy ball.

Still, they were good enough to pass muster in an ordinary way.

Enveloped in these, our young friends felt very much hampered in their movements, but it was a first-rate disguise.

After a few words of adieu with Ina, they were put ashore, and side by side sauntered into the streets, assuming as well as they could the stealthy walk of a holy father.

They kept their cowls drawn pretty close, but they could not quite hide their young faces, and many cast a quick glance at them as they went by.

The streets and shops were well lighted, and a great number of people abroad on gaiety bent.

From some of the *cafés* came the strains of music, the pattering of feet, and voices rich with laughter.

Occasionally the two friends exchanged a few words in a quiet way.

"I say, Donald, did you see that woman stare?"

"Yes, Jack; she suspects us. So does that fellow. Don't make any show of hurry, but get along as quick as you can."

Presently a woman came up and tapped Donald on

the arm with her fan.

"Friend," she said, "have you a spare ticket for the ball ? If so, I pray you give it to a poor senorita."

Donald muttered something—he never knew exactly what he did say—and nudged Jack to get along.

The woman followed them a short distance, and then, finding she could not get either a ticket or their companionship, muttered a few words not exactly complimentary to them, and turned away.

"Jack !"

"Yes, old fellow."

"We are in luck's way. There is a ball to-night, and we shall not be bothered if we keep moving."

They walked with a bolder step now, and, as Donald said, were not troubled by inquisitive persons.

There were other monks abroad, but they were, for the most part, as unreal as our friends, being on their way to one of the frequent public fancy balls of Monte Video.

Up and down street after street went our friends, stopping to look at many a building that bore some resemblance to a prison, but speedily finding it was the residence of some grandee.

Fortunately, they had brought some biscuits and wine with them, and at a late hour sat down in a doorway in a narrow thoroughfare to partake of needed refreshment.

"It's weary work," sighed Jack, and then whistled two bars of " Nancy Lee."

"Hush ! Jack—a whistling monk won't do," said Donald. "We shall find what we seek, yet. There is a prison at Monte Video I am sure. It is not a large place."

"Donald," said Jack, "how about the old forts ?"

Now Monte Video—as every school-boy knows—stands on a peninsula, and on two sides of it are forts which were of some use half a century ago, but now practically useless. Until Jack thought of it, Donald never associated these forts with a prison.

Now he saw it might be so ; and giving Jack a slap on the back worthy of the jolliest of jolly old monks, he thanked him, and after ook round they made tracks for the southern forts.

The streets ran right up to the inner walls, but there was a roadway round. The forts themselves were of low structure, with here and there a solid tower.

Between the towers sentries paced to and fro.

Our young adventurers could hear the rattle of their arms as they moved about, and could see their forms dimly limned against the starry sky.

Two of the towers they passed were as dark as pitch, but in a third several lights were burning.

This tower was near the sea, and the softened roar of the increasing tide fell upon the ears of Donald like the boom of far-off guns.

There was a gateway to this tower, facing the spot where Donald and Jack stood—and on either side of it were two narrow slits in the wall.

Around, all was quiet save the sound made by the sentries as they tramped to and fro.

None of the city revellers were near the spot. It was a corner away from the hum of busy life.

" I feel," interposed Jack, " as if we had dropped on the right spot at last."

They crept across the road, moving as stealthily as cats, so as to avoid the challenge of the sentry, and got up close to the gate of the archway.

It was made of some hard wood, studded with nails, and held together with iron clasps, very stout and strong.

They could never hope to force it, and when Donald applied his ear to the huge keyhole, he could hear armed men, some distance inside, walking to and fro.

" It seems to be a beastly place, Jack," he said, with a sigh.

Jack began to whistle, and had only got out two notes when Donald clapped a hand over his mouth.

He did not whisper a warning to him, deeming this action sufficient, but he was prepared to hear a challenge from one of the sentries.

They, however, kept up their steady tramp, but from somewhere on the right hand side of the gate an answering whistle came back.

" What's that ?" said Donald, in a hushed way, as he

set Jack's mouth free.

"I don't know," replied Jack. "It sounded like a late echo to my whistle."

Again was the sound heard, and this time it clearly came through the niche in the wall, which was about seven feet from the ground.

"Give me a leg up here, Jack," cried Donald.

Jack did so, and Donald got his face level with the niche.

"Anybody here?" he whispered.

"Oh ! Donald, old man, is it you ?"

It was Danby's voice, and Donald's heart fairly jumped within him.

That whistle of Jack's was a repetition of history.

It was like Richard Cœur de Lion and Blondel over again.

"Yes," he said, "it is me. Jack's here, too. We have come to rescue you."

"Oh ! my dear boys, Heaven bless you ! But you can't do anything this side. This cell runs right through the tower, and there is a barred window opposite. I could soon cut through with a file. Frosby is on the other side of the tower."

"Who goes there ?" sung out one of the sentries aloft, in the dialect of the place.

Neither Jack nor Donald understood the words, but they knew the meaning of them, and Donald slipped down.

"Lie flat and close," he whispered to Jack.

Again was the challenge repeated, and the sentry, getting no answer, fired his rifle.

Immediately the walls above were alive.

Quick footsteps, challenges, cries, and words of command.

"Run," said Donald. "Keep under the wall until we get to the next tower, then skedaddle across.

Away they went, and carried out their programme successfully so far as to reach the next tower and get across the road.

But there good fortune deserted them.

Instead of getting into a main street they got into a

short, blind thoroughfare, with a dark archway at the end of it.

Inside this archway was a stout door, locked and barred on the otherside.

"Oh! blow it," said Jack. "What a beastly job!"

"Keep quiet," whispered Donald; "and get ready to use your revolver if necessary."

By the walls of the fort the soldiers were now searching, and they passed up and down in front of the short street a dozen times.

At last two men entered, one bearing a lantern.

Discovery now seem inevitable, for the men came right up the street.

Donald and Jack curled themselves up and lay close.

Their dark dresses saved them, for the two men just flashed their lantern into the archway, saw nothing, and passed on.

So far all was well, but our friends were practically prisoners for the time.

All night long sentries paced the thoroughfare at the end of the street, and they dare not come forth.

They had not only themselves to think of, but of Captain Frosby and Danby.

If they could once get out of the city and back to the Fairy, the rescue of the prisoners was not only possible, but probable.

But all that night they had to remain where they were, hardly daring to move, and only now and then exchanging a whispered word.

At length the dawn came, and with it the sentries were withdrawn to the forts again.

Then our friends came out, and with their cowls well over their heads, sauntered down the street, turned the corner, and got into a main thoroughfare.

There they found many people stirring, and among them was a man with two mules, with their gaudy trappings.

He espied our friends and saluted them.

"Holy fathers," he said "after the ball you have lost your way. Whither would you go?"

Donald pointed towards the sea.

"Mount. fathers. and ride." said the man: "a dollar

for two, and tie the mules to the first post when you have done with them."

Donald had been provided with money, in case of need and hastily thrusting a dollar into the man's hand, he mounted a mule.

Jack did the same.

The man gave the brutes a bang with his stick, and away they started.

A holy father on a mule was a common sight there, and nobody heeded them.

All went well until they came to an old stone archway, beyond which was the quay and the sea.

They sniffed the very air of freedom when a sentry stepped out and barred their way with his bayonet.

"Senors," he said, "whither go ye? Stay and give your names."

CHAPTER XV.

QUICK WITS AND QUICK BLOWS—AGAIN ON BOARD THE FAIRY—PLANS TO RESCUE THE PRISONERS—VAMPA'S RAGE.

THE challenge of the sentry fairly took Donald's breath away.

It was so sudden, and came at a moment when all things seemed so favourable to their getting clear of the town.

As for Jack Johnson, his eyes fairly bulged out of his head, and mechanically he screwed up his mouth to whistle.

Nothing came forth but the first two bars of the " Dead March."

"Senors, your names?" cried the sentry again.

Two or three people had stopped to stare, wondering what the challenge meant.

In a minute or two there was quite a little crowd.

Donald, recovering himself, promptly replied—

"We have no names that you would know. We are wo sailors who have been to the fancy ball."

"You were not there," said the sentry. "Don Venuezlar stopped it owing to the illness of the senora, his wife."

This was another floorer; but Donald was not yet defeated.

"Here is a dollar; let us pass," he said.

"Senors, I arrest you—"

Donald lost all patience, and now, being close to the sentry, he dealt him a blow on the side of the head that laid him full length in the street.

"Ride on, Jack—quick!" he cried.

Jack urged on his mules, and, strange to say, the usually obstinate brutes were willing for once to bestir themselves.

They sprang forward, and galloped on to the quay.

Donald and Jack pulled up by a huge pile of empty boxes and baskets between themselves and the astonished spectators of the scene.

Quick as lightning they dismounted.

"Off with your disguise, Jack, and stuff it into that basket."

Off came both their dresses in a twinkling, and then they ran to another lot of things—baskets, boxes, and what-not—and from there looked towards the landing-stage.

"Whoop!" cried Jack Johnson. "Look! she is there!"

"Don't make that row," said Donald.

Yes, the boat was there, with four sleeping sailors in her.

It had been lying there all night awaiting the return of the young adventurers.

A shake and a word or two aroused the seamen, and Donald told them to pull steadily, like seamen, for the Fairy.

He and Jack took off their caps, wrapped themselves up in a tarpaulin that was in the boat, and took their seats in the stern.

Donald steered.

"Don't look back, Jack," he said. "Don't do anything but sit quiet. That is our one great chance of getting away. All together, men, and put your weight into it."

Meanwhile, the sentry, who had been half-stunned by the blow he received, lay in the street with half-a-score amazed people staring at him.

It was quite a minute before it occurred to one of the spectators that he ought to be picked up, and by that time he could sit up without assistance.

His hat had been knocked off his head, and his first ac was to feel for it.

Finding it was not in its usual place, he looked about, and saw it lying in the road, a few feet away.

"Curses !" he exclaimed. "Who did this ?"

"The holy fathers," replied one of the lookers-on.

"Ha ! them," cried the sentry ; "which way did they go ?"

The direction was pointed out to him, but he could not leave his post without summoning the guard.

"Run !—stop them !" he cried.

But nobody stirred.

"By the saints !" said one man, "I have no taste for blows from an iron fist. The holy father deals in hard knocks."

So time was lost, and when the guard was summoned and went on the track of the offenders, nothing was found but the two mules, tethered to a post.

Donald and Jack had just reached the Fairy, and were safe on board.

Ina, who had passed a long night of deep anxiety, gave them eager greeting.

"What news ?" she asked, lifting up her wistful, pale ace to Donald's.

"We have found them," he replied, "and rescue is not impossible ; but it cannot be done in the daylight."

"And must we pass another day here ? Is it safe ?" Ina asked.

"We will stand out to sea ror the day, and return after dark," said Donald ; "but there must be no haste. Let us do nothing to attract attention."

He was so cool and steady that he inspired both Ina and Jack with confidence.

For a while they kept their eyes on the shore without speaking.

They saw the guard, consisting of half-a-dozen men.

running about the quay, poking their bayonets into corners containing packages, and fussing about in an amusing way, in search of the men who had dared to knock a Monte Video sentry down.

It was very amusing, and for a few moments the watchers forgot their other troubles.

"Sharp lot that!" said Jack Johnson.

"Let us be thankful they are no sharper,' replied Donald.

After searching the quay, the guard returned to the town, and then Donald thought he might safely stand out to sea.

Without a challenge from the forts, or, indeed, being observed, save by some lazy sailors on other craft, they got clear away.

By the time Monte Video was fairly awake the Fairy was a spot on the distant sea.

Donald steered north until the land was simply a cloud on the horizon.

Then, with shortened sails, she gently tacked to and fro throughout the day.

It was quietly spent by those on board in preparing for the rescue that was to be attempted that night.

Donald's plan was to stand in towards evening, and as soon as it was dark to anchor off the mouth of the harbour and pull ashore, landing on the south side of the fort, and make his way to the prison of Captain Frosby and Danby.

He carefully thought out the position of the tower in which they were confined, and, on comparing notes with Jack Johnson, believed he was correct in most of the details.

"Still," he said, "there will be much to trust our wits to in the dark. Above all, we must not make any mistake about the tower."

He had a stout rope-ladder prepared, with hooks at one end, for he reckoned that the land on the sea side of the tower would be lower, and it might be of use.

Six of the best men were selected to accompany him, and Jack would be of the party, of course.

Vampa did not volunteer his services, which made Ina

angry with him.

She was not often unkind to her " watch-dog," but of late she had occasionally shown signs of irritation when speaking to him.

Perhaps she did not exactly relish his distrustful way of treating Donald.

The night seemed as if it would never come ; but evenng, its herald, came at last, and the Fairy was headed for the shore.

A fair north breeze carried them swiftly over the water, and it was barely dark when they saw the lights of Monte Video shining a few miles away.

About ten o'clock they anchored off the point of the promontory, and a boat was lowered.

Very little passed between Ina and her friends by way of adieu.

" Go, and Heaven help you !" she said.

" We will either return with our friends," replied Donald, " or share their captivity."

The boat departed, the men rowing with muffled oars, and Ina watched it until it was lost in the gloom.

A sigh escaped her, and it was answered with a low growl behind her.

Turning, she saw Vampa.

'' You need not be so watchful here,' she said ; "and what was the meaning of your exclamation a minute ago ?"

" Senorita," he replied, "you think too much of these Englishmen."

" And what is that to you ?" she demanded, with flashing eyes.

" To me—nothing," he replied ; "to you—much. What do you know of them ? Is it not a fact that one has already been found out. What he is may not the others be ?"

" Vampa," said Ina, "these things are not your affair. You forget yourself by speaking in this way to me."

" You despise your watch-dog now," he said, sadly.

" No," replied Ina ; "but if my watch-dog forgets himself, I must send him away."

She turned from him as she spoke, and rushed to the

companion, down which she disappeared.

Vampa remained quite still for a while. Then, in a slow, hissing way, there came a few words from his lips—

"Send—me—away—for *them!* Ah! it—will come to that—after I have killed *him.*"

He snatched a knife from its sheath at his waist, and, leaning over the side of the vessel, stabbed the air—once, twice, thrice.

"A blow for each," he muttered. "Ah! then—when they are dead—she may, if she will, send me away. What did I say of him—he—the pirate? Ah! and what might be said of me? Who will come here to declare it? If they should—

He stopped short and shuddered.

"She would hate—despise me!" he groaned. "Ah! that would be worse than all."

CHAPTER XVI.

THE ATTEMPTED RESCUE — DONALD AND JACK ARE DRIVEN FROM THEIR POSTS, AND GET INTO A VERY AWKWARD SCRAPE.

ALL was still and dark on the shore, although a short way off the town was lighted up.

Under the shadow of the fortress crept Donald and Jack, with two of the seamen in close attendance.

Donald kept his mind fixed on one thing—the plan of the fortress as he had mapped it in his mind; for any mistake as to locality might be fatal.

The beach just there was covered with shingle, and they had to step cautiously lest they should be heard and challenged by the sentry on the walls.

The night was clear, and the stars shone, as they do in that latitude, most brilliantly.

The outline of the walls and towers could be clearly seen.

Donald reckoned the third tower was his destination, and on reaching it he stopped.

About twelve feet overhead were two openings, protected by heavy iron bars, one on the extreme right and the other on the left.

To reach one of these windows, and ascertain if the prisoners were there, was the first thing to be done.

The two men bent their backs, and Donald stood upon them with a foot on each.

Jack climbed up and stood on Donald's shoulders, with two files in his pocket and the rope-ladder in his hand.

"Are you there ?" Jack softly asked.

"Right !" replied the cheery voice of Danby. "Have you rescued Frosby ?"

"Not yet.'

"Go to him first, said Danby, "and make sure of a good man before you do anything for a bad one."

"Here is a file and a piece of hard fat," said Jack. "I reckon you know what to do with them."

He thrust them through the bars, and, after a word of caution to Donald, slipped down.

They all shifted their ground to the next window.

In a few moments Jack was up, and holding on to the bars.

"Captain Frosby !" he whispered.

"Who's that ?" asked the startled prisoner within.

"I—Jack Johnson."

"Heaven bless you, my dear boy !" said the captain. "How came you here ?"

"We will tell you all that by-and-bye," said Jack. "Here is a file and some grease. Cut through the upper bars and squeeze yourselves out ; you will find a rope-ladder hanging to the lowest bar. Don't make more noise than you can help, as there are sentries overhead."

Down slipped Jack, leaving the rope-ladder hanging to the window ; and the men, having rendered all the service they could, were sent back to the boat.

Then Jack and Donald sat down upon the shingle, to wait for the full fruits of their enterprise.

Overhead they could hear the soft sounds of the well-greased files biting their way through the iron bars, and it was sweet music to their ears.

But some other sounds broke upon their ears—the voices of men, and the trampling of feet upon the shingle close to the walls.

"Whither go ye, senora? I give you names," he cried.

"Goodness !" exclaimed Jack ; "what is that ?"

"A patrol going its round, perhaps," said Donald.

Whoever or whatever it might be, to remain there was to be discovered, and they had to shift their ground.

At first they thought of moving towards the boat, but this would necessitate their going into comparatively open ground and the possibility of their being seen, so, instead of doing that, they hurried inland, keeping close to the walls.

But ere they had gone far they found, to their dismay, that the ground between the walls and the sea grew narrower, until it was only a few feet in width.

Still onward came the men, as yet unseen, with a steady tramp—tramp.

"We ought to have made for the boat," said Jack.

"It is too late to talk of that now," replied Donald. "We must go on."

"I didn't reckon on this," said Jack.

And then he screwed up his mouth to whistle, but fortunately thought of the consequences in time, and checked himself.

The narrow land did not extend more than two hundred yards before it began to open into the country, and again the hearts of our friends beat with hope.

They drew away from the forts and lay down on the ground, hoping to hear the advancing men pass by.

But to their dismay they halted at the very neck of the narrow land, and so cut off the retreat of our friends.

Donald could see the outline of their forms, and they were certainly not soldiers.

They had more the appearance of fishermen or rough, sea-faring men.

Gathering together they talked in a low tone in a *patois* neither of the listeners could understand, and their conference was a long one.

At first there was not more than a dozen, but as time passed at least fifty gathered together, and their conference threatened to be interminable.

If it had been a question of themselves alone Donald would have risked trying to pass them.

But there were the prisoners to think of.

They wanted time to get through the iron bars, and anything in the nature of an alarm might prove fatal.

So Donald lay close with Jack among some sedgy grass impatiently waiting for the time when the party in conference would move on.

Donald's ears, ever on the stretch, were, after a time, aware of another sound indicating further trouble.

It was the lapping of water against the walls of the fort.

The tide was coming in, and their return to the boat promised to be entirely cut off, for that night, at least.

He whispered the nature of the new peril to Jack, and a few hurried words were exchanged.

"We shall have to go inland," said Donald, " and take our chance. If Danby and Frosby get out they are sure to make for the shore and find the boat.'

"Will they go away without us?"

"I hope so. Common prudence ought to dictate to them to go on board for Ina's sake."

They were conscious now of the tide creeping up to them, and they had to shift their ground.

Rising cautiously and picking their way further inland, they put another hundred yards between them and the group of men still conferring together.

"I think I can see trees not far from here," said Jack. "I suppose we shall have to hide somewhere, unless we can get round the town and—"

"Impossible, to-night, at least," said Donald. "We are cut off from our friends and there is an end of it. I only hope they have got away."

"Of one thing I am sure," said Jack. "They will never entirely desert us."

As it was useless to remain in the open, they bore away to the left, where Jack fancied he saw trees, and found he was not mistaken.

To the right and left spread quite a wood of tall, straight-trunked trees—a species of palm, as far as they could judge.

Here they were sheltered from the dew that was falling, and they could have lain down and slept, if they had so chosen.

But sleep was impossible under the circumstances.

The town was now in almost complete darkness; but out in the harbour they could see lights belonging to various ships lying at anchor.

"It's a beastly sell!" muttered Jack.

"And shows the difference between going the right way and the wrong one," returned Donald. "But keep up your spirits, Jack; all will be well yet. I reckon, by not hearing any disturbance, that our friends have escaped."

Well, it was a long night for those two young fellows.

Not knowing what else to do, they passed it under the shade of the trees, sitting down, strolling to and fro, and cheering each other with hopeful prognostications of the morrow.

But their hopeful view did not take any definite shape, and each in his heart admitted that things had decidedly gone wrong.

The morning came, and they saw the sun rise out of the sea, spreading its light over the expanse of water, the shipping, and the town, and the land near them.

There were the ships at anchor, but, scan them as closely as they could, no sign of the Fairy was to be seen.

But Monte Video was awake, and on the walls of the fort near the town, where the two prisoners had been confined, there was a slight commotion.

Presently the watchers saw that the rope ladder was gone, and the windows of the two cells had a blank look, which showed that the bars had been cut away.

"They have escaped," said Donald, "and I am thankful."

It would not do to linger there, for it was too near the town.

The better course would be to get away from the place, and from some high point near the sea watch for the Fairy.

That they were really deserted neither believed for a moment.

Without food the prospects of the day were not cheering, but healthy natures bear up slight gastronomical inconveniences, and they staved off the keener pangs of hunger by eating a few berries, which had a wholesome appearance and flavour.

The wood was of limited extent, and a quarter of an hour's easy strolling brought them to the open country.

As they stepped out of it, not thinking of the presence of a possible foe, a number of ruffianly armed men leaped from the ground, where they had been lying and apparently sleeping.

Uttering fierce cries they dashed at the two friends, who were fortunately armed with their cutlasses.

Donald warded off a blow aimed at him by the foremost ruffian, and on the impulse of the moment, in self-defence, cut him down.

The man fell to the ground stunned, if not killed, by the force of the blow, and the others drew up short, dismayed by Donald's vigorous action.

For a few moments they remained staring and snarling at Donald and Jack, who remained quietly on the defensive.

Then one was heard to mutter the word " Englese," and it was followed by a general growl of execration.

Donald was of opinion that these men were some of the party he had seen under the walls of the fort of the previous evening, but he could not be sure ; nor had he time to think it out, for his position was one of peril. If these fellows had the courage to attack he and Jack would have but a poor chance with them.

To shift his ground or show a desire to retreat would give to the men the courage they lacked.

The friends were in the position of a man who meets a wild beast in the forest, and holds it with a dauntless eye. While that eye did not shift the beast would do nothing, but to make the least movement of retreat would bring the enemy on with a rush.

The man whom Donald had cut down speedily exhibited signs of returning life, and began to groan. The sound had a magical effect upon his fellows. It infuriated them, and with yells they dashed at the dauntless pair.

"Don't be taken, Jack," cried Donald ; "fight to the last."

"I hear," replied Jack.

Instead of retreating before the rush they stood their

ground, and used their cutlasses so manfully, although a little wildly, that once more the foe began to waver.

A second of their number had bitten the dust, and Donald saw that a bold rush might scatter the rest.

"At 'em, Jack!" he cried.

"Here goes," muttered Jack. "Victory or death!"

Side by side they rushed on their foes, who broke asunder like a bundle of sticks when the cord is cut.

Victory seemed assured; but, alas! for the hopes of our friends.

A shout was heard behind them, and, taking advantage of a clear space between him and his nearest antagonist, Donald turned his head.

Only for a moment could he look, but that was enough.

Fully a score of men were bearing down in his direction, and at the head of them was his old foe, Carker.

"Jack," he said, "we must run for it now. It's no use waiting here to be slaughtered. Run!"

CHAPTER XVII.

JACK AND DONALD HAVE A VARIABLE TIME WITH THEIR FOES—A RUN TO THE SHORE—RESCUE.

WITHOUT a doubt there is a time to run as well as to stand and fight.

When a man finds himself opposed by hopeless odds he has a right to get away as speedily as possible.

If he does so no man has a right to call him a coward.

Donald and Jack ran.

Both were pretty nimble on their legs, but they gained no fictitious activity from fear.

Prudence dictated their "advance movement to the rear."

Donald did not like doing it, but he was not disposed to put himself in the power of an old enemy, who, he had good reason to believe, would, if occasion served, be remorseless. Of course, there was a general pursuit.

The moment the two friends swung round and dashed away to the right both gangs began to follow, yelping like curs.

But the majority could yelp better than they could run, and they soon began to tail off.

One of the first to do so was Carker himself.

Either he thought it beneath his dignity to run, or he was not in condition.

But the fact remains that almost as soon as he entered into the pursuit he abandoned it.

But he encouraged the men who were his followers with shouts, offering them a reward for the capture of the two friends, dead or alive.

The foremost were soon out of hearing, and as Donald bore away to the right a knoll of rising ground hid him and his pursuers from view.

His intention was to make a semi-circle and get to the sea.

It was possible that some signs of the Fairy might be seen.

But first he must shake off those who pursued him.

Looking back over his shoulder he saw that they had been reduced to half-a-dozen, and two of them were blowing like grampuses.

"Jack," he said, "how's your wind ?"

"All right," replied Jack. "Whistling made that right years ago."

"Put a spurt on, then. We shall break the hearts of those fellows."

Jack spurted as if finishing a race for the championship of the world.

Donald made his effort, too, and those in pursuit followed suit.

The result was that four out of the six dropped behind, and only two remained.

The country here was much broken up, earth and rock and bush being intermixed.

Donald doubled in and out among all sorts of impediments until he had lured the leading pursuers well away from the rest.

Then he called on Jack to stop.

"There are only two left," he said. "Let's go at them, Jack."

The two brave lads, who had retained their cutlasses in

their hands, wheeled about, and the arduous pursuers came to a sudden stop.

They were well-knit half-castes, and they had the half-caste's failing—a soft spot in their hearts.

The determined look on the faces of the two friends made them shrink back, and as Donald dashed forward a pace or two they fairly turned tail and bolted.

"Ha—ha !" laughed Jack, throwing himself down on a bank of earth. "What an ending to a promising tragedy."

And then, although pretty well blown, he whistled, with good effect, the "Rogue's March," as a fitting one for the occasion.

Donald sat down to rest, too, but only for a brief space of time.

"We ought not to linger here," he said. "Carker is sure to try what craft will do."

"It will be murder this time," said Jack. "What do you propose to do ?"

"We must get to the shore somehow," said Donald. "I am sure our friends will be looking out for us."

"If they have got away?"

"And if they have not Ina will not desert us."

They moved on, climbing about the broken ground and keeping as far as they could behind anything that would hide them from the foe.

Both suffered from hunger and thirst, but not to any great extent.

Nothing more was seen of their pursuers just then, and in an hour, or thereabouts, they came to a wide stretch of sandy ground leading to the sea.

On the left, about ten miles away, lay the town of Monte Video, and a number of craft of various sizes were dotted about the sea.

"There is the Fairy," cried Jack, pointing south.

Donald looked in the direction he indicated, and saw a trim yacht tacking towards the shore.

"My eyes are not so good as yours, Jack," he said. "I should not like to stake my life on its being the Fairy."

"Well, *I* only FEEL it," said Jack. "We had better show ourselves on the off-chance. If it is the Fairy they are sure to be looking for us."

After a glance round, and seeing nobody in sight, the two friends ran side by side down the slope towards the sea.

They took off their hats and waved them as they ran.

To their great joy an answering white flag was speedily run up, dipped twice, and lowered again.

The helm of the yacht was put up, and she was brought to dead in the eye of the wind.

"It is the Fairy!" cried Jack, overjoyed. "See! they are lowering a boat. Oh! Donald, I am overcome now. Dash it! I shall cry like a baby in a minute."

He brushed away a tear as he spoke, and Donald's vision was a little misty.

The joy he felt would have overwhelmed many a strong man.

It was like being brought back from the jaws of death to life again.

Near the beach the sand made a sudden cliff-like sweep downwards.

It had been formed into banks of twenty feet high by stormy seas.

Jack and Donald slid down like playful schoolboys to the shingle below.

And now they could see that the boat was manned by a dozen men, with a figure like that of Danby in the stern.

There could hardly be any doubt that it was the man who, in spite of the evil they heard of him, they looked upon as a dear friend.

"But why all those fellows with him?" asked Jack.

The answer was given by a noise above, and, looking up, they saw Carker and some of his men coming over the edge of the sand-bank.

Not only had Donald and Jack been seen from the yacht, but their foes bearing down upon them also. Hence the number of men in the boat.

"Stand your ground, Jack," said Donald, "the boat will be here in a minute."

"To take our bodies on board," laughed Jack. "Hang it all! I wish those fellows at Jericho."

But "those fellows," armed with cutlasses, knives, and, in some cases, with revolvers, were coming upon them.

Carker's face was pale, but it was rather with joy than with fear.

He looked upon Donald and Jack as the authors of the reverses which had befallen him, conveniently forgetting that he had himself to thank for it if such was indeed the case.

"Give yourselves up, you cubs !" he cried ; "it will be all the better for you if you do."

"Not with life," replied Donald, "while I can defend myself."

"At them, boys !" cried Carker.

But the boys received a slight check.

A shot was fired from the approaching boat, and the bullet, whistling past Carker's head, lodged in the heart of a man behind him, who fell gasping to the ground.

The others pulled up, and Carker advanced alone.

His face was distorted with passion, and, notwithstandng his being really a good-looking man, the demon-like ook upon him made him repulsive.

"I have hoped a curse could kill you," he said to Donald, as he drew a revolver from his pocket ; "but I will make short work of you now."

As he spoke he fired, and Donald instinctively threw up his cutlass. The bullet of the revolver struck the blade.

Ping !

It was another bullet from the boat, and Carker, with a terrible malediction on the hand that fired the rifle, tumbled in a heap upon the sands.

How easy for Donald or Jack to have slain him then, and, for a moment, it flashed on both that it might easily be done.

But they could not butcher a helpless man, although he was a cruel, remorseless foe.

As for his men, they had began their retreat, when he gasped out—

"Would you leave me here, you curs ?"

That they held him in fear, if not in reverence, was clear, for they hurriedly returned, and dragged him back to the sandy hill. Neither of the young fellows interfered.

Nor was another shot fired from the boat. And others of the band lending a hand, Carker, gasping with pain, was dragged up the slope and borne away.

It was magnanimous on the part of Danby, and Donald, and Jack not to interfere ; but in the truly brave magnanimity is ever found.

The boat touched the sands, and Donald and his friend leapt in. Danby was there to give each a hand.

"How we have suffered !" he said. "We feared you had fallen into the hands of the blackguard authorities nere, and have been devising all sorts of schemes to find ut where you were."

"Is Captain Frosby safe ?" asked Donald.

"Safe, so far as being on board the Fairy," replied Danby ; "but it won't do to hang about here."

"Why did you stay for a moment ?" asked Donald, impetuously.

"Because it was our duty to risk anything for two of the bravest lads that the sun shines on. Give way, men."

———

CHAPTER XVIII.

THE FAIRY GETS BACK TO HER HOME—VAMPA AS A WOULD-BE ASSASSIN—ARRIVAL OF THE WATER FIEND.

"No reference ought to be made to the charge against him. Let him tell his story in his own chosen time."

It was Captain Frosby who advised Donald thus, and t may easily be inferred that it was Danby they were speaking of.

"For my part," Donald replied, "I do not want to hear it—in the form of explanation. I shall take him as he i:. I am sure that whatever errors he may have committed his heart is sound."

So Donald undertook to deliver a message to Danby, which he did directly after he parted with Captain Frosby.

It was a moonlight night, and Danby was on deck in charge of the watch. The Fairy was two days out from Monte Video, and hitherto had not been pursued.

There was a quiet, sad demeanour in Danby that was touching, especially to Donald, who had learnt to know him as he might a faithful elder brother.

He went up to him and offered him a cigar from some Captain Frosby had given him.

They lighted up, and walked slowly to and fro.

"Danby," said Donald, "why are you so sad?"

"My dear boy," replied Danby, "you expect me to be happy?"

"Why should you not be?"

"Have you not heard the story of the cause of my imprisonment?"

"Of course I have, and I am the bearer of a message from Frosby, Ina, Jack, and myself. It is that we forget all that we have heard or will not think of it. If ever you choose to explain or tell the story of your life previous to our meeting we will gladly hear it, but you are to do it simply to satisfy our curiosity."

"My boy," said Danby, laying his hand upon Donald's shoulder, "I have no words to answer you. My heart is full. I cannot tell my story now, nor do I consider it expedient. You will take my word that I am not quite so black as I appear to be?"

"Yes, and believe it apart from your word."

"And the others will believe it, too?"

"Implicitly."

"Enough," said Danby. "I am myself again. Away with all sadness." He sent out a cloud of smoke as if that were his sorrow, and the wind carried it across the sea. "I am happy."

Donald kept watch with him, and a long and interesting talk they had of the future.

They were going back to Carita, where Captain Frosby was assured of the loyalty of the inhabitants, and preparations would be made to resist any further attempts on the lives and liberty of any of them.

Captain Frosby admitted that he had been taken by surprise; anyhow he had expected that sooner or later the base mongrel rulers of Monte Video would make some attempt to get at the secret of his wealth and extort it from him.

What better conduct could be expected of a people who borrowed money from the old country, and then callously refused to recognise the debt, or to so surround the payment of interest with evasion as to practically amount to the same thing?

Stored in a secret place in the wood behind his house, Captain Frosby had long kept the means, not only of defending Carita from a foe of moderate strength, but also the guns and ammunition to turn the Fairy into a smart little gun-boat.

That was to be done immediately on their return, but not in the harbour of Carita, as it would take time, and a cruiser might be sent by his enemies to seize it.

Some miles down on the Patagonian coast there was a place where the work could be done in secret.

Meanwhile a watch would be kept, and if a force too strong to resist was sent a retreat by way of the woods was easy.

It would be practically impossible for anyone not well versed in the intricacies of the lone land to follow and capture them.

"So if the worst comes," said Danby, "we shall have only to find a new temporary home inland, and all I ask is that when the Fairy is fitted out I only hope that Carker may be sent with the Water Fiend into our district. We will then be able to settle off old scores with him."

It was a delightful prospect for Donald, and he longed as much as Danby for the time to come when the respective strength of the vessels might be tested on the sea.

Meanwhile, of course, Carker might die of his wound; but Danby did not think so.

"I dropped him," he said, "with a bullet in the leg, and by his after movements I do not think it was broken. It was only a severe flesh-wound."

The run back to Carita was accomplished in safety.

Great rejoicings of the inhabitants showed how gladly they hailed the return of their chief. It was like a people being awakened from a trance.

Everything in the houses was found intact, and everything in the way of stores being taken out from the Fairy, she was entrusted to Danby's care to be taken to her hiding-place to be fitted out with the armaments of war.

Jack and Donald took possession of their house, and shared with the inhabitants the task of watching for a foe.

From the hiding-place in the forest Captain Frosby brought out rifles and ammunition, and every man in the place was armed.

A warlike spirit took possession of even the women and the children.

The latter were not very numerous, and it was estimated that in case a retreat into the interior became necessary that they would not prove to a very great encumbrance.

Only one discontented spirit was in the place, and that was Vampa.

He hated Donald with a bitterness that could not be expressed in words, and he watched his every movement when with Ina with the jealousy of a lover.

And the secret of it all was that Vampa loved his young mistress.

When a child the grizzled old Mexican had only been a faithful attendant, but when womanhood dawned upon her another feeling laid hold of him.

It was a hopeless passion.

It was the love of an old fool, whose position shut him out from the faintest prospect of success.

And therein lay the bitter sting of it.

He had become a dog in the manger—what he could never win, others should not have.

There was a dark spot in the history of his life which had left its mark behind. At a pinch Vampa could become a murderous ruffian.

It was three days after their return, and Danby was still down with the men, getting the Fairy into her quarters for alterations. It was a hot afternoon, and Donald, seated in a rustic seat which the servants of Captain Frosby had made for him, fell asleep.

Jack had gone off to the village about some small matters, and Donald was alone.

Vampa, moving about with his mind moodily dwelling upon the absorbing subject of his thoughts, came up and espied Donald asleep.

In a moment the dark passions within him were bubbling over.

He fought against them, for he knew that the crime he was prompted to do would result in his being promptly punished unless he fled away and hid himself from all there.

He tried hard to turn and go away. Prudence prompted it, but the evil within him bade him do the deed and take what followed.

There was the possibility that he might not be suspected, or if suspected not convicted.

Yes, he would kill him !

The delay brought about by these contentions within him saved Donald's life.

Jack was hurrying back from the village with news of great importance when he saw Vampa stealthily stealing up to Donald with a keen stiletto in his hand.

The intent of the old villain was but too apparent, and Jack, in a frenzy of anger and fear for his friend, dashed over the sandy soil to the rescue.

He was just in time.

The weapon was uplifted and would in a moment or so have been plunged into Donald's heart, when Jack grasped Vampa by the arm with one hand and with the other struck him a blow between the eyes.

A desperate struggle ensued, and Donald, awakening, saw Jack and Vampa rolling on the ground in a struggle as fierce as that of two Indian warriors.

Jack's blood was up, and Vampa, foiled of his prey, was half mad, and would have killed Jack if he could have got him fairly in his power.

But Donald was there, and he, guessing something more than an ordinary quarrel was afloat, pinned Vampa's shoulders to the ground and held him fast.

"Get up, Jack," he cried, "and tell me what all this is about."

"Stop a minute," said Jack. "Let me see if he has any more weapons about him."

Jack had already got possession of the stiletto, and as Vampa had no other weapon about him he was allowed to rise.

Then Jack accused him of attempting to take Donald's life.

"It's a lie!" hissed Vampa. "I was but passing by when you sprang upon me like a hound and dashed me to the ground."

"That is your story," said Jack. "We will see which of us Captain Frosby believes."

"Oh! he will believe you," snarled Vampa, "and I shall be condemned to death—that is, if I stay here; but I am going away. And remember this, you Englese dogs, you have not heard the last of Vampa."

With these words he stalked away into the wood, and when he was gone Donald began to wonder whether they had been wise to let him go.

Vampa had all the makings of a dangerous man in him.

Openly they did not fear him, but from the stealthy assassin who is safe?

"I wonder what I have done to the fellow," said Donald, "that he should hate me so?"

"Oh! black-blooded brutes of his stamp hate for hatred's sake. Never mind him, Donald, I have other news for you. The Water Fiend is in the offing, and standing in. Frosby has ordered all the women and children into the wood, and the men are arming."

"Has Danby turned up?" asked Donald.

"No; but he is expected some time to-day," replied Jack. "We had better shut our crib up and join the captain."

"Has Ina gone?" asked Donald.

"Yes. She is in command of the women," replied Jack, "if I may put it so. That girl has a cool head! She inspired them all with courage. Frosby says that if any men attempt to land he will not parley with them for a moment."

They armed themselves, and having shut up their abode, set off at a trot for the captain's home.

Below, half-way down the cliff, a rough sort of fort had been constructed, which was now occupied by a dozen armed men.

The Water Fiend was standing in, and in half an hour would be at anchor.

That she came on a message adverse to peace was certain, for with the aid of a glass Captain Frosby had

E

already made out that men were standing by the guns, and a number of soldiers were assembled on deck.

"They have come to take us openly and by force," he said, grimly; "but they have not got us yet."

He had a score men with him on the cliff, and among them were his servants, six in number. Every man had a rifle, and the great part swords and revolvers also.

But the question how they would use them remained to be answered, for Captain Frosby had never tested them in a fight with disciplined soldiers—or, indeed, with any formidable foes.

But they were all devoted to him, and devotion goes a long way towards inspiring men with courage.

Boom !

A gun, with blank cartridge, was fired from the privateer, probably as a hint that the captain was not going to be trifled with.

Donald, with Captain Frosby's field-glass, was scanning those moving about the deck.

At last he found the man he sought.

"Carker is on board," he said, "limping about and giving orders. Ah ! if the Fairy were but ready."

"She won't be for a month," said Captain Frosby, "as everything has to be transported to her. Here comes a boat-load of soldiers."

"And another one is being lowered," said Jack Johnson.

The ruffians stood at bay behind their comrades.

CHAPTER XIX.

THE ATTACK ON CARITA—REPULSE—CARKER MAKES AN EFFORT, AND FAILS—CARITA DESERTED.

CARKER could be plainly seen by all limping about the deck of the Water Fiend. He had not yet quite got over the wound inflicted upon him by Danby.

He was not one of the party that came ashore in the boat. These were soldiers of the republic, with an officer, apparently on the level with our sergeant, in command.

Neither he nor his commander had realised the fact that there would be armed resistance, and on landing the officer was leading his men up the winding way on the face of the cliff, when a voice was heard—

"Halt!"

He halted, and looking up, saw the barrels of a dozen rifles pointed at him by the men in the impromptu fort.

"Go back!" cried the same voice; "or I will fire upon you."

Realising his danger, the officer ordered his men back to the boat, and in the meantime Carker became aware that something unexpected was happening on shore.

He came to the side, and with a glass took a rapid survey of the land. Then, with angry gestures, he gave orders for another boat to be lowered.

Into this he got himself with twenty men, the majority of whom were sailors.

This was rather promising, as Jack Johnson said, and the party on the cliff lay down upon a sloping ridge and prepared to discomfit the foe.

Carker landed and joined the inferior officer he had sent ashore.

Though he limped, he moved without exhibiting any sense of pain, and, as far as fighting was concerned, he was as good a man as ever.

On board the Water Fiend there was still a number of men. She was evidently well manned—over-manned rather than otherwise.

For the comparative handful of inexperienced men of Carita the chance of a successful defence did not seem to be very hopeful; but they had a good leader in Captain

Frosby, and he in his turn was well supported by Donald, Jack, and Danby; the latter of whom had appeared, as he often did, just when he was wanted.

The men below had their orders, which were to do what damage they could to the foe, and if they could not hold the little fort to retreat to the summit of the cliff.

There the fighting could be kept up until retreat was imperative.

Carker, at the head of all the men he had ashore, now began to ascend the cliff road.

It was zigzag, as all such roads or paths must be, and it laid the invaders open to the rifles of their defenders for some time, say ten minutes, ere it came to a hand-to-hand conflict.

Carker, as he approached, was in his turn challenged to halt; but, waving his sword defiantly, he urged his men on.

" Fire !"

The rattle of rifles was heard, and three of Carker's men fell back upon the road. One tumbled over the narrow coping that fringed it, and rolled and bounded down to the beach, where he lay quite still.

The ardour of the rest was considerably damped, but Carker, by ferocious threats and violent gestures, urged them on.

" There are only a handful of men," he cried. " On, and avenge your comrades !"

He had pluck, without a doubt, and his words and air inspired his men. Limping and shouting he hurried on, and again the rifles of the defenders poured out their leaden hail. But this time with less deadly effect.

Probably the defenders were getting flurried, as men unused to warfare are apt to be—or they did not make allowance in aiming for their foes being nearer and more under them.

From what cause, however, matters not, only one man fell, and the rest, with Carker at their head, darted up to the fort.

Perhaps it would be better to call it a stockade, as it was really no more, but it played its part well as a means of defence.

Carker could not clamber over it, and his men hesitated to attempt it without a leader.

They paused but a moment, and that was fatal to them.

From the stockade came a third volley, and a well-directed fire from the summit of the cliff.

This was fatal to five of the Water Fiend men, and these tottered back into the arms of their comrades more or less seriously wounded.

Carker saw that the attack had failed, and not only gave the word for a retreat, but set an example by hurrying down as fast as his lameness would permit him to go.

It was a most ignominious movement to the rear, and the shouts and laughter of the victors must have sounded very galling in Carker's ears.

High above all the noise was heard Jack Johnson shrilly whistling " Rule, Britannia !"

Never before had he been in such whistling voice—at least, that was what he afterwards declared.

The wounded were left to take care of themselves, and they crawled and limped after their comrades, acting as an involuntary shield to them; they partly covered those who were unhurt, and Captain Frosby gave the command to " cease firing."

"We have thrashed them," he said, "and that is enough. They can now go home and tell what story they like. As for Carita, it is a doomed place, and we, my lads, are outlaws.

This may appear very dismal intelligence, but his listeners took it very lightly and even laughed.

"I am sorry," said Frosby, after a few moment's silence, "for I liked Carita; and now all we can do is to take away what we can and leave the rest to our foes or destroy it."

"Destroy it," said Danby; "leave them nothing. There goes Carker in the first boat. It does me good to see him running away like a dog. If he had not been lame I would have gone down and met him; but I felt it would be mean to attack a lame man. But we shall meet again some day."

A similar feeling had led the others to practically

ignore Carker. Donald did cover him with his rifle, and would probably have brought him down, but he turned the muzzle aside, muttering—

"Hang it! I can't. A lame man is half a one. Only a coward would take advantage of a man being crippled."

Carker was not aware of the generosity of his foes. If he had been told of it he would have laughed at it as a jest.

The chivalric feeling shown by them he had bitterly wronged was a fable to him. He did not believe it existed.

On returning to his vessel he opened fire on Carita with two guns, which threw small shell of great explosive power. The Water Fiend was now armed better than she had ever been before.

But being so near shore the guns could not be elevated sufficiently to do harm to the houses or reach those on the cliff above.

His only course was to stand out to sea and fire at a much longer range. Seeing this, he had the canvas set and the anchor raised. With a light wind on the beam he bore away.

There is such a thing as true courage which knows when to retreat; only the foolhardy stand their ground when death is inevitable without being serviceable to any person or causes.

Captain Frosby saw that Carita was now untenable.

Half an hour at the outside would elapse before the Water Fiend got into position and trained her guns for firing, and what he had to do must be done speedily.

The men were sent to fire the place—each man to destroy his own house, and Captain Frosby was the most active man in preparing his own place for the conflagration.

Necessarily Jack and Donald had to sacrifice theirs.

Accompanied by Danby they hastened thither, packed up all that was portable, and having piled up the rude furniture, set it on fire.

"This," said Donald, "is the end of my pleasant dream."

"Yes, bother it!" replied Jack. "When we first

came here I thought we were going to have a taste of Paradise."

"My dear boys," said Danby, "a life of adventure is really more to the tastes of both of you. A week or two of pleasure alone would have clogged you. It is all for the best, take my word for it."

They were willing to take his word in this as in anything else, and each with a bundle under his arm, and armed, as the old writers used to say, "to the teeth," they turned out of their home upon the cliff.

It was getting late now, and night would soon be there; but darkness would not fall upon pleasant little Carita for many hours, for a score fires were blazing.

The wood and thatchwork in the structures burnt merrily; but there were sad hearts among those who gathered on the summit of the cliff watching the Water Fiend.

She was in water too deep to give her anchor ground. Carker had laid her too, and the men were busy preparing to bombard Carita.

A sharp report and a shrill scream was heard as a shell came hissing to the shore.

It struck the cliffs a little below the stockade, exploded, and tossed broken columns of sand into the air.

"Well aimed," said Danby.

Carker had good gunners on board.

Another sharp report and another scream, and a shell plunged fairly into the heart of the village.

It exploded, and brought one of the burning houses down at a run.

Captain Frosby ordered his men to take shelter in the wood.

They gladly obeyed, for the shells were uncanny things in their eyes.

He waited with Jack, Donald, and Danby until a third shell struck the summit of the cliff, twenty yards on the right, leaving a big gap in the earth, and exploding with a deafening sound.

Jack Johnson heard the whiz of a piece of shell as it flew over his head, and thought the noise it made was the most unmusical sound he had ever heard.

"It is time to move," said Captain Frosby. "Only a fool or a madman would stay to be shot at like a target Farewell, Carita, where I have spent so many happy hours. Come, my friends, let us away."

They sauntered into the wood, and Carita was left to fire and shell to complete its destruction.

For two hours—and darkness came before the expiration of that time—the Water Fiend wasted its ammunition on a deserted place, and those who once inhabited it were by that time out of the sound of the guns.

The night passed, and when morning came Carker saw that the place wasleft to itself, and he sailed away south-ward.

He had not the number of men, nor the right men, to scour the country and arrest the men he had been sent to capture.

But he did not abandon the idea of capturing them.

They were few, and he could get many to aid him.

In a country periodically uninhabited the trail of so many people travelling together could soon be discovered and followed.

CHAPTER XX.

SCENE IN THE RUINS—VAMPA AND THE STRANGER—DONALD PUZZLED—A HUNT ARRANGED.

"How came such a place as this in the heart of a forest?"

It was Donald who spoke, and he was addressing Ina, with whom he was walking among the ruins of an old building, strangely like the old abbeys of England.

The similarity was not complete, for the ruins among which Ina and Donald were wandering were of cruder form than those glorious pieces of masonry which have beautified our country.

It had been erected at a much earlier age; but by whom?

Ina, woman-like, was not disposed to speculate on the subject.

She had other thoughts in her head.

"Nobody knows," she said, indifferently; "and I do

not suppose anybody will ever find out. Donald, there is one thing I wish you would not do."

"And what is that?" he asked.

"Go so much into the forest alone," said Ina.

"I only take my turn seeking for game," he said, lightly; "and I am very fond of shooting."

"Yes—yes; but you should take your friend with you."

"Jack is helping to make the waggon for the women and children. Now, Ina, what cause is there for fear?"

"Have you forgotten Vampa?" asked Ina. "You would not tell me that he had attempted your life, but I *screwed* it out of your friend Jack."

"Jack is very fond of you," said Donald, with a side glance at her.

"I cannot help that," said Ina, with an impatient toss of her head. "It has nothing to do with what I am saying to you. Beware of Vampa! He has been a good watch-dog to me in his time, but I always knew since I was a little girl that he could be dangerous in his hatred of others."

They were standing in a part of the ruins close to a gap in the wall, and Ina stopped. Donald took her hand.

"Ina," he cried, "I ought to be more grateful than I am, but I do not wish to encourage your fears, which I feel are groundless. Vampa slunk away like a whipped dog, and his threats I fear no more than the yelpings of a brute."

"You do not know, I say," returned Ina.

As she spoke she raised her eyes to his, but only for a moment. They were drawn away by a spectacle that for the moment froze her heart with terror.

Two men were crouching by the gap, looking at Donald with faces distorted with hatred.

The other was standing back a little, and exhibited no weapon.

Donald saw the expression which came into her face, and, observing her gaze was fixed on something behind him, he wheeled round, and was just in time to see the two men disappear.

They went so suddenly that at first he was not sure he had really seen anybody at all.

Then he had a faint idea one of the faces was that of Vampa.

And last of all, he had a still fainter idea that the other face was familiar to him.

But whose it was he could not tell.

Nor had he time to reflect just then, or as he made a movement in the direction of the gap Ina grasped his arm.

"No—no," she said; "there are two of them."

"What would it matter," he said, "if there were a dozen? I must see if it is Vampa. We are not far from the outpost. Ina, do not detain me, *please*."

She did not leave go of him, but she moved forward with him. It was already too late; Ina's detention had enabled the men to get away.

Within fifty yards of the ruin was the forest, into which they had doubtless plunged.

"You see what Vampa is—a cur!" said Donald." "Although he had another with him he ran the moment he was discovered."

"He is secret and cruel," said Ina; "and he came to kill you. Promise me you will not go into the wood again alone?"

"Who was the other man?" asked Donald, by way of evading the promise. "Do you know the face?"

"No," replied Ina.

"I only caught the merest glimpse of it," said Donald, "but I am sure I know it."

They did not linger in the ruins, but set off across the country, until they came to a point from whence it sloped down to the river.

Then they arrived in sight of the camp—a very busy scene.

Only the rudest of erections for shelter had been put up, because it was known they were only to be temporary, and everyone was busy.

The women were washing clothes in the river, the children running to and fro, and the men engaged in making various things—from a large waggon downwards.

Captain Frosby, Danby, and two men were engaged in

breaking-in some horses which had been found wild, and captured by means of the lasso.

Jack Johnson, who was handy with tools, having in his boyhood shown a leaning towards amateur carpentering, was as busy as the rest of them.

"Hallo, Donald!" he said, cheerily. "Don't you feel ashamed of yourself idling about while others are earning their bread like true descendants of Adam?"

"I have had a bit of an adventure, Jack," said Donald.

"Is that anything new?"

"No; but this has an odd side to it. I can't remember a man's face I have seen."

Ina did not linger there. She was a ruler among the women, and had constantly to assist them with much-needed advice. Ready in resources, she helped them over many a difficulty, showed them how to make the best of everything, and was idolised by them.

Donald told Jack his story, and the volatile whistler looked very grave.

"I quite agree with Ina," he said. "You ought not to go about alone."

"On my word," replied Donald, impulsively, "one would think I was a child or in my dotage."

"Nothing of the sort, dear boy," said Jack. "But with a sneaking foe like Vampa we can't be too wary. It is only care, dictated by common-sense. Look here! I will take a day off my job to-morrow, and we will have a hunt around for Vampa. I shall have very little compunction in shooting him now."

"But who is the other fellow?" exclaimed Donald, with a puzzled face.

"Oh! hang him!"

"By all means, Jack, when we get him. I would not bother about him, but I know the face, and I am sure it is one I have cause to dislike."

"It must be somebody we have seen here."

"I don't think so. Besides, who is there missing? No, Jack; that idea won't do."

"It will have to do for me," said Jack, philosophically, "for I have no other."

Danby at this moment rode up on a small, stiff-built

mustang, which exhibited a deal of white about the eye, and evidently objected to the bridle, but was under the control of a firm hand, and had to submit to it.

To him, also, the story was told, and he listened to it as his steed moved from this side to that, reared a little, bucked a bit, and exhibited all the idiosyncracies of a half-tamed steed of a wild waste land.

"I don't like that yarn," said Danby. "If there are two—"

"And there *were* two," interposed Donald.

"Beg pardon; of course," rejoined Danby, "as there were two, there may be more. In a country like this, adventurers in search of gold or silver may drop down at any time, and they are always dangerous. If they can get what they come for they are peaceable enough; but if they don't they will take what they can get and in any way they can."

"I have it!" said Donald. "I know who it is."

"Out with it, then, for goodness' sake," said Jack Johnson.

"Mike Barlow," said Donald. "That's the man—I can swear to it."

"Almost impossible!" said Jack.

"He is altered," said Donald; "much thinner than he used to be, and had other clothes; but Mike Barlow it is, I am sure."

"As for the possibility of it being him," said Danby, "a man might cross such a country as Patagonia, although, of course, the odds are terribly against him. The natives of the interior are veritable devils. Why, they would *eat* him!"

"Eat Mike Barlow!" exclaimed Jack. "Well, if they would do that, all I can say is—no, I won't say it."

"It is dangerous to have such men near us," said Danby, "and I will speak to Frosby about it. If he takes my advice he will have a hunt for them to-morrow."

"Meanwhile, they may get away."

"Let them go, then. I, for one, don't want the job of hanging anyone or anything, not even a wild dog."

He rode back to Captain Frosby, and they conferred together for a time.

CHAPTER XXI.

₁AN-HUNTING—ON THE TRAIL AND BEING TRACKED— DARING DANBY DOES A COOL THING.

ALL night long a watch was set round the camp, and if Vampa had been daring enough to seek them he hated beneath its shelter, he would assuredly have paid the penalty with his life.

But he held aloof, and the sleepers were not troubled with any sounds of alarm. Early in the morning all were astir.

Arrangements for scouting the **wood had already** been made.

Half of the available men were to start early, make-a circuit of it to the other side, and then spread out to beat the bush, just as they do a pheasant covert at home.

As soon as the two men were espied a shot was to be fired, and everybody bear about in the direction of it.

Danby, Donald, and Jack had to play the part of "sportsmen," advancing so as to meet the beaters. The lower camp was to be the charge of Captain Frosby and the rest of the men.

Now, the wood was of great extent, and could only be beaten in detail—the men would have to take it in slices, working up and down, as it were; and they received instructions to do their work quietly.

Before the light of day had fairly arrived the beaters set out, and an hour later the three friends faced for the wood.

A few words of adieu to Ina from Donald, and a caution from Captain Frosby not to stray far from each other, and they were gone.

Ina was sorrowful at heart, but she was made of the stuff that shows little external grief, and, with a cheery face, she went about the business of the day.

The three friends did not keep close together, but walked a few yards apart, generally within hail of each other. They walked to and fro, disturbing many a wild creature in its lair, among them a species of puma, that at first threatened to show fight, but finally slunk away snarling.

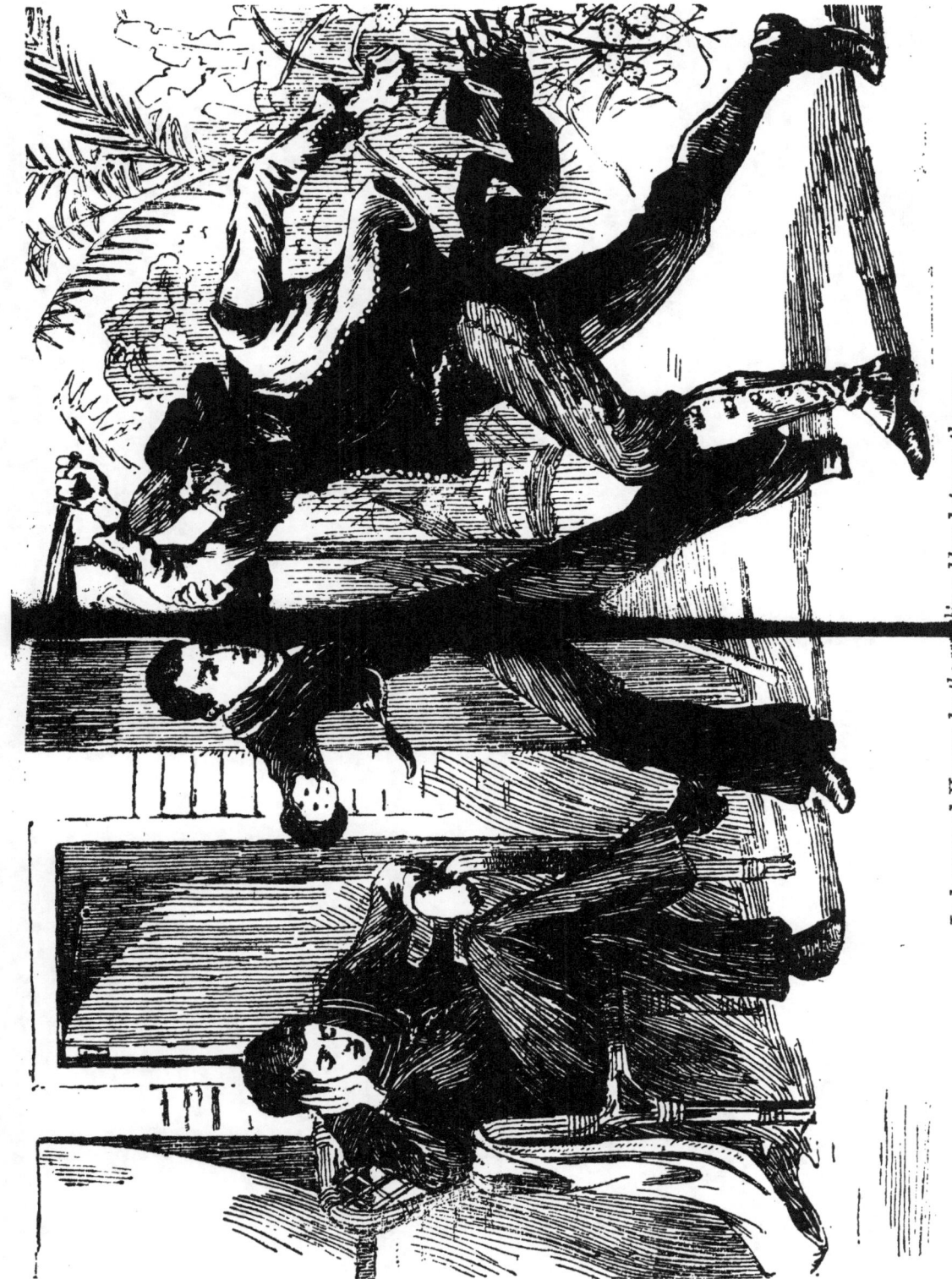

Jack grasped Vamira by the arm ... him a blow between the eyes.

There were parts of the wood that were quite inaccessible to men not provided with implements to cut through the brushwood. Our friends had nothing of the sort with them. Where Vampa and Mike Barlow could go, there they could go also.

Steadily to and fro they tramped for hours, and had not yet met the beaters. When half the morning was passed they struck a trail.

Danby knew more of such things than either Jack or Donald, and he was sure that it was the trail of two men.

"They are walking in Indian file," Danby explained; "the hindermost one keeping in the steps of the foremost."

They followed it here and there, losing it in places and finding it again, and after bearing generally away for the time it turned back towards the camp.

"As I thought," said Danby; "they do not intend to leave us."

But a little further on the trail was lost, and all their attempts to find it were futile.

Being in a dense wood they were now somewhat out of their reckoning, and not one of the three were at all sure that they were in a way to meet with the beaters, who would march straight through the wood without a halt until they came to the other side.

They stood still and listened for the sounds of movement, but there were none that could be traced to human beings.

"Dancing about after this trail," said Danby, "we have got right out of the track of our friends."

So it appeared; and, as all were tired, they decided to halt, and partake of some of the food they had with them.

The wood here was so dense that very little sunlight penetrated it, and there was upon it the chill of night as it is known in warmer countries than ours.

Jack's proposal to light a fire was not negatived.

"It may serve to attract our friends," said Donald. "The little breeze there is blows in their direction, and it may carry the smoke to them."

Although he did not like to confess it, Danby had lost his way.

Winding about here and there, turning this way and that, he had entirely lost his reckoning.

As for the wind, that was no guide, as it might have shifted since they started.

Jack got a lot of dry wood together and made a fire, before which they sat and partook of the bread and meat they had with them.

For drink they had cold, strong tea, which has to a healthy person all th advantage of a stimulant, without the unnerving after-effect.

Jack was disposed to talk, and not being checked, he rattled away on various subjects, wondering, among other things, what had become of his old master, Basil Bennett.

He also spoke of his ward Isabel.

Now, Danby had never heard the full story of Isabel's disappearance, and Jack, at his request, enlightened him.

He was deeply interested, asking for a description of her, and when he learnt that she was as beautiful a girl as one could wish to see, his interest in her was not in any way lessened, you may be sure.

Jack was on the point of finishing his story when a slight rustling sound, about twenty yards away, fell upon Danby's ears.

He did not exhibit any signs of having heard it, but continued to ask questions of Jack, while his eyes and ears were busy in endeavouring to detect whether the sound arose from man or beast.

He had the knack—rather an uncommon gift—of seeing things at a short distance pretty clearly without apparently looking at them.

He was assisted in this respect by the long lashes that fringed his eyes, and he now sat quite still, with the lids drooping, but with his gaze fixed ahead. In front of him — say, fifty feet away — there was a huge tree, from behind which the sound, he was convinced, had come.

On that tree he fixed his eyes.

" So you think, Jack," he said, " that the girl was really drowned ?"

"I have no doubt of it," replied Jack.

"And that it was her corpse you saw?"

"There was a ring upon the hand, exactly like that described in the bill."

"Well, there is no knowing," said Danby; "but in this world you can't tell. I am going to smoke. Phew! Don't you feel how this fire draws the damp from the ground?"

"No," replied Donald, "I don't feel it.'

"Nor I," said Jack.

"That is the advantage of having very young bones," said Danby, rising; "but I can detect damp instantly, and, as I have had swamp fever once, I don't think I'll run the risk of having it again."

As he spoke he started to his feet, stretched his arms, and, drawing out his cigar-case, extracted a small cigar from it.

Sauntering to a tree close by, he leant his back against it and lighted his cigar.

"How could the world get along without tobacco?" he said, "as it undoubtedly did once upon a time."

"One might ask," said Donald, laughing, "how it got along without steam or gunpowder, or how it gets along without some of the things which will be discovered by-and-bye."

"Something in that," said Danby, as he put his hand into his jacket pocket. "Of course, it is no use speculating on such things."

He drew his hand out and put it behind his back.

A faint click was heard.

"What's that?" asked Jack.

"Only an old trick of mine," replied Danby, "of making a noise with my tongue when I feel I am shut out of an argument. By the way, boys, I've had enough of this wild-goose chase. What say you?"

"Enough of it?" exclaimed Donald, opening his eyes.

"Yes; those fellows are much too cunning for us, and this wood is a regular maze. I vote we get back to the camp without delay."

"Oh! dash it," said Jack, giving vent to a dolorous whistle.

"Will you tell me what else is to be done?" asked Danby.

"No; we look to you," said Jack.

"Then I say—go back!" said Danby, calmly; "but there is no hurry for a few moments. I have a little job in hand."

As he spoke, he suddenly brought his arm out from behind his back, disclosing the fact that he had a revolver in his grasp.

Leaping forward a pace he pointed it towards the tree and fired.

A wild scream was heard, and Jack and Donald leapt to their feet. Writhing and twisting on the ground, holding his head between his hands, was Mike Barlow.

At the same moment another man was heard to dash away, and Danby sent a second bullet after him.

A fierce cry responded to the shot but nobody fell, and the second man got away.

"I hoped to get the two," said Danby, coolly; "but one bird is better than no game."

As he spoke he strided towards Mike Barlow, who continued to clasp his head, writhing and moaning.

The three friends ran up to him.

"Get out of this," cried Danby. "What are you barking about? You are not dead."

"Oh—oh!" groaned Mike; "my skull is rent in two."

"Not it," said Danby, as he jerked off his hat; "but it's been a close thing for you. I've ploughed off a lot of hair and a bit of the scalp. Get up, I say."

"My head's red-hot!" shrieked Barlow.

But he got up and stood before the author of his present anguish with a sullen face, twitching with pain.

"Now you'll tell us," said Danby, "how you came here?"

"Mostly on my legs," replied Barlow.

"Listen to me, Mike," said Danby, with all the suavity of a nobleman; "this is not the deck of the Water Fiend, and Carker is not here to encourage your insolence. Give me another reply like that and I will shoot you as I would a worthless dog—for a worthless dog you are."

"I tramped part of the way and was dragged some of

it," said Barlow. "I came through fire, water, and a land of devils."

"Patagonia?" said Danby.

"Yes," replied Barlow, "the pal I had with me—well —he is *eaten*. Yes, it's a fact, and it's shocked you to hear it. What must it ha' been for me to SEE it?"

"Where did you get those clothes from?" asked Danby.

"They belonged to a man as was eaten, too," replied Barlow. "Lor'—oh! my head. The devils had half-a-dozen of us—all but me and my pal picked up on the coast. We was inland, making our way as well as we could to civilisation, when they dropped on us. We were all skin and bone, and I'm blessed if they didn't take us to their camp and *fatten us* for a feast day as was coming on."

Danby looked keenly at him. There was no doubt he was telling the truth, although, as a matter of habit, he would rather have lied.

CHAPTER XXII.

MIKE BARLOW'S TRIBULATIONS—HOW HE MET VAMPA —HE IS GIVEN A CHANCE OF LIFE.

"AND so you were all fattened and saved to be eaten?" said Danby.

"That was it," said Barlow; "and I'm a poor hand at spinning a yarn, so I'll just get through it sharp. They had us all out one morning and stripped us stark naked. I stood next to a Yankee pedlar chap who prayed and cussed in turns, and snivelled through both. I felt sick, for I knowed pretty well what was coming. They fell on my pal first, danced round him, knocked him on the head, and hung him up by a fire.

"I can't tell you no more about it," said Barlow, turning white; "you must guess it. I ain't no saint, and I've eaten rough vittles in my time, but that was a settler. Then they went for another, and such a tumbling and banging of metal things, like gongs, you never heard. We was all surrounded by them warmints, and getting away seemed hopeless, but I thought I'd try; so I makes a grab at the pedlar's clothes as happened to be nearest, and run for it.

"Lor'! how I DID run," said Barlow. "Wild cats and dogs wouldn't have overtaken me. But then, very few of the beggars gave chase You see, as I reckon, they were afraid of losing the rest and not catching me. So, naked as I was born, I bolted along. Two only chivied me into the wood, where I had to tramp along, through thorns, and all sorts of vegetable knives and scissors—I was almost as much cut up as if I'd stopped to be eaten."

He perspired now as he thought of that time.

No doubt he had suffered keenly; but he could not expect much sympathy from his hearers, who were all grimly smiling.

"You got away?" said Danby.

"Yes, and led the life of a wild beast for a fortnight or more, eating roots or anything I could get, and never at rest for fear I should be dropped on. Oh! I have suffered; but I got clear o' that devil's home at last."

"And where did you meet Vampa?" asked Donald.

"Oh! Vampa—him what I've just parted from?" said Barlow.

Danby quietly cocked his revolver again, and Barlow hastened to say—

"In course his name is Vampa, if YOU say it is; but he never told me so. I was drawn to the coast by the smoke of a fire, and when I got there I saw a whole village in a blaze. Vampa was there, and we palled up. He said he wanted a pal, being lonely like, and kind o' swore me in. So we chummed, and in course, I felt bound to do as he did; but kill me if ever I thought it was old friends he led me on the trail of."

"At least you knew it yesterday," said Danby.

"I did," replied Barlow; "but I'd got thick with him and didn't see any way to swear off. You can't do it when you've got mixed up with a chap like him."

"Donald," said Danby, "what shall we do with him?"

"As far as I am concerned, nothing," Donald answered. "I think he has paid a pretty dear price for his former villainy, and now, perhaps, will try to behave like an honest man."

"Gimme the chance," said Barlow, "and two or'nary honest men won't be a match for me. Lor'! how my head do smart. But you was allus a clean shot, Mister Danby, I'll say that for you."

"No soft sawder required, thank you," said Danby. "Now, understand me. Your life is spared on condition that you give us no trouble, but do just what you are told."

Barlow was beginning to swear that he could do all and more than any man could tell him to do, but Danby checked him.

"That will do," he said. "Go wrong again, and you may make your will. Now, where does Vampa hang out?"

"Anywheres and nowheres," replied Barlow. "We've slept in the open, just where we happen to be."

"How have you lived?"

"There was some provisions left in the village—we got em out of the captain's house—but they are all gone, and we was thinking of making a raid on that camp of yours to-night."

"Put your handkerchief round your head and follow me," said Danby. "Jack, Donald, you boys, keep behind him; if he shows any tricks drop him."

"You may leave that to me," said Donald, quietly.

Danby's ears now caught the sound of men breaking through the wood, and as he darted off loud shouts and cries for help were heard.

"Vampa!" he cried. "Boys, keep your eye on Barlow! Hurry up there!"

Danby sprang forward, and Barlow kept up with him.

When he HAD to yield there was no man who bent with more readiness than this worthy.

The cause of the commotion was soon discovered.

A short distance on Danby discovered one of his men writhing on the ground with a cruel wound in his chest, and a little further away Vampa was struggling with two more.

The others, attracted by the cries, were coming up—heard, but as yet unseen.

Danby sprang forward, and with a blow of his fist laid Vampa sprawling on the ground.

He dropped a knife as he fell, and he was speedily disarmed of every other weapon he possessed.

Means to bind a prisoner in case of capture had not been forgotten, and a few feet of rope, expertly knotted, secured him.

He speedily recovered from the blow, to find himself captive, and he made an effort to release himself.

Finding it was of no avail, he sulkily yielded.

From under his bushy eyebrows he looked at Donald keenly, not only then, but during the entire march back to the cave.

He seemed to have no eyes for anybody else, not even for his late companion Barlow, at whom, indeed, he did not so much as glance.

The success of the searchers was rewarded by the acclamations of those in the camp, and Captain Frosby and Ina came out to meet them.

Sternly the captain looked at Vampa, who hung his head and shivered.

He did not look at Ina. He was completely cowed in her presence.

The story of the capture was soon told, and Barlow was told to join the men in the camp.

Ina was desired to go back to the women-folk, and a court was formed to try Vampa.

Captain Frosby was the judge, and Jack and Danby were the accusers.

The story of his attempts on the life of our hero need not be repeated.

They were briefly told, and Vampa was asked what he had to say in defence.

"Nothing," he said; "it would be useless. The English liars have your ear—I have lost it."

"Vampa," said Captain Frosby, "there was a time when I trusted you; but of late I have doubted whether you are the man I supposed you to be. Do you remember how I first found you?"

"Yes. I was hanging to a tree."

"Where you had been left, as you told me, by a party of horse-thieves. Was that true?"

"No," said Vampa, defiantly; "it was I who was the

horse-thief. I have been all things in turn—pirate, brigand, thief, murderer! See! I confess the worst. Now do all you can. I have killed none of yours, but you may take my life. Forget the faithfulness of years, and hang me because the accursed Englese wish it."

"What is to be done with this man?" asked Frosby, turning to Danby.

"I cannot be his judge."

"And you, Donald?"

"No; I cannot sentence him."

"Then I must," said Captain Frosby; "for the man is dangerous, and cannot be trusted. I think I can guess his secret. Go away, you three of the tender heart, and leave him to me and my men."

They obeyed, for, despite their repugnance to take a fellow creature's life, they felt that he was right. Vampa was as dangerous as a wild beast, and, like a wild beast, he must be put out of the way.

They retraced their steps to the camp, from whence the spot where Vampa had been tried could not be seen.

Jack Johnson went back to his usual work, Danby strolled up and down, and Donald joined Ina, who was standing on the river's bank, thoughtfully watching the flowing water.

She heard Donald's footstep, and awoke from her day-dream.

"Well," she said, "what have you done with him?"

"*I?* Nothing," replied Donald. "By your father's desire we have left him to be judge."

"He was a good dog once," said Ina, "but, like the Cuba hound, he is not to be trusted always. For the sake of others he must die."

"Against me he was especially bitter," said Donald. "I wonder why?"

Ina looked up at him with a faint flush upon her face

"You do not know?" she said.

"No," he replied.

"Nor guess? But how should you? I only guess it rom things which I remember, and which I did not notice at the time. I cannot tell you what it is; it does not matter. Here comes my father and the men. Vampa is not with him, and we need not trouble ourselves more about him."

As the captain did not approach them Donald left Ina and joined him near where Jack Johnson was busy.

"We have hanged him," said the captain. "As I found him years ago so I leave him. There was too much black blood in his veins for me to spare him.

Turning to the men with him he bade them let Vampa hang an hour, and then dig a grave and bury him.

Then all went about their various avocations for awhile, and Donald gave Jack a hand with his work.

Danby and the captain returned to horse-breaking, and so an hour passed.

At the expiration of that time, or thereabouts, half-a-dozen men sallied forth with pick and spade to pay the last offices to the dead, and although it was but a knave—and a sorry one, also—who was to be buried, a strange quietude fell upon the camp.

All labour ceased, and speaking only in whispers the men and women watched the six men go up the slope and disappear.

Then they talked a little louder, but work was not resumed.

A few minutes elapsed, and then one of the men reappeared, and came bounding back to the camp.

"What's wrong now ?" asked Jack.

He and others ran forward to meet the man. He was stopped and surrounded by quite a crowd.

He was nearly out of breath with running and excitement, but presently he got out a word—

"Vampa !"

"What is it ?" asked Donald, pushing his way to the front. "Is he not dead ?"

"He is GONE !" the man almost shrieked.

"Gone? Impossible !"

"It is too true. The tree is there, the rope is there, the very noose is there ; but Vampa is NOT ! He is the very devil !"

Captain Frosby and Danby had now joined the group, and on hearing this they both set off for the scene of execution.

All the men followed, leaving the wondering women behind. Ina had strayed on down the bank of the river.

She had no desire to hear any more of the pitiful story of her once faithful watch-dog.

The story of the man was quite true. He had told the truth, and nothing but the truth.

There was the tree, rope, and noose, but Vampa was gone.

" How did he get out of that ?" was the general query.

Had he received help the rope would certainly have been cut, but the inference was clear.

He had succeeded by some means in wriggling out of it.

For some time they stood wondering, walking round the tree, and doing many useless things, after the manner of men when nonplussed.

" Yes ; he got out of that rope," said Captain Frosby. " But how ?"

" Perhaps that is not a very important matter," replied Danby. " The chief thing we have to consider is that he is *gone ;* and in my opinion it would be better to have half-a-dozen wolves prowling around."

They moved off slowly, and not a little troubled.

The wolf that has once been snared grows wary, but it does not abandon its ferocious instincts, but rather brings them more into play.

Vampa would not abandon his revenge.

They sauntered back to the camp, where orders were at once given for none of the women or children to stray, and Captain Frosby looked around for Ina.

She was not in sight.

Hurriedly he asked where she had last been seen, and they pointed down the river.

It wound about a good deal until it disappeared round an arm of the wood about half-a-mile away.

Surely, Ina had not gone beyond that point ?

Sudden, terrible fears took possession of him, and he set off in the direction Ina had taken.

He reached the bend, and then found that the trees grew down to the very water, so that the bank came practically to an end.

"Ina!" he cried.

His voice reverberated in the wind, but no answering cry came back.

"Ina—Ina!"

And all the reply he got was a mocking echo.

"Oh! my child—my darling!" he cried, clutching the branch of a low-growing tree for support. "Can it be possible that you have met with so terrible a fate as to fall into the clutches of that monster?"

CHAPTER XXIII.

THE TRACKING OF INA—MORE MYSTERY—NEWS OF THE WATER FIEND—A RESCUE PARTY.

CAPTAIN FROSBY could do nothing alone, so back he staggered, rather than walked, to the camp. He was seen approaching, and many went out to greet him, Donald among the number.

"My daughter!" was all he could say at first, as he pointed to the wood.

It was enough.

A cry burst from Donald's lips, and it was taken up by all there.

No more words were needed.

Everybody grasped what was in their leader's mind.

Not only had Vampa escaped, but he had succeeded in carrying off his master's daughter.

And now, for the first time, the nature of Vampa's devotion flashed upon all there, and awful possibilities rose up before them.

Such a man would destroy anything he loved rather than another should possess it.

Men of his nature are more cruel than the beasts.

There was no time wasted in discussing matters.

The men who were armed at once made for the wood; those who were not ran back to the camp to procure weapons.

Among the foremost to reach the wood was Donald, and he was plunging wildly into it when he was checked by the voice of Danby.

"Steady, Don, old fellow! Let us find the trail."

There was need of a cool head then, for blind anger only leads men astray.

Donald paused, and Jack and Danby joined him.

The latter had been casting his eyes around, and on a bank hard by he saw the fragment of a torn garment.

"This way," he said, "and go easy and silent for awhile. Poor Frosby! he is quite overcome."

The ground was too hard to leave any footprints; but there were bent twigs and crushed flowers to guide them.

High above their heads grew the giant trees; around them was all the tangled foliage of a virgin forest.

Already they were ahead of the rest, and, with Danby to the fore, they hurried on.

It was impossible for any man to break through such a forest without leaving some signs that would serve for practised eyes.

So many ferns and flowers, so much bush, and in places the ground was strewn with rotten twigs and branches.

"We are on the right trail," said Danby; "but step lightly and speak low. If he finds us gaining upon him he may kill her."

Donald made no answer.

His eyes were blood-shot, and his cheeks had lost all their colour.

The intensity of his emotions had entirely changed the look of his face.

Jack was amazed and terrified; for the time he appeared quite ten years older.

Vampa—if it were indeed he ahead—had made good headway, and, although they proceeded at a rapid rate, they travelled for an hour and came no nearer to him.

The trail, as they judged, and rightly, too, led straight back in the direction of the the sea, and suddenly they came upon a spot where the earth was softer.

There they found not only the footmarks of one man, but many, and, what was stranger still, the signs of a struggle.

In one place there was a stain of blood upon the ground, which showed that a man had been injured.

"What does this mean?" exclaimed Danby.

They all stopped in sheer amazement, from which they were aroused by Jack springing forward and picking up something from the ground.

It was a small piece of white linen, part of a lady's handkerchief.

Now there was only one woman that was known to carry such a thing as a white handkerchief in those parts, and that was Ina, and it flashed upon Donald that she was tearing up her handkerchief and using it as boys use paper for the chase.

Without wasting any time in vain speculations over the indications of many footsteps, Donald and his friends hunted around for signs of the continuation of the trail, and speedily found them still leading seaward.

Twenty yards further in the forest they found another piece of white linen.

Now all surmise was at an end. Ina was helping those who might possibly pursue by giving signs of the route taken.

With set lips and eager as a bloodhound, Donald now led the pursuit, and was so quick in his movements that his friends could hardly keep up with him.

On through that virgin forest they went, winding here and there to the line of the trail, which deviated to avoid fallen trees and other obstacles.

They came to a slowly flowing brook, and Danby saw that it was still muddy with the crossing of men— assuredly, then, they were not far ahead.

The bank on the opposite side was soft clay, and there the footmarks were so numerous that Danby was sure there could not be less than a dozen men.

This was a fact that had to be made a note of.

" Donald," he said, softly, " we MUST be cautious now, or we may defeat the end we have in view. Listen for a moment." ·

They stood still and listened.

Behind them there was no sound of movement, so that they must have far outdistanced their friends ; but ahead a faint clanking was heard.

" Armed men," said Danby.

" What of that ?" said Donald. " Let us get on."

"My dear boy," said Danby, "you know I am not troubled with childish fears, but we must be cautious."

"Cautious," said Donald, "and Ina's life and honour in peril !"

"Can we help her," asked Danby, "if we madly rush into a horde of foes who may be too strong for us ?"

There was no gainsaying this question, and Donald, with a gesture of despair, said he would be guided by his cooler friend.

Danby did not waste time, but moved on at once, and now their way was clearer.

The party ahead had abandoned their in and out progress among the bushes, and were cutting a passage here and there.

Danby's experience told him that the men were using cutlasses.

"They are sailors," he said, "and they are going in the direction of the bay where the Fairy is lying."

"Can it be Captain Frosby's own men who have committed this outrage ?" asked Jack.

"No—I think not," said Danby, pursing his lip ; "but one cannot tell. Ina is a very pretty girl, and these half-caste fellows cannot be trusted."

"So the theory of Vampa falls to the ground," said Donald, bitterly.

"I fear so," returned Danby. "Hush !"

He stopped short, and the others pulled up beside him.

Ahead was heard the voices of men, one louder than the rest.

"Come on," said Danby, suddenly warming up, "neck or nothing. If we make a sudden dash upon them we may be victorious. If not—exit Danby, Donald, and Jack the Whistler. Not another word, dear boys."

They were all active and light of tread. With the speed and quietude of greyhounds they pursued their trail until they suddenly came upon open ground.

It was simply a space in the wood about fifty feet across, and it was occupied by a dozen men.

Bound and gagged, Ina lay upon the ground, a pitiable sight that fairly maddened Donald.

The men were resting after their journey through the wood, and were passing sundry wine bottles around.

They had no inkling of an adversary being near, and when the three friends dashed into the open they were completely taken by surprise.

They carried cutlasses and pistols, but ere they had time to use either a third of their number had fallen writhing on the ground.

The rest drew their cutlasses and revolvers, and made an effort to defend themselves ; but the attack was too sudden for their nerves, and with a few cuts and thrusts, and a wildly aimed shot or two, they fled.

Five of their number lay seriously wounded on the ground.

One, indeed, who had been cut down by Danby, was past all hope of recovery.

Donald went at once to Ina's assistance, cut her bonds, and raised her in his arms.

"My darling !" he cried.

She could not answer him, save by a look.

The excitement of the last hour, and the suddenness of the rescue, had quite overcome her.

Jack and Danby disarmed the wounded men, and proceeded to attend to their injuries with all the assiduity of surgeons on a battle-field.

Danby was binding the arm of a man, who muttered a few words in broken English.

"Who are your your fellows ?" Danby asked.

"Seamen of ze Watare Fee—end," was the reply.

"What are you doing here ?"

"Mister Carkare send us to do vat mischeef ve can."

"To a woman ?"

"No, sare—ve hurt not ze vooman ; ve only steal her."

Without entering into any discussion as to the palliation of his offence, Danby asked him where the Water Fiend was lying.

"About two miles south of ze Carita," was the reply.

This was disquieting news, as it was not far from where the Fairy lay hidden.

A close search of the coast would inevitably lead to her discovery.

But he did not question the man on this point.

It would not help the Fairy in any way.

Having bound up the wounds of two men, and finding Jack Johnson had attended to the rest, he returned to Donald, who was leading Ina gently to and fro to assist her in regaining the full use of her limbs, and said—

"We had better get back now."

"And these men ?" said Jack.

"Oh ! they can return to their ship," said Danby.

Dropping his voice, he asked—

"What the deuce can we do with them ?"

Nothing, absolutely nothing, unless they killed them in cold blood, which would go sorely against the grain with our friends.

"Now, you fellows," said Danby, "your lives are spared, and you can get back to your ship. But don't hurry—travel slowly."

He turned to the man who was mortally wounded, and was now on the point of death.

"Ah ! here is one who will not travel at all. Can I do anything for you ?"

He stooped over the man, who glared at him like a wounded beast, and hissed out a few unintelligible words.

Then he made an effort to rise, and fell back again.

All was over.

"He is your friend," said Danby to the other men. "You have no means to bury him, but cover his face."

One of the men drew a coarse handkerchief from his pocket, and covered the still features of the dead man.

Ina, Donald, and Jack were already going back, walking very slowly ; for Ina was stiff and sore.

Danby had the cutlasses of the wounded men under his arm, and all their revolvers stuck in his belt.

He looked a most formidable being, quite a pirate of the old school.

But there was compassion on his face as he looked at the dead man.

"You were a babe once," he said, in a low, musical tone, "and a mother loved you. What visions had she of your future when she held you to her breast ? Surely, she saw nothing of such an end as this ?"

"It is a good thing," he muttered, as he turned round and walked slowly away in the wake of his friends, "that those who brought us into the world had no insight into our future. Oh! mother mine, so loving and kind, merciful was the hand of death when it took you away and shut your eyes to the future of your son."

For a moment he was quite overcome by some memory of the past.

His head drooped, and something suspiciously like a tear fell from one of his eyes.

Then in a moment he was erect again, and striding up to Jack Johnson, who was whistling "The flag that has braved a thousand years."

Donald and Ina were moving on a little quicker ahead.

"We may call this a lucky business," said Danby; "but how the deuce this fellow came to drop exactly upon us is more than I can make out."

"Perhaps they have been playing the spy upon us all the time."

"It may be so, Jack, and I am a fool not to have asked them. But perhaps they would have lied."

"What has become of that blackguard, Vampa?" said Jack.

"That is what we shall have to find out," replied Danby. "Phew! what a noisy, ramping, tearing thing is life! I don't care for land. If the Fairy hasn't got into the clutches of the Water Fiend she must be almost ready now. I vote we get away to sea."

"Will Frosby go?"

"Not without Ina; and as to having a woman on board—well, it wouldn't do, Jack. We have two or three accounts to square around—above all, with Carker."

"I can't understand why it is, but I am always thinking about old Bennett. I dreamt of him last night. I thought—"

But what Jack thought was cut short by an exclamation ahead, and, looking up, he saw Captain Frosby holding Ina in his arms.

He had just met them on his way to assist in rescuing her.

Behind him were half-a-dozen of his men

Great was the joy of that meeting, and when the captain heard all he was, as the others had been, more amazed than ever.

So it was not Vampa. Where, then, was that nefarious and very slippery malefactor, who seemed to be born to die some other death apart from the rope?

And Carker had not, as they hoped, sailed away, but for some reason had kept about the coast.

As regards the peril the Fairy was in, he quite agreed with Danby. Lying as she was without the means of defending herself, or, rather without being in order for defence, she was at the mercy of any foe strong enough to assail her.

No time ought to have been lost.

"It alters all our plans," Captain Frosby said. "You must go at once with all the men I can spare, and see whether so great a disaster as losing her has befallen us."

CHAPTER XXIV.

STRONG IN DEFENCE—HELPLESS TO ATTACK—A MEETING IN A LONELY PLACE—THE DUEL.

"AND if the Fairy is still safe?" said Danby.

"Proceed with completing her fighting arrangements, and await my coming. There are two things I must do first. Find Vampa, and place the women and children, with sufficient men to guard them, in a place of safety."

"Suppose Carker finds the Fairy after our arrival, and attacks us?"

"I leave everything to your judgment. Do the best you can in my interest and your own. I give you *carte blanche*. You command, and here are your officers, Donald and Jack. They have a fair idea of sea-work now."

There was no delay between, and no fuss over parting so soon.

Donald was sorry to part with Ina and she with him, but a touch of the hand, and a glance into each other's eyes, was the only adieu.

Danby took the men that were there, and Captain

Frosby promised to send others from the camp to join him.

Good-byes were exchanged, and the party for the Fairy turned back, and keeping to the trail, once more hastened through the forest.

All were eager to know the worst or best ; and three of the band, at least, were anxious to get at Carker.

"I want a brush with the fellow," said Danby. "If I get the opportunity I will sink that accursed Water Fiend. The guns of the Fairy are small, but they are A 1 in make."

"There is one thing we have all overlooked," said Jack Johnson. "A rendezvous for all."

"Frosby will look out for us," said Danby. "He must come after us. We cannot come back to him. Our place, is on board the Fairy—that is, if the Fairy is left to us."

They reached the spot of the recent encounter, and saw a pile of branches and leaves, under which the dead man lay.

It was not a pleasant sight, and they hurried on.

Again they were in a part of the wood unknown to them, and had to rely on the trail of their foes to guide them.

In half an hour they overtook the wounded men crawling back to the coast, who, on seeing Danby and his followers, thought that their last hour had come.

They feared that he had repented of his clemency, and returned to slaughter them.

"Mercy !" they cried, throwing themselves on their knees.

"There is nothing to fear," he said ; "we are bound for the coast," and passed on.

They cried out after him that he and those with him were "angels," and begged that he would take them as servants, slaves, anything so that they had no need to return to Carker's service, which they hated.

He bade them follow him as speedily as they could, and he would see what could be done for them, but he could not linger.

It was painful and ludicrous to see the efforts they

made to keep up with the party, but it could not be done. One by one they fell back to the rear, bewailing their hard lot.

On Danby hurried, with Donald and Jack beside him, and in another half-hour they were clear of the wood.

A wide stretch of open ground had to be traversed, and then there was another belt of wood, and beyond that the sea.

Without a rest they kept on, walking hard, across the plain, through the wood, and so on to the rocky coast, where Nature had excelled herself in piling up fantastic stonework.

On the right there were two jutting arms of rocks, running out about half-a-mile to seaward, and then bending round to each other until only a very narrow opening was left for any vessel to pass through, and even then the white caps of the waves showed that the passage was dangerous.

In that land-locked bay the Fairy had been taken, and the question that troubled our friends was, "Is she there still?"

The Water Fiend was not in sight, which was not reassuring. Perhaps she had already entered the bay.

On they hastened over the rocky ground until they came to an almost perpendicular slope, at the foot of which the mouth of the river—the same beside which they had recently camped—ran into the bay.

By the mouth of that river, well hidden rom view by some large mahogany trees that grew upon the promontory, lay the Fairy, to all appearance safe.

The impulse to shout was very great upon Donald and Jack, but Danby checked them.

"Warily there," he said. "One thing you have not noticed. Look yonder."

Following the direction of the arm he extended they saw the Water Fiend lying at anchor in the middle of the bay.

"It looks as if Carker has already won the prize," said Donald. "I fear we are too late."

It may be imagined with what feelings of doubt and fear our frends saw the position of things.

It looked, indeed, as if Carker had triumphed, and the Fairy had been his prize.

But Daring Danby was not the man to waste his time in vain speculation.

"Let us go down and make sure that all is lost," he said.

So down the broken cliff—a mixture of rock, sand, and trees—they went, all silent, and making as little noise as possible.

Two-thirds of the way they came in full view of the Fairy's deck, and then, to their intense delight, they saw Bob Bitters, who had been left in command, hurrying his men to assume the defensive.

He, therefore, had seen the boat approaching through a gap in the trees, which had been previously cleared to command a view of the bay.

But, while hurrying them, it was also manifest that he was urging them to be as quiet as possible in their movements.

From this Donald and the others inferred that the Water Fiend had no knowledge of the Fairy being there, and the boat was coming ashore for some other purpose than that of attack.

There was about thirty yards of water between the Fairy and the shore, and for our friends to get aboard it would be necessary to send a boat for them.

To attract Bob's attention, Danby picked up a stone, and hurled it as far as he could in the direction of the craft.

It fell about midway between, and the splash of it attracted Bob's attention, as it was intended to do.

He first looked at the water, then raised his eyes and espied his friends.

Bob, as a rule, was very far from being a demonstrative man; but, on seeing those he most longed to see, he could not refrain from cutting a caper.

Five minutes later the new arrivals were all on board, and a quiet shaking of hands was indulged in.

"It's about the time for you to be here, gentlemen," said Bob; "for, although I would have fought to the last, I'm not strong enough to stand against the Fiend lot."

"When did she arrive in the bay?" Danby asked.

"An hour ago."

"And they don't know you are here?"

"Not they. They've got some casks in the boats, and I reckon they are coming for water."

"They shall have fire instead."

Donald looked round the deck of the Fairy, and was delighted to see how she was equipped.

Some of the minor arrangements had yet to be attended to, but she had half-a-dozen nice little guns ready for action, and the men were armed with cutlasses and revolvers.

There was also a double stack of rifles, twenty in each, ready to hand.

"I've got 'em all loaded," said Bob, "and I think we ought to pretty well empty that boat."

It had shot out of sight now, but they could hear the sounds of the oars in the rowlocks getting louder and louder each moment.

In two minutes the boat would enter the mouth of the river, and be both in sight and within range.

"I don't know that we need stand on any ceremony with these fellows," said Danby; "they are walking, or, rather, rowing into an unintentional ambuscade, and they must take the consequences.'

"Carker is in the boat, I think," said Donald.

"He is."

"Leave him to me."

"No, me," said Jack.

"Excuse me," said Danby, "but I look upon Carker as my especial property. In his case, I gladly undertake the task of public executioner."

The bow of the Fairy pointed to the mouth of the river, and there the trio gathered with half-a-dozen men, each armed with a rifle.

Bob Bitters mistrusted himself as a marksman, and played the part of spectator.

"At close quarters, with the cutlass," he said, "I can cut about a bit, but them popguns ain't in my line. It's no use shooting at the stars or moon."

Click—click came the sound of the oars, and then the

nose of the boat was seen. Another moment and it was half in sight.

The bow oarsman happened to have his face in the direction of the Fairy, and immediately espied her.

With a yell of astonishment, he dug his oar into the water and partly stopped the boat.

But it came into full view, not with broadside on, as it would have done if the rowers had all continued to pull, but with the bow to the Fairy.

This was a fair mark, in its way, but the men rowing acted as a shield to Carker in the stern.

He had cast off his old attire of ship's officer, and was dressed like a stage grandee—flap hat, short jacket, velvet breeches, and silk stockings.

For one moment they saw him, and then he stooped down to avoid the fire of those on board the Fairy.

They heard him yell out two or three commands in Spanish to the men, who began to vigorously back their oars.

They kept the boat end on, which gave little to aim at ; but a volley from the Fairy dropped the bow oarsman and ripped two or three holes in the boat.

Then she was backed out of sight.

" That villain has the luck of the evil one," said Danby. " Well, ere it comes to a fight in the bay, Bob, we will get the Fairy out at once."

" Good Heavens !" exclaimed Bob ; " it can't be done. The tides are uncommon low the last day or two, and she's aground."

" Aground ?"

" Only just touching, but the water ahead is shallower still. She's shut in here until we get a higher tide."

" And when will that be ?"

" When the wind blows from the shore."

" Then here we are caged," said Danby, " and that fellow can pepper us with his guns."

" The same as we can pepper him," said Bob, " and one pepper is as good as another, and mebbe better."

" We ought to have the best of it," said Donald, " for we have the trees to protect us, and if some could be cut down—they are very thick—so that they fall against others, I think we shall be pretty safe."

"A good idea," said Danby.

A dozen men were promptly sent to the front with axes, and Donald took command to direct which trees should be cut down.

The wood had some enormous mahogany trees in it, but between grew many straight species of pines, with very fine foliage on their crowns.

To the latter Donald directed his attention, and the men setting vigorously to work on their comparatively thin stems, a number were soon half down, forming a very good means of defence from such shot and shell as the Water Fiend was capable of firing.

Strange to say, it was fully two hours before she commenced to bombard the Fairy in her retreat, which might be accounted for, Carker not having his guns ready for action.

Possibly he had them removed from their carriages, or out of order in some way.

Whatever it may have been, he certainly did not think that he would have occasion to use them just then.

By the time he set to work the rough means of defence was as good as it could possibly be under the circumstances.

Our friends on board the Fairy heard the bombardment and the crash of the shell as it struck the timber. Now and then they saw a little cloud of splinters fly into the air, but they were well shielded, and busied themselves in getting the Fairy ready for a possible night attack.

Everything that could give a sailor a chance of climbing up to the deck was hauled in, arms were prepared, and those on board divided into two watches.

Those who were off duty were to lie down in their clothes, and have their arms ready for immediate action.

Danby took command of one watch, and appointed Donald to the other, the former going first on duty. He insisted on it, and when he insisted there was no gainsaying him.

Donald and Jack went below, and lay down on the seats in the chief cabin. Not being troubled by any particular fears they soon fell asleep.

An hour later they were both aroused by the rattle of

firearms on deck. Leaping up and having secured their arms they hurried up the companion.

In the bow was quite a host of men on watch, with Danby near them. He was in the act of lighting a cigar.

" All right, dear boys," he said ; " sorry to disturb you. They came, as I expected, but the patter of half-a-dozen bullets has made them sheer off. Silence forward—listen !"

All stood still, and then the voice of Carker was heard cursing, and calling on the men to rally and renew the attack.

But the sound of oars and his voice gradually softened down. The cowards were mutinous, and declined to renew the attack.

" He hasn't much command over those fellows," said Jack.

" I hate a fizzle like this," said Danby. " To-morrow we will try to turn the tables on Carker, and cut HIM out."

The attack was not renewed, but two or three senseless shots were fired from the guns, and after that there was silence.

Donald and Jack returned to the cabin, had another short sleep, and then began their watch.

It lasted until daylight, and then Danby returned to the deck. A boat was lowered, and he was taken round the point to study the exact position of the Water Fiend.

It was gone.

Carker had to all appearance looked upon discretion as the better part of valour, and sheered off.

But knowing how cunning he could be Darby was by no means disposed to accept the idea as a certainty.

Very likely the Water Fiend was only just without the bay, making preparations for some cruel attack upon the Fairy

To ascertain this it was necessary for somebody to scale the cliff and make a survey. There was a point half a mile from the bay which would command a very clear view of the sea for a long way up and down the coast.

Danby could not go himself, being in command, so he entrusted the task to Donald and Jack.

To all appearance there was no danger whatever in the mission. Had it been otherwise he would not have permitted them to go without an escort.

They were landed, and owing to the nature of the ground they had to make a slight round inland. When half their journey was performed they suddenly came face to face with Carker, who appeared from behind a clump of bushes. He was accompanied by a sinister-looking man, with whom he was in close conversation.

The Water Fiend was not far away, and he had even coolness to spy out the exact position of the Fairy, with a view to attacking her from the land side.

Only for a moment was he unaware of the presence of Donald. Then their eyes met.

He whipped out his sword, and Donald and Jack drew theirs, but the sinister-looking stranger did nothing.

"Would you leave me to fight the two?" hissed Carker.

"Pardon me," said Donald, "but one will suffice. Just leave him to me. If I fall get back with all speed, and tell Danby that I died like a man."

"Ah! this is interesting," said the sinister one—"an office of honour for an old friend."

"He is my cowardly foe," cried Donald. "Carker, defend yourself!"

"One moment," said Carker's companion. "Let all things be regular. If any of you fall there is an end to this meeting."

"You coward!" hissed Carker, between his set teeth.

"Not at all," was the cool reply. "It is the way with you Englese. You think all are cowards. I know not these young men. In a general fight I would try to slay them, but not now. No. Senor, let me stand apart and see fair play."

Jack was a bit distressed on account of his friend, for he feared that Donald would be no match for the more expert Carker, but he would not interfere.

It was with an apprehensive heart that he stood aside with the stranger, and Donald and Carker advanced and began the fight.

Donald knew that the chances were against him, but

his hatred of Carker was intense, and he burned to avenge the wrong he had suffered at his hands.

He thought also of Ina and her father, the destruction of Carita, and his arm was nerved thereby.

Carker was a master of fence, and was considered so by good judges, but he had not been trained to the use of the cutlass, as Donald had been.

Each fought according to his knowledge of the weapon, and the result was confusing to Carker.

It is well known that a mere novice with the steel, if he is resolute, will puzzle a master. The accepted cuts and thrusts are well known, and the practised man can guard against them, but when he is face to face with one who uses his weapon in a novel and neater manner, he in turn becomes a novice.

Donald's attack was so fierce and resolute that Carker could do nothing but defend himself.

He had for the first few moments no chance of dealing a deadly cut or thrust, and he had to back a little.

A sarcastic laugh from his sinister friend did not improve his temper, and that being lost he was more abroad than at first.

Blind with rage he exposed himself to a cut from Donald which laid open his sound arm just below the elbow, but it did not disable him.

He could have fought on, and perhaps have won the day, but for his rage, which was now his master.

With a bitter oath he drew out a revolver with his left hand, and, presenting it at Donald, fired.

Our hero darted aside just in time, and with a sweep of his weapon, cut through the hat that Carker wore and laid him bleeding on the ground.

It was in his heart to kill him then, but the sinister second was already on the spot.

"It is all over," he said. "You have beaten him, and honour should be satisfied."

"Honour be hanged with such a cowardly scoundrel," cried Donald.

"His honour is hanged—destroyed," said the other. "But, pardon me, I am his second, and act for him. I declare the duel over; my brother second must support me."

Two men were crouching near and looked up with faces distorted with hatred.

"I don't know much about those things," said Jack, looking flurried and bewildered; "but if it is the right thing, of course, I agree with you."

"You hear?" said the sinister one.

"Oh! I am satisfied," said Donald, thrusting his weapon back into its scabbard. "But I appeal to you if he has not acted like a dastard?"

CHAPTER XXV.

THE FAIRY AFLOAT—OUT AT SEA—CHASING THE WATER FIEND—AN ENGLISH VESSEL IN DISTRESS.

"HE has," replied the sinister one calmly, "and as a man I despise him; but as his second I cannot stand by and see him killed like a wounded dog. You have a sense of honour—I see it in your face; you yield to my view?"

"I do," said Donald. "You are right. Take him away; he is not worth killing."

Carker meanwhile lay upon the ground holding a handkerchief he had drawn from his pocket to his wounded head.

Blood-stained, covered with dust, and completely cowed, he was a sorry plight.

Donald bent over him, and, looking into his shifting eyes, said—

"Carker, you are a pirate, thief, and a coward! Go, get the better of your wounds, and remember that when we meet again, *no matter where it may be*, I shall call you to account. Senor, Good-day. We know now all we came to discover—the Water Fiend has not left, and we shall be prepared for you."

He raised his cap, the sinister one returned the compliment, and Donald and Jack turned back to retrace their steps to the Fairy.

* * * * *

"H'm!" said Danby. "So that is what has happened? Donald, you have come out of that affair very well indeed."

The three friends sat upon the deck indulging in coffee and cigars, they had been discussing the meeting and the fight.

Two hours had elapsed, and a breeze was blowing inland—the very thing they had been hoping for.

Bob Bitters was getting a cable ready to tow out the Fairy if the water rose high enough.

The process would be very simple.

The boats would take out a small anchor and the cable, drop it, and then wind in so as to draw her into the deeper water.

By repeating this process two or three times they would be able to get into the bay, anchor there, and when the wind shifted, as it generally did towards sunset, sail into the open sea.

"I suppose I was lucky," replied Donald, laughing. "I just chopped away at him and took my chance of what he might do to me."

"That won't do a second time," said Danby. "The act is, old fellow, you *must* leave him to me."

"I won't."

"Then if you fight again, it must be with pistols. I can soon teach you the trick of shooting quick and straight. It is more a matter of instinct than the eye. If you go taking aim in the ordinary way, you will be shot down before you can press the trigger. Here, you see that small loose bolt on the capstan there. Now see this. Here is my revolver. I take it out of my pocket, raise it like this. Pop."

The crack of the weapon instantly followed, and the bolt toppled over.

"That is only about seven paces," said Danby; "but when you can hit a bolt at that distance, what chance would a man stand at fifteen?"

"None," replied Jack; "no more than a windmill."

There was plenty of amunition on board, brought from the stores Captain Frosby had kept in a hut in the forest, and Donald, having first studied the knack of holding the weapon, fired a dozen shots.

He knocked the bolt off at the fifth fire, then again at the twelfth.

"Very good for a beginning," said Danby, approvingly; "you have a quick eye. Now, Jack, you try your hand. It may be useful one day."

So Jack had a little practice, and succeeded in hitting the bolt once in twelve times, with which he was satisfied.

By that time the tide was almost at the flood, and Bob Bitters was exulting, in a boat at the side, on the prospec of the water rising high enough to get the Fairy out.

"She'll just float, Mr. Danby," he said; "if she doesn't, take a pop at my head with one of your shooting-irons, and let daylight into it."

"Would THAT float the Fairy, Bob?" asked Danby, smiling.

"Well! no, sir, but it would let me know whether we touched bottom or not. Now, you lubbers, give way!"

The "lubbers" gave way, and carried out the anchor to the chosen spot. It was dropped into the water, and half-a-dozen men at the capstan were ordered to turn.

"Go slowly!" cried Bob. "Let the anchor get a good grip before you open your shoulders."

The cable became taut, the anchor got hold, and then there was a moment of suspense.

The cable was strained as tight as a fiddle-string, and then a yell came from Bob in the boat.

"She moves!" he cried. "Round you go! Put your weight into it!"

Slowly the Fairy slipped from the sandy bed below.

"Keep a-going!" yelled Bob. "That's it. She runs now! She rides!"

The Fairy was in deeper water, and a cheer burst from all on board.

The rest was easy enough, and before the tide began to ebb the gallant little craft was anchored safely in the bay.

"Give us a wind on the beam or off shore," said Danby, "say an hour before sundown, and we shall be at sea."

There are occasions when Nature is especially kind to man, and this was one of them.

As the sun neared its western bed, the wind veered right round, and blew off shore.

It was not by any means a breeze in that sheltered spot, but it was enough.

The only question concerned the depth of water at the entrance of the bay.

The Fairy was built so as to be ot light draught, and there was one spot, and one only, where she had a chance of getting through.

It could be plainly seen—a comparatively dull piece of water between the breakers, not more than forty feet in width.

"It is enough, and more than enough," said Danby. "Shake out the sails, my lads. Ready there to heave the anchor! I'll take the helm myself until we are throug' the way. Now, lads—smart there!"

The men did not clearly understand all he said, but gestures sufficed to make his commands comprehensible.

The canvas filling, the anchor was raised, and the Fairy bore away, with the wind well aft.

With his eye on that dark spot, Danby stood by the helm, and everybody on board watched the white line ahead.

To strike them was to be wrecked, and it some were apprehensive they were to be pardoned for it.

They KNEW their peril; but when they looked at Danby's calm face they were reassured.

He encouraged no fears.

In any case they could not help him.

On went the Fairy, with her head going as straight as an arrow to the narrow way.

Whirr!

She was, to all appearance, among the breakers, and then the full force of the breeze was felt.

A cloud of spray made all things on deck misty and ghost-like.

A touch—a slight touch—against a hidden rock, and the neat little craft was in the open sea.

"Bob," said Danby, joyously, "take the helm. Head her north, and I will see what has become of the Water Fiend."

The only thing that could possibly be the vessel he sought was a dark speck, five miles away, at least.

Not even with the glass could he make sure it was a ship at all; for the sun had now dipped behind the rocky shore, and the subdued sheen of twilight was on the sea.

But the course the Water Fiend had taken was pretty clear.

She would, in case she had now departed, assuredly head for Monte Video.

"I will pursue her for the night," said Danby, "and if I see nothing of her in the morning I will return."

After taking careful observations of the speck ahead, he gave Bob directions which way to steer, and with Donald and Jack went down to dinner, which one of the seamen - an excellent cook—had prepared.

The viands were plain but good, and as there was a small store of wine a bottle was opened to drink confusion to their enemies and good fortune to all honest men.

There was a late moon that night, or part of a moon, for it was on the wane, and when it arose there was, in that clear latitude, plenty of light upon the sea.

The breeze had fallen after the sun went down, and they made but little headway.

With a night-glass Danby, after dinner, scanned the sea.

He turned it first in the direction of the speck supposed to be the Water Fiend, but could find nothing.

"He can't have got clear away," he muttered, "for the Fairy is as good, and better, than the Fiend, any day."

Turning his glass to the east he carefully scanned the sea, and, finding nothing, casually looked to the south, and there he beheld, within a mile of him, a ship with all her canvas set.

"Bob," he cried, "you've passed her."

"Not me," said Bob. "That's a trader, and handled by a lot of lubbers. She's going along anyhow."

"Bob," said Danby, after a close survey of the vessel, "there is something wrong aboard there. She looks like a deserted vessel. See there, how she pays off. Why, the helmsman is drunk, or she has broken her rudder; we will see what is the matter."

The Fairy's helm was put up, and she stood away to sea; and then, bearing southwards, came up close behind her.

The vessel was behaving in a most eccentric manner, just as if her helm was loosely handled, and now they were near enough to see if there were any men on deck.

None were visible, but standing on the bulwarks, and holding to the ratlines, was the fragile figure of a girl or woman, waving a handkerchief as a signal of distress.

"I knew it," cried Danby; "something IS wrong there. Bring her round, Bob; with this breeze we may safely run in close and board her. Ready with the gig there."

Donald and Jack had now come up from below, and were standing beside Danby, staring at the figure—now not more than thirty yards away.

The moonlight fell upon it, and they could all see that it was a young girl, and apparently very beautiful.

On Jack Johnson the sight had a petrifying effect.

He had good eyes, and as the two vessels neared each other he made out the features of one he thought was dead.

"It's a haunted ship," he cried, hoarsely; "and that's a ghost!"

"Nonsense," replied Donald, "it's no ghost—they don't talk. Can't you hear her voice? She is crying for help."

"I tell you it IS a ghost," insisted Jack. "I ought to know, I knew her alive. It is the ghost of old Basil Bennett's ward. She was drowned in the Thames; didn't I see her hand with the ring on it? Don't go any nearer, it's a haunted ship I tell you!"

But nobody there believed in ghosts, and the Fairy having taken in some of her canvas the gig was lowered, and Donald was directed to go on board and see what was the matter.

There was no difficulty in approaching the craft, for she now broached to, and lay like a log with her canvas flapping

The girl leaped down upon the side and tossed a rope over to the boat.

It mas made fast, and Donald nimbly climbed upon the deck.

CHAPTER XXVI.

SAVED FROM THE WRECK—A STRANGE STORY.

HIS first care was to rescue the girl, who was in an exhausted condition from the efforts she had made to attract attention.

She was conveyed on board the Fairy, and Danby carried her down into the cabin, where he gave her a little wine.

Never before in his life had he, in his opinion, seen so beautiful a creature.

She was very pale and somewhat thin; but her figure was graceful, and her face beautiful, tender, and sweet.

Meanwhile, Donald and Jack, acting on Danby's orders, had gone over the vessel.

They found it was the White Rose, a trader from London to Chili; but everything on board was in a wrecked condition.

She had been boarded by pirates, and robbed of everything worth taking away.

There were also signs of a deadly struggle which made them shudder.

It was easy to guess what had taken place.

But how was it that the girl had escaped?

That was what puzzled Donald and Jack.

The former had seen her and spoken of her beauty; but Jack as yet had not clearly seen her face.

One of the men on board with them said he thought the vessel was slowly but surely going down.

He pointed out that the vessel was deep in the water, and had positively no cargo on board.

His surmise was correct.

She had been scuttled; but the work had been done in a hurry, and the water was coming in but slowly.

For all that the vessel was doomed.

The pirates had destroyed the pumps, and there was no chance of getting the water out of her.

They returned on board the Fairy to report, and found Danby on deck.

He told them that the girl had so far recovered as to be able to tell him that the vessel had been attacked and plundered by pirates.

The crew had been butchered and thrown overboard, while she had escaped by hiding in an old locker and covering herself with a bit of tarpaulin.

"They actually drew a part of it aside," said Danby

"and seeing her dress said, ' Oh ! it's only a rag-bag,' and went in search of more promising booty."

"And when did all this take place?" Donald asked.

"About noon. But she will tell us the full story to-morrow ; to-night she has great need of rest. Excitement has worn her out."

"That this crime is to be added to the full list of similar perpetrations by Carker," he added, "I do not for a moment doubt. Oh ! for the day of reckoning with that villain. It will surely come—it must."

Danby asked about the vessel, and was made acquainted with her condition. He saw that nothing could be done except to remove anything that might be of service to prove her identity.

The log-book was about the best thing, but on arriving on board Donald was unable to find it.

It had been removed or destroyed.

So he was obliged to content himself with a few odd things on which the name of the vessel was stamped or engraved, and with these he returned to the Fairy.

They stood off and on for awhile, until the good ship was on the point of settling down. Half-an-hour later her bows began to rise as greater weight of the water settled in the stern.

Up, up she went, until her bowsprit was almost erect, and then, with a rush, she went down under the blue waters, to make another item among the missing things of the sea.

The fair stranger on board slept in the cabin undisturbed, and about an hour after sunrise came on deck, where she joined the three friends.

The moment Jack Johnson caught sight of her his eyes came nearly out of his head.

He stepped back and clasped Donald by the arm.

"Why, it IS HER," he exclaimed.

"Who ?" asked Donald.

Jack did not answer, for the charming stranger was close to them, uttering thanks for the service rendered her in a tone of voice that was like the ringing of silver bells.

"I am sure," she said, "that I can never be sufficiently . grateful to you all."

"You can make us a good return," said Danby.

"How?" she asked.

"By never naming it again."

"If you wish it," she said, "I will not; but I can never forget it."

Up to this moment she had only just glanced at Jack Johnson, but now, as she turned her face towards him, an exclamation of surprise burst from her lips,

"Mr. Johnson!" she exclaimed.

"Oh! you have not forgotten me," said Jack, "although you never saw me but once before."

He felt flattered at the idea of being remembered, but there was more than that behind the meeting.

In the person of this sweet girl he saw the ward of Basil Bennett, the merchant, who was supposed to be drowned.

But he felt he could hardly introduce the subject just then, as he thought it advisable to consult Donald before saying anything on the subject.

"Meeting you here," she said, "it is very strange—1 may say marvellous."

"And meeting you is more so to me," returned Jack. "It is miraculous."

"How came you to leave the office and go to sea?"

"I was pressed."

"Pressed!" she exclaimed. "I thought it was never done now."

"Not in the ordinary way, for the navy," said Jack. "It was Carker who took me to sea."

"Oh! that man," she exclaimed, with a shudder; "how loathsome he was to me! What has become of him?"

They told her what Carker really was, and that it was more than probable that he had been the man who attacked and sank the White Rose.

This was another marvellous link in her history, and she pondered a few moments before commenting upon it.

"To that man and to that old wretched hypocrite, Basil Bennett," she said, "I owe much suffering. To escape them both I fled away. But it is a long story, and must be reserved for a little while."

"Until after breakfast," said Danby. "May I ask what was your destination?"

"Chili," she answered. "But it mattered little to me where I went so that I got quite out of the way from the persecution I suffered."

He told her that the vessel had been put about in the night, and they were going back to some friends, among whom was a young lady who would act as a friend and protector to her.

He hoped to reach his destination, if the wind was favourable, about sunset.

Breakfast was prepared by this time, and, by the desire of all, served on deck.

She told them that her name was Isabel Meriton, which was familiar to all, for Jack had often told her story as he knew it, and she hoped they would call her Isabel.

"I have never before known a brother," she said, with charming *naïveté*, "and now I feel that I have three."

Danby thought the word was rather a bold one, but he did not say so, and he felt the slightest possible amount of jealousy about the position Jack held towards her.

She treated him as an old friend, and there was much laughing and chattering going on as the Fairy sped over the glistening waves.

After breakfast cigars were introduced, and Isabel laughing at the idea of her objecting to them, they entered into a full revelation of events that had taken place since their one meeting at home.

Isabel was surprised to hear that a bill had been out, offering a reward for her. She had never seen or heard of it.

"I hid away, and worked as a seamstress for about six months," she said. "Then one day as I was going to the warehouse in the City where I obtained my work I saw that man Bennett on the opposite side of the road. He did not see me, but I felt that I should never be safe from him in England, and determined to go abroad. The captain of the White Rose was the brother of an amiable woman I lived with, and he offered to place me with some other relations in Chili."

"And were you the only lady on board?" asked Danby.

"Yes," replied Isabel; "but good old Captain Farnly was a father to me"—Danby was very glad to hear that he was old—"and I had every comfort. He was so kind to me."

"May I ask," said Donald, "why you were obliged to leave your guardian?"

"The old hypocrite wanted to *marry* me," replied Isabel, with an angry flush in her face; "and I was persecuted also by that man Carker whenever he was in England. They wanted my money, which I do not care for. All I wanted was peace."

"You are rich I have heard," said Jack.

"All I have is with me," said Isabel, with a merry laugh. "Oh! they may keep my money."

"Perhaps," said Danby, significantly.

Jack was now anxious to know how he could have made a mistake about the ring he saw on the finger of the woman drowned in the Thames.

He observed that Isabel no longer wore one, but felt delicate in alluding to it. She might have parted with it as others have to with their jewellery for bread.

"I hope you will pardon me," he said; "but you had a ring, a peculiar ring."

"Oh! yes," she said. "I meant to keep it, for it was my mother's, but I gave it away."

"To whom?"

"One night—the third after I ran away—I was out for a walk when I met a poor creature as young as myself crying most bitterly. I asked her what was the matter, but she would tell me no more than that her life was hopelessly miserable. I thought she must be very poor, so I gave her my ring. I knew my mother, if alive, would forgive me, and dead she could never know anything about it."

Then Jack told her what he had seen in the river on morn—the hand protruding from the river with the ring upon it, which had led him and others to think that she was drowned.

The natural inference was that the poor girl, whoever she was, to whom Isabel had given the ring had drowned herself.

Why?

Ah! there was the rub, and it was not a subject they could discuss. Isabel was very grave for a time, thinking of the lone creature who, with some mighty anguish in her heart, had sought a watery grave.

CHAPTER XXVII.

THE RETURN TO THE BAY—THE SECRET OF CAPTAIN FROSBY'S QUEST—IS IT A DREAM?

THERE was little more to be told, but it was impressed upon Isabel that she must not allow a man like Basil Bennett to enjoy her wealth, which she could rightly claim.

Had she known the laws of the old country it would have been easy for her to have gone to a good lawyer and obtained protection from her unworthy guardian.

The Court of Chancery would have taken the matter up, and prevented him making unjust use of what was not his own.

That much could be done by-and-bye, when she went back, so Danby told her.

"And when will you take me back?" she asked, with laughing eyes.

Poor Danby for a moment hung his head.

He feared there were reasons for his never setting foot in the old country again.

How far he was justified in this idea we shall see anon.

To Jack Johnson the discovery of Isabel, alive and well, was like a dream.

Remembering her sweet face, which had only to be seen once to be impressed indelibly on the mind he had often sighed over her presumed untimely end.

And now there she was, alive, well, and more beautiful than before—a rare treasure-trove from the sea.

Jack was not exactly in love with her.

Admiration and reverence were the more prominent feelings in his heart.

When Danby paid her attention—which he did at every opportunity during the day—he was not at all jealous.

He even remarked how well they looked together, and Donald assented.

The wind was kind, and, growing stronger as the day passed on, took the Fairy back to the bay soon before the sun went down.

She was being looked for by anxious eyes.

Captain Frosby and Ina were on the cliff awaiting their coming ; and, the anchor being dropped a quarter of a mile ashore, a boat was sent for them.

They came on board, and reported all well.

Mike Barlow had behaved himself with commendable propriety, and nothing had been seen of the Vampire.

In addition, one of the men had made what promised to be a great discovery.

Wandering about, he came across signs of an old well-laid road, running southward, in the forest where Ina had been dragged away, and the first assumption was that, if it could be traced, it would lead to some place or building worth exploring.

"It is very, very old," Captain Frosby said, "and much broken up by the growth of roots of trees and the action of worms and insects ; but I think we can follow it."

Then came the question—would it be safe to leave the Fairy ?

Captain Frosby was of opinion that it would be, for the authorities of the Argentine Republic were very dilatory, and it would be a month at least ere Carker could return with other vessels to assist him.

It was just possible that they would never send at all.

"My plan is this," he said—"let us get her into the bay and place her where she was before. If they return sooner than we expect, it will be the last place they will look for her, and, in addition, they will be wary in entering the bay themselves for fear of some trap. We have three weeks ahead of us at least."

Ina and Isabel were friends the moment they met. Both had found what they so long had needed—one of their own sex, age, and disposition to confide in.

They left the men to themselves, and went down to the cabin to have a long talk together.

Coffee and cigars were put on deck for the use of the sterner sex.

While enjoying these things Captain Frosby unfolded a part of the story of his life.

"I did not come here," he said, "merely as a settler, and I do not need wealth; but I am in search of something which will be worth money and more than money to me. Guess what it is."

They guessed all sorts of things, and, of course, guessed wrong.

They could not imagine what he sought.

"I have been seeking some armour that was hidden away centuries ago," he said. "It is of silver, and gold, and steel, and, unless the old manuscript where I found the story of its hiding lied, it is worth the trouble of a lifetime to find."

"Where was it hidden?" asked Danby.

"Ah! there's the rub," said Frosby. "The armour belonged to some of Pizarro's men, who forged it from the metals they found in the land of the Incas. There were sixty suits in all, each for a captain of note, and the whole were stolen away by a body of negroes in the night. They got clear away, and were never heard of for many years, until one returned and offered to reveal the secret of its hiding-place. He had quarrelled with his friends and wished to betray them."

"And what was his story?" asked Danby.

"He told them that the armour was hidden in the temple of the god Tishnah," said Captain Frosby; "but the Spaniards had never heard of such a god or such a temple. They told him he lied, and roasted him alive."

"But surely they endeavoured to find the place?" said Donald.

"Perhaps," replied Frosby; "I do not know. If they did it was in a half-hearted way."

CHAPTER XXVIII.

IN THE DEPTHS OF A DARK FOREST—THE BROKEN ROAD—IS THIS THE TEMPLE?

" So you have been seeking their armour?" said Danby.

"I seek the temple of the god Tishnah," replied Frosby; "and in looking for it I have found many temples around the coast—strange places hidden away from mortal eye among the mountains, and in the depths of forests, but never the one I sought. But it will be found yet—it will be found."

He rose up, excited in his manner, like some enthusiast who sees the hour of the fulfilment of his dreams approaching, and walked away forward.

"Seems to be a bit of a wild goose chase he is on," said Donald.

"I don't know," replied Danby. "Men have been led by a fancy to discover many strange and wonderful things."

Ten days have passed, and the scene is the depths of a vast forest, where for centuries Nature's work had gone on unseen by man.

The trees were for the most part gigantic; mighty trunks that were like towers rose up straight and solid, spreading out branches aloft so as to form a lace-work roof above.

Between these timbers and under the lace-work grew smaller trees and tangled masses of undergrowth.

Through the latter Captain Frosby and our heroes, accompanied by a dozen men, had cut their way.

The broken path through the forest was with infinite pains traced, lost here, found again; then a winding way forming, as the adventurers believed, a tracing of mystic words of a forgotten tongue.

In the old, old days men were given to make a symbol of anything.

Nothing was done without a meaning being attached to it, and those learned in such things can read a story in the very structure of an ancient building.

It was so in this instance beyond all reasonable doubt.

or what could be the object of laying out a path in fairly level ground winding about in semi-circular, square, and other forms?

In ten days the party had travelled about twenty miles, but, making allowances for the fantastic windings of the road, they did not think they were more than five miles from their friends.

Bob Bitters had been left in charge of the rest of the community, with orders to keep a good look out for strangers—a needless injunction with such a man.

By night and day a watch was to be kept up, although only Vampa was to be feared, he was now known as a dangerous, revengeful man.

Even Ina, Isabel, and the other women were armed.

They were camped near the Fairy in a grove that commanded a view of sea and land, and very little apprehension was felt for their safety by the adventurers in the forest, with whom we will now keep for awhile.

It was a hot, sultry day, and the air in the forest was stifling. The hour noon, and the party at rest after several hours' hard labour cutting their way through the interwoven bushes and creeping plants.

Seated on a huge trunk which had fallen from old age, the leader of the party reviewed the situation.

As yet they had seen no signs of life, save that of wild animals—monkeys, a species of leopard, snakes, and so on.

One whole day a horde of monkeys had accompanied them, keeping to the tree-tops and watching their labours with a grotesque interest.

At last they began to pelt the adventurers, and a rifle was fired.

It shook their nerves, and they disappeared to return no more.

"How much food have we left?" asked Captain Crosby.

"Enough for about two days," said Danby; "but it can at a pinch be divided into four."

"Then we have three days more to go on," returned the captain, hopelessly.

"And one to return," said Donald.

"Unsuccessful, as you fear."

"I am not so hopeless as you, Captain Frosby; but I am ready to go on with you to the end."

"Bravely said," replied the captain. "I have a fancy that I am on the verge of success. I dreamt so last night. Ah! you smile. *Some* dreams have a meaning in them, and a few come true."

"That is so, nobody can deny," said Danby. "Dreams by night and dreams by day."

"The old road," said Captain Frosby, "has for the last day and a-half assumed a more puzzling form. It is like a passing flourish at the end of a long word. Now if it should be that we are near the finale the prize is ours."

"Yours," said Danby.

Donald and Jack repeated the word, but Captain Frosby with a deprecating motion of his head and hand expressed his disapproval of their suggestion.

"As we have shared the labour," he said, "so we will share the spoil."

They did not agree with him, for they felt that it was like counting chickens before they were hatched.

An hour passed by in rest and conversation, and it must be confessed with occasional dozing, for the sultry air had a somnolent effect.

The followers indeed all had a sound sleep, from which they were awakened by their energetic captain's voice.

"Up lads and onwards!" he cried.

They aroused themselves and resumed their way.

Foot by foot the ground was examined, and the traces of the old road followed.

Two hours of their labours ended in their arriving at a part of the forest so dense that it threatened to completely bar their way.

Here trees had fallen as reeds shattered by a storm—mighty trees of mahogany and other precious woods leaning together like loose sticks tossed and tumbled about.

The intervening spaces were filled with the prevalent climbers as thick and as tough in the vine as moderate-sized rope.

And into this dense mass of wood and creepers the road abruptly plunged.

Vampa and his companion meant mischief.

The men looked at their leader and each other in despair.

"Here is the end," said one.

"No," was Captain Frosby's answer, "I go forward, if I do alone."

He raised the axe he, in common with the others, carried, and hacked away with the energy of a giant.

Donald and his two friends followed his example, and the men, inspired, renewed their labours.

It was almost as bad as tunneling through the earth, and in some ways more objectionable.

The multitude of creeping things were enough to chill the blood of man. Huge beetles, insects of strange form and colour, snakes a foot long, no thicker than the finger, others of great length, as stout as the leg of a man, were disturbed by their work; and the axe was often employed in destroying those that were pugnacious and disposed to check the progress of the invaders of their haunts.

Had they not been inured to the sight of the strange creatures of this country it would have been impossible to go on.

So they laboured on, with intervals of rest, until the day was almost spent, and a dreadful gloom was gathering upon them.

"Can we pass the night HERE?' was the question each man asked himself, but none uttered.

The word for a retreat to more open ground must come from their leader.

And he went on—dogged, determined, dauntless.

It seemed to them that night was on them at last, when Donald thought he observed daylight returning.

He asked himself if it were possible that they had toiled through the dark hours to another day.

The explanation of the phenomenon came from the lips of Captain Frosby.

"We are coming to a clearer part of the forest," he said.

"I hear a murmuring ahead," said Jack. "It is like the rumbling of a distant train."

"A railway here," remarked Donald, "will be a staggerer."

A shout from Captain Frosby startled them all. He cut through half-a-dozen vines, and quite a flood of daylight, in comparison to what they had known that afternoon, poured in upon them.

A few more blows of the axes of all and they had the full daylight of a late afternoon upon them.

Ahead was the strangest and most inspiring scene they had looked upon for many a day.

First of all they saw a broad cascade, only a few feet in height, tumbling over a line of rocks, like a weir at home ; then a broad barrier of water, and in the centre of it a a great building of stone.

In shape it was oblong, with towers round and square dotted about the roof.

There were a score of them at least, and in the centre, on a high pedestal, squatted a figure carved in stone, as ugly and repulsive as anything ever seen in a dream.

It was neither man nor beast nor bird, but a compound of all three.

The head was that of a tiger, the body that of a man, and his lower limbs were of the shape of half-a-dozen serpents entwined. On its shoulders were huge wings, like those of a monster bat.

It had four arms, with claws at the end in place of hands, and three rested passive, while one was raised in the air grasping a huge club in a threatening manner.

So realistic was the attitude that for a few minutes all who saw it expected to see some furthur demonstrations of hostility, but, recovering themselves, they exchanged glances of profound astonishment.

"Found at last !" said Captain Frosby, in a low, thrilling tone. "This is the temple of the god Tishnah."

They could not confirm his assertion nor confute it, and so were silent until he spoke again.

"It is not far to swim," he said. "Who among you can follow me?"

"One moment," said Danby. "Let us not forget that this pool may have deadly monsters in its depths. To me it seems made for the home of the cayman."

"Having risked so much to get here," said Captain Frosby, "I fear nothing."

He would have plunged in, but they held him back; and Danby pointed to some bubbles which had just risen to the surface of the water.

"Wait," he said.

Then from out of the depths of the pool came the head of a cayman, that vicious species of the crocodile tribe known in South America.

The amphibious beast, unconscious of the presence of its great foe, man, swam towards the cascade.

Suddenly it turned towards the shore, and saw the intruders on its long-deserted domain.

It was almost ludicrous to see the expression of astonishment that sprung into its sleepy eyes, to be followed by a look of ferocity.

Bent on mischief it approached the shore.

The majority of the party had rifles slung upon their backs, and there was a hasty unstrapping of the same.

"Keep cool," said Danby. "One at a time, and aim at the eye."

Half-a-dozen rifles were bent upon it.

"You, Donald—fire!" said Danby.

Donald fired, and the light of one of the furious eyes was gone.

The beast stopped short, and turning over exhibited its leaden-coloured repulsive stomach, soft and impregnable.

One convulsive movement, and it lay still.

"Well done!" snid Danby. "Never was a charge of powder and lead better spent."

So far well; but the fact remained that the pool was the haunt of the cayman, and there might be scores in its depths or skulking about the sedgy banks of the pool.

To venture to swim out to that strange temple in the midst of the water was to court death.

It was hard, after all their labours, to have the apple of success so near, and yet not be able to grasp it.

Only one thing would avail them—a raft.

"But we have no ropes or nails to bind the logs together," said Captain Frosby, despairingly.

"Nature has given us ropes galore," said Donald. "Some of the vines I cut through were as tough as the cable of a ship."

The thought was a happy one, and hope once more brought joy to all.

After partaking of some food the men went to work cutting vines and selecting branches which would serve from the taller trees.

Common prudence suggested that fires should be lighted, and Jack Johnson, having appointed himself to the work, speedily had four blazing on the banks of the pool.

There was no lack of well-seasoned fuel.

There were hundreds of tons of it within reach.

No cayman or beast of the forest would approach the blazing logs, and there was both warmth and security for them during the night.

When darkness came they chatted for awhile by the glowing fire, and then, having appointed a change of watchers and replenishers for the night, the weary toilers lay down and slept.

CHAPTER XXIX.

THE RAFT—WITHIN THE TEMPLE—SUCCESS—AN ALARM.

THE morning came bright and fair, and the first ray of light found the adventurers at work.

In two hours a raft that would bear them all was ready.

It was rough, but it was strong.

The tough vines admirably served as binders, and as the supply was prodigious they used them freely.

Danby was of opinion that the Atlantic could be covered upon it, with sufficient provisions and "barring being washed off."

Several sapling trees, springing out of the undergrowth, were cut down and shaped to use as propellers, and then half the party embarked, and two of their number propelled the raft.

The pool of water was, as they expected, not very deep —except here and there, where there were holes a few feet in width.

Jack Johnson, who was working one of the poles, nearly fell off the raft on coming to one of them. It made him more careful, and he covered his momentary alarm by whistling "'Way Down the Kiber" at his hardest.

The temple rose out of the water, having its foundations on the bottom of the pool. On the side nearest to the raft there was a flight of a dozen steps, but at the top no door was visible.

There was a circular opening in the wall, near the ground, about three feet or rather less in diameter, and that was the only visible means of egress to the place.

It was not exactly inviting, for on landing and mounting the steps the adventurers found that the interior was as dark as night.

The probability was that the temple was closed so that no daylight could penetrate.

Captain Frosby and Danby were disputing the question as to who should explore it when Donald settled matters by quietly stepping into it.

Jack Johnson followed him, and the pair were masters of the situation.

"Come back, you two!" cried Danby.

There was a very distinct echo to his voice and to the answer Donald cheerily gave him—

"By-and-bye, when we have had a look over the premises."

"Phew!" sneezed Jack; "what a beastly lot of dust. There hasn't been a broom about here lately. What's that?"

"A fine specimen of the native toad," replied Donald.

"Ugh!" said Jack, "it's as big as a tom-cat, I say, Don, this hole is getting wider."

"We are through it," said Donald, as he stood up. "Come on, Danby—it's all right."

Danby was already on the way, with Captain Frosby immediately behind him. In a few minutes all were standing together.

The place was at first as dark and chilling as a vault. The building had, without a doubt, been closed up, saving for the opening through which they had just passed.

But after awhile the faint light admitted revealed to them that they were in a vast chamber which echoed their voices, and was of too great an extent for them to see its full size.

The dust lay thick—so thick that it was like a carpet to their feet—and they had to move cautiously, for every step raised a little cloud of it.

"This is not ordinary dust," said Jack Johnson, after a violent sneeze ; "it has quite an aromatic odour."

"I should say that the floor was once thickly strewn with herbs and spices," replied Danby, "which rotted away, and, having no means of escape, the dust has quietly settled here."

"If we could only get a little daylight in," said Donald, "it would be a blessing."

"And a little fresh air would not be objected to," added Jack.

"Keep still here for a few minutes," said Danby. "I will go out and reconnoitre."

He went out cautiously, and the others kept where they were until they heard Danby's voice.

"Stop there. I think I can give you a little light," he cried.

In a few moments the report of a rifle was heard and a few pieces of stone came rattling down from above.

Looking up they saw an opening about the size of a man's hand.

"The walls are very thin," said Jack.

"It is an opening—a window," replied Donald, "which has been closed with a comparatively thin slab of stone."

A second report was heard, and now there was an opening fully eighteen inches in diameter. It was about eighteen feet above the circular entrance.

A beam of light streamed in and the nature of the chamber fully revealed.

It had an arched roof of stone, elaborately carved, and the walls were covered with fantastic figures and tracing of the most beautiful and elaborate description.

Jack Johnson, overcome with astonishment, turned slowly upon his heel until he faced the other way, and there found cause to utterly bewilder him for a few minutes.

Clasping Donald's arm, he gasped—

"Look there ! Behind you."

Donald and Captain Frosby turned at the same moment and beheld as rare and wonderful a sight as man ever looked upon.

Raised on a pedestal was a copy of the figure on the roof of the temple, the only difference being that the interior god was at rest, sitting with his four hands or claws passively clasped and, marvellous to relate, a benignant smile upon his tiger face.

And what did it smile upon ?

A hundred armoured figures, standing erect, with their drawn swords raised in the air as if saluting.

Covered with dust, as they were, nothing could be more majestic and more imposing than this array.

They stood in two semi-circles, arranged by a gifted, artistic mind, the attitude of each slightly altered so as to give a natural effect to the whole.

On Captain Frosby this spectacle had the effect of overwhelming joy.

He had not dreamt in vain—his labours were requited. The prize so long hoped and yearned for was won.

He said not a word, but quietly sank upon his knees, and remained there until the voice of Danby was heard again.

It was a cry of glad surprise that burst from his lips as he re-entered the temple, and then followed mutual congratulations on the success which had followed their labours.

They went up to those effigies—grim mockery of past glories—and saw, to their amazement, that each suit of armour was fitted on to a figure of stone.

What an amount of labour was here represented !

Who were the sculptors, and what had become of them ?

On this all known history is silent.

" Let the men all come in," said Captain Frosby, " and feast their eyes upon this scene."

The raft had already been sent back for the rest, and the men had all gathered on the steps, wondering what was to be seen within.

As soon as summoned they came in one by one, and gazed open-eyed on the dramatic scene before them.

There was something fascinating in that inanimate group, and they stood for a long time exchanging comments, while Captain Frosby and his three friends went from figure to figure, examining the exquisite workmanship.

The armour was of silver and gold, with jewels in the hilts of the swords—a rich, a wondrous prize.

At last the men began to return to the open air; for the temple impressed them as something uncanny.

The first to emerge immediately began to call for his comrades, and they poured out, to look upon a spectacle that struck them dumb.

A brown column of smoke was rising from the shore. *The forest was on fire !*

CHAPTER XXX.

THE ESCAPE BY THE RIVER—A DESOLATE WASTE— BOB BITTERS MAKES A BLUNDER.

AT first none assembled in that strange temple seemed to realise the full meaning of the startling announcement—

The forest on fire !

It was a blow—a tremendous blow—and in silence they stood looking at each other for a few moments until the crackling of the flames reached their ears.

Then there was a movement towards the outside landing steps to see the full nature of the threatened disaster.

" It may be only a few bushes burning," said Captain Frosby.

But Donald, as he emerged from the circular entrance, saw that it was a more serious thing.

A long drought had dried the undergrowth and the herbage, and the flames were running about below and aloft with wondrous rapidity.

Already some of the tree-tops were flaring like huge torches, and right and left upon the ground there was a fast-spreading flood of flame.

And with it there was a rising wind which favoured the conflagration in the direction of the forest.

"We did it ourselves," said Danby, bitterly. "It is strange that none of us thought of the possibility of our little fires making a big one."

"All our thoughts were HERE," said Captain Frosby, with a groan.

"Well," said Jack Johnson, cheerfully, "all the old timber will soon burn, and then we shall have a pretty clear road home."

"You forget," said Danby, "that the ground will have to cool first. Look at the mighty trees, and think of the number that have fallen. Why, Jack, the whole thing will smoulder for WEEKS."

"Unless we get rain."

"It is not the time to look for it," said Captain Frosby. "And the rain would have to be heavy indeed. In that case the ground would be a *swamp* of ashes and mud. Have you an idea of the fatigue of wading through it?"

"Then we are boxed up here," said Jack, dismally.

"Not at all," remarked Donald, "there is the other side of the river."

"An unknown land," said Captain Frosby.

"Or the river," said Donald. "Surely we can get along on the raft—or half our number?"

"And meanwhile," said Captain Frosby, "all our provisions are destroyed."

Loud roared the burning forest.

It was amazing and somewhat nerve-shaking, even to those hardy adventurers, to see the rapidity with which he fire spread.

The heat from it was soon felt across the water, and if the wind had blown towards them it would have been unbearable.

Their position was bad enough in any case; but Donald's suggestion anyhow was good—some of them ought to get away at once.

As for the great prize, that would have to be abandoned for the present; but it was hard work persuading Captain Frosby that it must be done.

Would not some other adventurer find it, and rob him of his prize?

This did not seem likely on the face of it, but then there was every excuse for him.

The majority of people would have experienced a similar fear.

The plan finally settled on was this.

The raft should be got down the lower cascade—it was only a water-shoot of a few feet—after all but Danby and Donald had been put on the opposite shore.

They were to navigate it with three or four men, who would be taken on board.

Captain Frosby and Jack's duty would be to forage ashore, keeping the river and the raft, as far as practicable, in sight.

Delay was dangerous, and the task was entered on at once.

First, all but Donald and Danby were landed on the opposite side of the pool, and then the raft was propelled to the cascade and allowed to float over.

Its strength was tested by the shoot downward; but it stood against it, and the water beyond was free from any further barrier.

After going a short way it wound inland, and then back into the forest again.

Fortunately they had ammunition and arms, and game was found in plenty.

Within an hour of starting they came in sight of a herd of deer, staring wildly at the burning forest, over a mile or so away, and ere they could fly Captain Frosby brought a big buck down with his rifle.

It was skinned, and what was left of the flesh after dinner was put aboard the raft, to be cooked when they halted for the night.

All that day they went slowly on, the raft moving heavily on the bosom of the stream.

At night it was tethered to the shore, and they all camped together on the soft, sandy soil.

For five days they followed the meanderings of the river, and then they found themselves on the verge of the huge forest.

Evidence of it still smouldering could be seen here and there, and the men on land could go no further.

Donald's attack was so resolute that [he] could do nothing but defend himself.

That the river led to the bay where the Fairy was moored was pretty clear, and some of the men were put on board the raft to get them there with all speed.

Captain Frosby remained behind with the rest.

"I shall not go further from my prize," he said. "Bring back with you two boats to carry away the spoil."

"I hope his men will remain faithful to him," said Danby, as the raft floated on, "but the sight of treasure often turns men into fiends."

"He has Jack with him," said Donald, "and he is a host in himself."

Danby said no more about his fears, which, indeed, only momentarily troubled him.

He was captain of the raft, and, as she was now pretty well loaded, the greatest care had to be exercised in managing her.

A more mournful sight than what was left of the burnt forest the eye of man had never looked upon.

The fire must have spread at a tremendous pace, for of the huge trees only the trunks were left, and many of them being partly hollow from old age were smoulde. ing pillars.

The main part of the fire had marched on northward, and in the far-off horizon a belt of dense smoke showed where it was still raging.

The destruction of valuable wood was so vast as to be appalling to the calculator of riches. Millions of pounds in valuable timber had been reduced to ashes.

The next day they were clear of what had been a wood, and floated by their old camping-ground.

Not a soul was in sight, but there were many little relics of their stay scattered about.

But for these they would not have recognised the spot.

Every bit of vegetation had been scorched or reduced to ashes.

Even the tree whereon they had hung Vampa was now no more than a blackened stump.

By the camp the fire came to an end. A wide stretch of the ground sheltered the other wood, and it had escaped.

By this the raft drifted on all day and night, and all the next day, and then they came to a view of the sea.

The Fairy was safe, for they saw Captain Frosby's flag fluttering at the mainmast, and this unexpected appearance nearly brought disaster.

Bob Bitters was on the look-out. At first, thinking they were foes, he opened fire upon them.

Luckily the shot was hastily aimed, and flew screaming over their heads.

Those on the raft took off their hats as a signal of their peaceful intentions, and Bob saw that he had made a mistake.

His contrition was very deep, and when the raft got near enough to see for certain who it was he hid himself below.

Ina and Isabel were both on board—in the cabin—and, hearing old Bob blundering down the companion, they asked him what was the matter.

He threw himself upon his knees and asked their pardon.

" What is the matter?" asked Ina. " What have you done ?"

" Killed 'em both !" gasped Bitters, " or nearly."

" Killed who ?"

" Your two young lovers," groaned Bob. " Why don't somebody kill me ?"

Both Ina and Isabel were thrown into a state of trepidation, but they did not show it. Ina took Bob by the collar and gave him a shake.

" How dare you talk about lovers ?" she said. " Who said we had any ?"

" Nobody," replied simple Bob. " Nobody need ha' said it, for anyone can see it."

Then Ina and Isabel looked at each other and laughed, although their cheeks were rosy red and they were somewhat confused.

The raft at that moment bumped against the side of the Fairy, and without waiting for further explanation from Bob the two girls ran on deck.

There they found living proof that nobody had been killed, although the escape was a narrow one.

Bob was fetched up from below and told that he **was** forgiven.

How was it possible for him to know that they would return in that fashion?

Their story was soon told, and Bob, with half-a-dozen men to row, started off with the two boats of the Fairy, taking with him sundry necessaries in the way of provisions and wine.

Danby and Donald remained in charge of the Fairy, and found compensation for recent sufferings in the sweet society of Isabel and Ina.

As boats can be propelled at a fair speed it was expected that the boats would be back by the morrow, bringing with them a portion of the treasure trove.

Meanwhile, the hold was put into order for its reception.

No signs of the recent fire had reached the Fairy, and Ina and Isabel were in total ignorance of it until the story was told by Donald.

They shuddered as they thought of its living creatures driven before the flames or destroyed, and were thankful it was no worse as far as their friends were concerned.

Now up to the present, since the alarm, not a word of love had passed between Donald and Ina.

It was not right and honourable that he should say aught concerning it, her father being away, but for all that the two couples sat apart when evening came, and there was much whispering to the soft music of a gentle breeze.

Isabel liked Danby, and finding him an agreeable companion encouraged him.

But did she love him?

As yet, not quite.

CHAPTER XXXI.

THE WATCHERS ON THE HILL—TWO STEAMERS APPROACHING—A SNAKE IN THE GRASS AND A FATAL SHOT.

WE pass over four days more, and come to the time when the first cargo of their great prize arrived at the quarters of the Fairy.

Jack Johnson accompanied it, and they heard his cheery whistling, long before the boats were seen—"Rule, Britannia"—on the air, and its spirited rendering won him a compliment from the charming Isabel.

The hold of the Fairy was prepared to receive the arrivals, having been cleaned out and strewn with a lot of dry brushwood in the place of straw.

Jack had brought ten suits with him, in pieces, of course, and at that rate it would require forty days to transport the whole of the treasures on board the Fairy.

"Too long," said Danby. "If Carker is coming back he will be here before the time has expired, and he will come prepared to blow us out of this hole."

"Frosby won't come away till the last is afloat," said Jack. "He says he literally *can't*."

"We must take our chance, then," said Danby, "but I would rather we had settled Carker before we took the armour on board. Suppose he licks us?"

"Impossible," said Donald.

"Impossible! But on the card," said Danby, coolly; " say that he does. What a prize for HIM."

"Rather than yield," said Donald, vehemently, "let us sink the Fairy."

"Right, if we are in deep water," replied Danby. "But he may turn up—as such knaves have a knack of doing—at an awkward moment.'

Danby was the last man in the world to give way to fear, but he had had experience, and when the welfare of others was concerned he was prudent.

Forty days was a long time, and a thousand things might turn up before the time expired.

And many things did turn up, as he feared.

Although things were very pleasant on board the Fairy the sterner duties were not neglected. All day long there was a look out from a high point of land not far from the bay set to watch for the approach of foes.

On the sixth morning after the arrival of Donald and Danby he reported smoke in the northern horizon.

That message was conveyed by signal, and Danby immediately went up to the look-out.

With the aid of a good glass he made out the hull of a steamer.

"Is it a friend or foe, or neither?" he asked himself.

An hour would answer the question, but it would be unwise to delay taking steps for defence. Much indeed had already been done in that direction.

The Fairy had been put into a state of defence, the largest of her guns being placed in the bow, so that any boat attempting to approach her from the bay would assuredly be sunk.

The men had also been drilled in the use of small arms, and were now, one and all, in a fair state of efficiency.

From the bay the attack was not much feared, as no ship of heavy draught could get in. The greater danger lay from the land side.

If a number of men were landed they would, if they had pluck enough, have a fair chance of capturing the Fairy.

But the Argentines were mostly cowards, as Danby knew, and he felt that he could, with the small force at his command, stand against two, or even three, to one.

His first care was to retire to the Fairy and get her out of her "dock" and anchor her at the mouth of the river, so that the grove of trees on the promontory would act as means of defence on the land side.

He stated the case plainly on his return, and Ina and Isabel volunteered to take the place of the look-out.

"I am sure you want all the men you have," said Ina.

That was true enough, and the plucky girls, each armed with a rifle, ascended the hill and sent the two men stationed there back to the Fairy.

They had the ship-glass with them, and the first thing they discovered on using it was that there was not one steamer, but TWO.

One was following immediately in the wake of the other, so that in the distance the pair seemed like one.

There was something ominous in this. Evidently a considerable force was being sent against them.

"Were you ever in a fight?" Ina asked Isabel.

"No," was the answer, "but I HEARD one once—on board the White Rose."

"To be sure. I forgot. How did you feel?"

"I was very much afraid. Then all my blood began to tingle with rage, and I wanted to come out and help the poor fellows who were being killed. But I had no arms—so I remained where I was."

"Quite right."

"You don't think it mean of me, I hope, Ina."

"No; it was prudent—especially as you are a woman. Well, dear, you will soon see what men call 'warm work.' I am sure those steamers are coming here to capture us."

"And if they do?" asked Isabel, anxiously.

"They won't!" said Ina, resolutely. "We will all die first. Only one thing I wish for, and that is that my father and the other men were here. We shall be in need of all our strength."

Isabel lost a little colour as she thought of possibilities arising out of the foe being too strong for them, but she did not quail.

Her voice was firm when she replied—

"We can die but once, Ina, and death is preferable to some things—isn't it?"

She turned away to conceal a sigh, and her eyes roamed over the scene inland.

From the point where they stood for two hundred yards the ground sloped downward. It was covered with long, coarse grass, in some places as high as a man's waist, but growing rather thin, it did not offer a great impediment to the watchers.

A peculiar movement in this grass attracted her attention. It was swaying right and left in a narrow line, as if some animal was creeping through it.

She touched Ina's arm and pointed it out to her.

"That is a puma creeping towards us," Ina said; "they are very dangerous. Stand still. If we run, it will bring death to one of us. Your rifle is loaded?"

"Yes."

The face of Ina was flushed, but that of Isabel was very pale. Different people have different ways of exhibiting signs of intense excitement.

"I may have to fire several shots," whispered Ina.

"Get ready to change rifles with me, and load them as fast as I fire."

Whatever it was that came near them was now not more than thirty yards away. Ina could just see a dark patch or two in the grass, and at this she aimed and fired.

Immediately, to her horror, a man leaped up and immediately fell again.

By the movement in the grass they could see that he was writhing and twisting about in pain.

"Oh! Ina, what have you done?" gasped Isabel.

"I don't know who it is," was the answer.

The report of the rifle was heard on board the Fairy, and every eye was turned to the summit of the hill, but as the girls did not make any signals for help it was assumed that nothing of great moment had occurred.

The girls' movements also gave colour to the assumption. Walking slowly down the hill, they bore a resemblance to two sportsmen about to pick up some game they had shot.

Let us return to them and see what sort of game they had " bagged."

Keeping the second rifle ready for action, in case it should be some dangerous foe, Ina led the way, until they came in sight of the man she had brought down.

He had made for himself in his agony quite a "wallow" in the grass, and now lay in the centre of it, gasping for breath.

An exclamation of pain burst from Ina's lips.

It was Vampa, her once faithful servant!

CHAPTER XXXII.

VAMPA'S DEATH—PREPARATIONS FOR DEFENCE—THE INVADING FORCES—THE MINE.

IF there had been any doubt as to Vampa's object in crawling towards Ina it was dispelled by the fact of his having a long keen knife grasped in his hand. It was his intention to have killed her and her companion also, the latter out of sheer malice.

And now, indeed, he had paid the penalty of his evil doing.

The mortal wound under which he was fast sinking had been given him by the woman he, in his way, madly loved.

The fact that she had shot him, unconscious of who it was, did not lessen the sting of it.

In his eyes were the smouldering ashes of the fire of a bold, bad man, with one green portion of his life to serve as a relief to the blackness of the rest.

That was the time when he was Ina's faithful servant—her watch-dog ; but he had wiped out all that was due to him on that score by his recent infamy.

" Vampa !" exclaimed Ina.

" Yes," he said, in a voice full of intense bitterness, " it is Vampa — dying by the hand of the woman he loved."

" I cannot even now," said Ina, " hear you talk of love to me. It is your own madness and folly that has brought you to what you are ; but I do not reproach you. Throw away that knife."

" Would that I had dashed it into your *heart*," he hissed, as with an effort he plunged it into the ground up to the handle. " It maddens me to think that I must go, and you will live—live—to be the bride of that English cub."

" Vampa," said Ina, " how can you talk so now ? If you are dying—"

" I am going," he interposed. " When a man feels SURE of his end being near he is past all human help. I feel that now. Oh ! the sting of it. I care not for death alone—if—I could have but carried out my purpose and killed you."

" This is horrible," exclaimed Isabel.

" And I once thought him a rough diamond," said Ina. " Truly it is hard to tell what is in the heart of some. Vampa, although you have no claim to mercy from me, I do not wish you to die like a dog. Is there anything—"

" No," he almost screamed, " nothing. If the curse of a dying man is of any avail, may you—"

But the impious curse never passed his lips. He suddenly stopped short, and every particle of colour fled from his cheeks.

He turned his eyes—dim with the glaze of advancing death—upon Ina, and with a groan expired.

Ina took the hand of Isabel and turned her gently round.

"Come away," she said, "this is no sight for you, dear. I am sorry that he died by my hand, but I did not know what I was doing. He was a dangerous man, and the world is the better for his leaving it."

"He knew you?" said Isabel.

"He was my faithful servant," replied Ina, "until a short time ago. Then he had the presumption to *love* me. Ah! think of being loved by that man. How much sweeter was his hate, bitter as that assuredly was!"

"Shall we go back to the Fairy?" asked Isabel.

"Not until we are relieved," replied Ina, with a faint smile; "we are on sentry here. Duty before everything."

Isabel said no more, and they returned to their post.

Both steamers were now well in sight, and the way they bore down upon the coast indicated their destination.

One was a cruiser and the other a trader, and both carried the flag of the Argentine Republic.

"There are a lot of men on board," said Ina, after a long inspection of the approaching vessels. "Yes, I expect we shall see some fighting."

"I suppose you will laugh at me," replied Isabel, "but I would rather not see it."

"So say I," said Ina; "but when it comes to a question of life and honour what would you do?"

"Fight," was the reply.

"Well said," answered a voice behind them.

They both started and faced about.

It was Danby who had come up swiftly and quietly behind them.

"You must both come on board at once," he said, "for you can do no good here. By the way, what did you shoot?"

"A man," replied Ina; "although I did not know it was one—Vampa."

"That villain here?" said Danby. "He is as persistent as the wolf. He fled, I suppose?"

"No, he died; I killed him," replied Ina. "I could

not neip it.   Bad as he was I would rather he had fallen by any hand but mine."

" Where is he ?" asked Danby.

Ina pointed out the spot.   Danby said—

" He must lie there for the present until we have the time and opportunity to bury him.   We must not linger here."

They left the hill and walked slowly to the cliff, down which the path to the river was fairly well defined.

Half-way down two of the men were just closing up a hole that had been recently dug.

" What have you buried there ?" asked Ina.

" A little surprise for our friends who are approaching," Danby replied.

The men quickly completed their work, and in five minutes all were again on board the Fairy.

She was now in a position that hid her from the approach on the north side of the river, and the path by which Ina and the others had recently descended could only be seen from the grove on the promontory.

There a man had been placed on the look-out.

Orders were now given for quietude on board the Fairy, and it became at once like a ship manned by the dead, so silent were all.

The men went about with bare feet, and the two girls, by Danby's orders—he had positively to order them— took refuge in the cabin.

But for the necessity of waiting for Captain Frosby and the others it would have been easy enough for the Fairy to have slipped out of the bay, and either met her foes in fair fight, or, finding them too strong, have shown them a clean pair of heels.

But there she was, held faster than any anchor could have done by the exigencies of the case.

Hour after hour passed, and there was no sign of the foe.   The day was almost done before they were sure that it was foes they had to dread.

There had been an off-chance of its being otherwise, but it was now rudely dispelled.

The look-out in the grove came down to the water's edge, and by signal reported men on the cliff above.

Danby asked Donald to go and see what they were like. Our hero landed, and, crossing the grove, came in view of those who may be called the invaders.

There were at least a score of them, and in their midst Donald saw his old enemy, Carker.

He was giving directions to the two men, and to others behind, invisible to those below.

They were hauling something heavy up to the verge of the cliff, and presently it appeared.

It was an ordinary ship's gun—one of the old sort—but without the carriage. Preparations were made to lower it down the cliff.

The object of their arrangements was apparent. It was intended to attack the Fairy in front and rear, her position having by some means been clearly discovered.

There were two men besides Donald at the look-out, and one of them was sent back for assistance—half-a-dozen seamen with rifles.

Donald and the other men opened fire without delay.

The first two shots wounded one of the foe, and the rest scuttled away like rabbits to their burrows, leaving the gun on the brow of the cliff

In a few moments from various points, and under cover, Carker's men began to return the fire.

It was responded to by one of the steamers which had come to anchor not far from the shore, and two shells came whistling over the grove, to bury themselves in the sandy bank on the opposite side of the river.

"They have made up their mind to make it warm for us," thought Donald.

He did not like the position of things at all, for the Fairy was fairly boxed in, and could not return the cruisers' fire. If once the gunners got the correct range the dropping shells would soon make a wreck of the Fairy.

Two more shots were fired from the sea, but the shells went far away to the left, and no more harm was done.

As for the fire of the party on the cliff it was very erratic, and mere guesswork.

Sometimes a bullet struck a tree near Donald, but by keeping on the right side of the trunks he and his attendants were safe.

The other men speedily appeared, and Danby with them to take stock of the situation. He smiled grimly as he saw the mouth of the cannon above.

"Let them fix it, Don," he said. "There is only one spot where they can do so, and that is *where we made our preparations.*"

"Ugh!" said Donald; "I don't like the idea of the thing."

"All is fair in love and war," replied Danby.

With some fallen trunks he instructed them to make a rough stockade, and then he prepared to return.

"Two pistol-shots from the Fairy," he said, "will be the signal for my work on board. By-the-way, *your* signal must be the flash of a dark lantern. I will send you one."

The sun went down and night came on. The watchers in the grove kept still as mice, and those on the cliff did not again show themselves while daylight lasted.

Nor did they make any apparent movement until the night was several hours old.

Donald, who kept to his post with sleepless eyes, judged it was about midnight when a scraping sound from the direction of the cliff reached him.

He judged they were cautiously lowering the cannon to some chosen position.

Now, there was only one projection on the cliff large enough to be of service as a place for a cannon, and it was where Ina had seen the men filling up the hole.

To this they were bringing the cannon, and a more suitable spot would have been hard to find.

Just then the path took a sharp angle, and a rock jutting out and rising about five feet made a splendid breastwork for the gunners.

The practised eye of Carker had seen the advantages of the place, and selected it for the purpose of fixing a gun wherewith to destroy the Fairy.

They went to work with all possible caution.

The gun was wrapped up in cloth, and he had at least fifty men to assist in lowering it.

Very little noise was made; but what there was sufficed to acquaint Donald of their movements.

He gave them an hour to complete their labours, and then he sent word to Danby that the time for action had come.

Danby immediately came to the grove, and he and Donald crept up to the very verge of the wood.

Resting beside the trunk of a fallen tree was a small box which Danby opened.

" A touch and it will be done," he whispered.

" It seems a horrible thing," said Donald.

" My dear boy," said Danby, softly, " it comes to this. We are outnumbered and overweighted ; we must either have resource to stratagem and to trickery if you like, or we shall be beaten. I ask you what is to be the fate of Ina and Isabel if these fellows get the upper hand of us ?"

" Give it to me," said Donald, resolutely. " I will do it."

He pressed something in the side of the box, and immediately there was a report as if a dozen ships had fired a simultaneous broadside.

Danby dragged Donald back, both half-blinded by one flash of vivid flame.

Yells, cries, shouts for help were heard from the cliff, and a shower of fragments of stone fell into the grove and into the water.

Some were heard to bounce upon the deck of the Fairy, where everybody, prepared for the explosion, was under cover.

Danby had fixed some dynamite in that hole above, and laid an electric wire to the grove.

The dynamite he found on board the Fairy while rummaging over her stores.

Captain Frosby, it seemed, had occasionally used some for blasting purposes.

It was the thought of the moment that led Danby to lay the mine, his original intention being to fire it in case of open attack.

As soon as the echoes and reverberation following an explosion ceased the footsteps of Carker's men hurriedly retreating were heard.

" We have settled them on the land side," said Danby, " and now we have only to fear attack from the sea."

"I wonder if Carker is among—THEM ?" said Donald, in a hushed voice.

"He may or may not be," replied Danby, "but the chances are that he is not. Fellows of his stamp have the knack of keeping out of mischief."

Nothing more was heard of the enemy that night, but when the daylight returned two shells were fired from the steamer. As before, they went wide of the mark and did no harm.

A view of the havoc done by the explosion was now obtained, and it was amazing to see the amount of mischief which, in a limited area, had been worked by the dynamite.

The action of that terrific compound is to explode *downwards*, and the lower part of the cliff was fairly scooped out, so that the upper part beetled over. The path was quite destroyed, and approach from that direction was almost impossible.

As for the gun brought there by Carker's men, it had completely disappeared.

It had either been tossed into the river or buried by the fall of earth.

The men who had charge of it had disappeared also, but here and there among the earth wreckage an arm or leg could be seen protruding in a significant and awful manner.

CHAPTER XXXIII.

AFTER THE EXPLOSION—ATTEMPT TO ENTER THE BAY —DONALD SHOWS GENERALSHIP.

"It was a horrible necessity," said Danby. "They will not attack us from landward again. Our great danger now lies from the sea."

The boat that morning came down with another load of armour, bringing Jack Johnson with it.

He came to see how things were getting on, and was not a little dismayed at the report he received.

"Why, hang it !" he said, "you will be under fire for a couple of weeks."

"Unless one of two things is done," Donald replied.

" Either the remnant of the prize must be given up, or the rest brought down at once."

" And how is that to be done ?" asked Jack.

" On a raft," said Donald. " The river is navigable, isn't it ?"

Danby and Ina approved of the idea, and Jack was sent back with a good supply of useful rope, nails, and axes.

The timber could be got from the side of the river which had escaped the ravages of the fire.

Fortunately for the Fairy, the tides were exceptionally low at the time, and a stiff breeze was blowing from the sea.

The entrance of the bay was a mass of breakers, and the commanders of the steamers were not likely to risk a passage through the dangerous rocks.

In four days, if all went well, the Fairy would have everything on board, and she might with a favourable breeze go out of the bay, and take her chance of what followed.

It was odd, as Danby said, that a raft for the armour was not thought of earlier, but it is so with the world all over. The right thing is generally only thought of at the last moment.

Now ensued a time of keen anxiety.

As hope grew stronger, so the excitement increased.

The only watch that Danby could set was a man in the top of one of the highest trees in the grove, and there one man was perched while daylight lasted.

He reported no movement on the part of the steamers. They kept their anchor ground, but that was all.

But preparations of some sort were going on aboard, the nature of which could not be ascertained.

For two days while daylight lasted the wind blew from the sea ; at night there was complete calm. The wind, as sailors say, followed the sun.

On the morning of the third day the cruiser was espied at the mouth of the bay, cautiously feeling her way in.

She and the Fairy were now face to face, and the latter was in a helpless position, the wind being dead on her bows.

She could not be towed out, and the boats fit for that service were away, and when the cruiser got inside it would, as it seemed, become a question of gunnery.

But here again Donald's native wit came again to their aid.

"A dozen men with rifles on the cliff, at the point," he said, "would keep off that steamer."

The land there was a mere ridge of rock—one of nature's rugged break-waters, requiring the agility of a cat to climb—and a few men posted on the summit could hold their own against five times their number.

"Go at once," said Danby.

The boat that was left for the Fairy's use was put into use, and Donald and the men he required were landed inside the bay, just round by the promontory.

The tide was low, and there was fairly level ground for them to travel on, so they got over the ground fast.

Meanwhile they had been observed by those on board the cruiser, and shots were fired at the party from the deck.

But they soon got the point of land between them and the vessel as a shield, and Donald and his men fairly raced for the place of vantage.

They gained it ere the steamer could push the passage through, and, having attained the summit of the rocks, they opened fire upon her.

The range was not more than a hundred yards, and the cruiser's deck was pretty well crowded with men.

The first shot sent half of them scampering below.

Carker was there—Donald saw him by the man at the wheel, directing his movements—and to him our hero turned his attention. Taking careful aim he fired.

A rocking movement of the cruiser saved Carker's life, or at least spared him a serious wound, but the man at the wheel tumbled over.

The steamer was brought broadside on towards the rock, and immediately there was a terrible commotion on board.

Carker seized the wheel, and, yelling out a few words of command, the engines were reversed, and she was put about.

Donald's men were now firing rapidly, but they were not exactly skilled marksmen, and in addition the moving of the steamer disturbed their aim.

They brought another man down, and then all but Carker joined those below.

It was ludicrous to see officers and men seeking safety under the deck. Carker was undoubtedly the bravest man there.

Donald would not shoot at him again, but let him go, and like an arrow from a bow the cruiser shot away seaward out of rifle-range.

Donald sprang upon a pinnacle of a rock waving his hat and cheering. His men leaped upon points of vantage and shouted derisively. An answering cheer came back from the Fairy.

Good generalship had succeeded. The cruiser would not venture to try to get into the bay by day, and at night it was an impossibility.

Of course there was the peril of a party being landed from the enemy's ships, say about midway down the sea-wall, and cutting Donald's party off, and it would have been done by men with an ounce of real courage in them.

The Argentines, however, were not the men to attempt it by daylight.

Carker brought the steamer round about half a mile from the bay, and his men having returned to their posts he began to shell the position taken up by Donald.

Ensconced behind a solid mass of rock, he and his men laughed at the efforts to dislodge them.

In an hour the firing ceased, and the cruiser sullenly steamed on to the trading vessel, which lay at anchor in its old position, and took in what appeared to be a further supply of ammunition.

He had evidently brought a good supply with him, and was able to squander it, to a great extent, with impunity.

"It will amuse them, anyhow," said Donald, as he lighted a cigar. "Let them blaze away."

CHAPTER XXXIV.

THE LAST LOAD—ALL ABOARD—A DANGEROUS PIECE OF NIGHT WORK—CARKER GETS A SURPRISE.

TIME was all that our friends wanted, and time was vouchsafed them. Carker made no further attempt to enter the bay, but stood off at a safe distance, keeping watch and ward over its mouth.

He judged all things by outward appearance, and he fully believed that the Fairy was not brought out because its commander was afraid of him.

The cruiser was a bigger vessel than his old craft, the Water Fiend—had more guns, and was in every way superior.

In point of build and armament she was fit to make a mouthful of the Fairy.

So he waited outside, in the full belief that ere long the little craft would endeavour to steal out, and then he could sink her.

Of the real reason for her delay he of course knew nothing whatever.

So the time for the return of the raft passed, Donald going to his hut at dawn, and remaining there until sunset, leaving Danby to act as cavalier to the ladies, which he did, considering his sentiments towards Ina, in the most impartial manner.

All day long the raft was looked for, but night came and it did not appear.

"Surely," said Danby to himself, as he was looking up the river from the stern of the Fairy, "it ought to be here!"

Ina came up behind him and stood there for a few moments quietly gazing in the same direction.

"Has anything happened do you think?" she asked, suddenly.

"I don't think so. I hope not," he replied.

"They ought to be here?"

"Yes; but to calculate the time necessary for the work is one thing and to do it is another."

The night came on and the usual little party gathered

together in the cabin to dine. The quartette of very close friends were not in their usual spirits and the conversation flagged a little.

They were all thinking or the raft that ought to have been there.

Danby felt that something must be done to raise their spirits ; moaning and groaning never helped anybody yet, so, with a laugh lighter than his heart, he filled the glasses of Ina and Isabel with wine and said he had a toast to propose.

As he got upon his feet a sudden shock to the vessel caused him to resume his seat with unwonted suddenness.

On deck there was the stamping of feet and a rifle was fired.

"Carker—to cut us out," he cried. "Keep here, ladies ; you can do no good on deck."

He and Donald snatched up their swords and darted up the companion.

On the top step Danby ran against somebody coming down and grasped him by the throat.

"Here—I—what's the row ?" cried a familiar voice.

"Jack Johnson !" cried Danby, joyfully, as he let go.

"Yes, it's me," replied Jack. "What's the cause of your spite ?"

"I mistook you for an enemy. Was that the raft which bumped against us ?"

"It was. All's well. Frosby will be here as soon as his precious armour is hoisted on deck. We got aground on a shoal, and it took us half the day to get off again. That is what made us late. How are you, Donald ?"

Ina and Isabel had heard all and came up quickly. All was joy on board, even in the heart of Bob Bitters, who had again fired at his friends in the excitement of their sudden appearance, fortunately without doing any mischief.

"What a blessing it is," he said, "that I couldn't hit an elephant ten feet off to save my life. I wonder where *that* bullet went to ?"

Nobody knew and nobody cared. They had other matters to think of.

The precious armour was hoisted on board, and Captain

Frosby was as happy and light-hearted as a boy. Leaving Bob Bitters to superintend its storage in the hold, he embraced Ina and exchanged congratulations all round.

Then, with an addition of two to the party in the cabin, the dinner was resumed, and went off merrily.

Immediately after it serious business was brought on the board, and after an earnest and all-round discussion, it was resolved to get out of the bay as soon as possible—that night, if feasible.

The latter was left to the decision of Danby, who said that, without a bit of a breeze, it was impossible.

"The wind has been veering round," he said, "and there is what we haven't had lately, a bit of it at night-time.

At eleven o'clock it was reported that the wind was in the south. This would give a wind on the beam to the Fairy in the bay, and, with a little light and skilful management, she might make the run of the narrow channel to the open sea.

At midnight the wind died away, and, all being awake and watchful, were awfully disappointed. Meanwhile Bob Bitters had seen to the storage of the treasure, and it was all safely stowed away in the hold.

"All go to rest," said Danby; "we shall not get out to-night."

It really seemed a hopeless case, and they turned into their bunks, the two girls, as heretofore, sleeping in Captain Frosby's cabin.

After many laborious days and nights of broken rest he was tired, and slept soundly, hearing nothing until a tramping of feet on deck aroused him.

Springing up, he saw that daylight was near, and hastily dressing, he ran up to the deck, to find that he was the last, save the ladies, up from below.

All the others were there, down to the last man of the crew, with their eyes ahead on the narrow channel, towards which the Fairy was sailing with a strong breeze from the south-west.

Danby was at the helm, and Captain Frosby furthermore saw that the guns of the vessel were ready for action and the men all armed.

He knew the reason of these preparations, and approved of them.

The Fairy, if she got into the open water, meant to try conclusions with the cruiser.

Some men might have desired to get clear away with such a prize as he had, but Frosby knew that there were many wrongs to settle with Carker, and he did not for a moment believe that the victory would be on his side.

A big ship and heavy guns go a long way, but they must have stout hearts behind them, or they are not worth a straw.

It was difficult to make out the channel, for the tide was meeting the wind, and the lashing of the sea at the mouth of the bay had churned the water into a body of foam.

Still, a keen eye could make out where the commotion was less marked, and the calm Danby, with his eyes on one spot, steered for it.

A mistake would be fatal, but those who have oft carried their lives in their hand are not easily daunted.

Not a word was spoken on board. All had their eyes fixed upon the one spot where danger lay.

With a rush the gallant little Fairy went through, throwing up the spray half-mast high. Without a touch she cleared the rocks and reached the open sea.

The men could have cheered then, but the possibility of their doing so had been foreseen, and they were instructed to be silent.

Gracefully the gallant little vessel bore round northward, and there before her lay the cruiser and her consort at anchor.

It was early, and whatever watch the men kept on board either must have been a poor one.

Not a man was in view.

So the Fairy bore down upon them unseen and unexpected.

"They are all asleep," said Jack Johnson.

"We will wake them up," said Danby.

And on his giving the signal two of the guns forward were fired.

The shot of one crashed into the cruiser's side, and

the other cut her bowsprit away. Immediately, all was confusion on board both vessels.

Men came tumbling up, and among the first to appear was Carker, hurriedly putting on his upper clothes.

They heard him calling to his men, who were running wildly to and fro upon the deck.

Boom—boom !

Again the guns upon the Fairy were fired—aimed, as directed, between wind and water. Both took effect— one near the mark desired, and the other just above it.

The men on board the trader hurriedly lowered their boats on the shore side and crowded into them ; and the word was given to let them go.

The trader, as a matter of fact, was not to be harmed in any way. With superb grace the Fairy passed on—tacked and came down with her other guns ready for use. By that time there was a semblance of order on board the cruiser.

As the guns of the Fairy were small, they were only available at a comparatively short range, so Danby steered boldly in and fired them at close quarters.

The cruiser returned the fire and a shell clipped the Fairy's bow, passing on to seaward.

Two more shots from the Fairy at close quarters completed the disorder of the men under the command of Carker. One of the guns was dismantled, and the steering wheel was shot away, while half-a-dozen men were injured or killed outright.

Once more the Fairy tacked, and was brought up right under the helpless cruiser's stern. Shot after shot was sent across the deck, which was fast being cleared of men.

Half of the crew had already jumped overboard and were swimming for the shore.

"Let them go," cried Captain Frosby. "Shall we run in now ?"

"Ay !—ay !" sang out Danby, cheerily ; and with a skilful turn of the wheel he brought the vessels together.

The grappling irons were ready and made fast. Donald and Jack, with half a score of the Fairy's men, leaped on board the cruiser, and charged at a group of the foe who appeared to be resolved to defend themselves to the last.

CHAPTER XXXV.

THE CRUISER RETURNED TO HER OWNER—CARKER IN A FIX—THE CHASE ASHORE.

SURPRISE no doubt had a great deal to do with the panic among the Argentine men, but as a body they did not show much pluck.

The party opposed to Donald numbered about thirty, and they were well armed, but their resistance was very feeble. Donald, on the other hand, was full of fire.

He was a bold fighter, provided he had a good cause to espouse, and his rush was irresistible.

Like the thin edge of a wedge, he pierced the Argentine group, and his men, to carry out the simile, acted like the rest of it, and clove them asunder.

With loud cries for mercy they dashed their arms upon the deck, and all resistance was over.

It was quite in harmony with the wishes of our friends that it should be so. They were not lovers of carnage, nor did they take delight in dealing death to men who until that morning were strangers to them.

All they wanted was Carker.

But he was nowhere to be seen about the deck ; and Donald, glancing shoreward, saw him in the stern of a boat carrying half-a-dozen men with him to pull for their lives.

The sight raised within Donald a feeling of the bitterest anger. The thought of such a man escaping when fairly within his grasp was naturally gall to him.

So it was to Danby, Captain Frosby, and Jack Johnson, who were now standing near him.

"I will follow him," said Donald. "Let me have a boat and half-a-dozen men."

"Not enough," replied Danby.

"The fellows with him will never show fight," returned Donald. "I must go."

They did not dissent any further, and, as half-a-dozen men were as many as they could spare, he started with that number in one of the Fairy's boats.

Jack Johnson wanted to go with him, but Donald said "No."

"All through the piece," he said, "I have resolved to settle with Carker alone. Do not, I beseech you, make it an unfair contest between us."

"Let him go," said Danby; "he can take care of himself."

So he went, and in two minutes the boat was being propelled towards the shore by strong-armed, eager men.

Carker's boat had not yet reached the shore, and as he turned his eyes backward he saw Donald coming in pursuit.

With vehement gestures he urged his men on to increasing efforts.

He had the start of the race, and his boat grounded on the beach while Donald's was yet midway between the vessel and the shore.

Immediately his boat touched ground his men sprang out and ran off inland as fast as their legs could carry them.

They took the direction of the bay, and Carker, for some reason, wanted to go in the opposite direction.

He wasted a minute or more in shouting after them, and finding they would not heed him, he fired a revolver in impotent wrath after them, and then sped along in the direction of the ruins of Carita.

It was fully five minutes before Donald leaped out of his boat upon the shore, and Carker was a third of a mile away, climbing up the cliff.

"Stay here," said Donald to his men. "I can go on alone."

Instead of following the line taken by Carker, he made a dash for that portion of the cliff just in front of him. It was very steep there and required sure foot and handhold. He possessed both, and scaling the cliff successfully, disappeared.

His movements were watched by his friends with the keenest anxiety, and after he was gone from sight Jack Johnson felt sorry that he had not insisted on going with him.

Danby said nothing, but there was a slight gleam of apprehension in his eyes, for he knew that Donald was open and impetuous, and Carker a secret, cunning foe.

Ho ever, the issue was not in the hands of any but Donald himself, and pending his return—if ever he did return—they busied themselves with other matters.

First there was the cruiser and trader to be dealt with.

These were to be dismantled to such an extent as to partially cripple them and yet leave them with the means of getting home again.

"I shall return them, with my compliments," said Captain Frosby, " to the contemptible Government that despatched them against us."

" And won't there be a bobbery about your attacking them?" asked Danby. "I understand it to be your intention to return to the old country?"

" I mean to go at once," replied Captain Frosby.

" Well, the British Government might be induced to take up a complaint from the Argentine Republic."

"Not if they get MY complaint first."

Danby laughed.

" Oh ! that is your game, is it ?" he said. " Not a bad move, either."

" As soon as I land in the old country I shall lay my case before the home Government," said Captain Frosby. " I was a peaceful settler here, and they sent a piratical scoundrel to attack me. They drag me from my home on a false charge, and afterwards destroy my property. All I did was in self-defence."

" You have a good case," remarked Danby.

" The papers will take it up," continued Captain Frosby. " British subjects are not to be outraged with impunity. I have justice on my side, and a strong Government to protect me. You may trust the Argentines not to make much fuss over this affair."

" And we can let them rest," said Danby. " Now, what is to be done with these vessels ?"

" First of all, make the fellows pitch their own stock of coals into the sea," said Captain Frosby. " That will leave them with only sailing power to get home with. You may also ask them to thin out their stock of canvas, leaving them just enough to keep before the wind. A fortnight ought to elapse ere they get back again. You understand ?"

"I think I do," said Danby, with a smile; "and I would give a trifle to hear the dons swear in good solid Spanish when they see their cripples in port. They had the best of the job at one time—now I think we are geting a little cream."

Danby set about the congenial task of ordering the Argentines to cripple their own vessels, and Captain Frosby returned to the Fairy.

CHAPTER XXXVI.

CARKER'S FLIGHT—BACK TO THE RUINS OF CARITA—IN HIDING—HAND TO HAND AND FOOT TO FOOT.

DURING all that had taken place, Ina and Isabel had remained below.

Whatever anxiety they might have felt at first was soon dispelled by the meagre sounds of conflict and the laughter that was heard afterwards.

The victors were in the highest spirits, and the ordinary sailors indulged in a little extempory dancing as they went about their work.

A little freedom of action at such a time was permissible.

Captain Frosby went down the companion, and joined them in the cabin.

"A ridiculously easy victory," he said. "There was not an ounce of real fight in the fellows."

"Anybody hurt?" asked Ina.

"Nobody to speak of."

"And that man Carker," said Ina; "have you secured him?"

"No—not exactly. He escaped in a boat, and got ashore; but they are in pursuit of him."

"Who are they?" asked Ina, steadily looking at her father.

"Donald, and half-a-dozen men."

"Why Donald more than any other officer?"

The whole thing had to come out, and Captain Frosby told it.

"He insisted upon going alone," he said, "and alone he is in pursuit of Carker."

"You said he had half-a-dozen men with him."

"He left them in the boat on the beach. Carker is ashore too. It will be a man to man affair."

"Donald is a man," said Ina, bitterly, "and that Carker is a tiger. Do you think HE will ever fight fairly? Donald ought not to have gone alone."

Hitherto, through all the scenes she had witnessed, Ina had never lost nerve, but now she fairly broke down.

It was wrong, it was cruel, she insisted, to let Donald go by himself to meet so crafty a ruffian as Carker.

Isabel said nothing. She fully understood Ina's emotion, which Captain Frosby did not.

"I really see no harm to fear," he said; "and if you look at the matter in the right light—"

"I cannot look at it at all!" interposed Ina. "Why are you all here, careless of what becomes of him. Go to his aid at once!"

"Ina, be reasonable!"

"I *am* reasonable. If you will not go put me ashore—"

"Really, Ina, I shall cease to imagine you are the plucky girl I had for a daughter," said Captain Frosby, reproachfully. "Would you have had Donald shirk a meeting with that man?"

"No," answered Ina, with a flash of fire from her eyes. "You are right and I am wrong. Donald will punish the villain for his misdeeds, and on his return we will give him a welcome. They used to do it with the brave men of old, Isabel. We will have a day of merriment—a feast. Ha—ha!"

And in this contradictory mood did Ina receive the tidings of her lover's pursuit of Carker.

Truly women, as the Northcountrymen say, are "strange critters."

.   .   .   .

There were times when Carker could be brave as any man, but on other occasions the whole of his heart seemed to go out of him.

The sudden and successful attack upon the cruisers he commanded had completely unnerved him.

It came upon him at a time when he felt that he had his foes within his grasp.

Assured of the strength of the escort he commanded, and misled by the apparent fear of those on board the Fairy, he went into a Fool's Paradise of thought.

At the moment of attack he was in his berth, awake, arranging in his mind what he would do with Donald and the rest—when he got them into his power.

Donald, Danby, and Jack Johnson were to be hanged right away.

He was not quite sure what he would do with Captain Frosby, for he wished to curry favour with Ina, for whom was destined the honour of becoming Mrs. Carker.

It was a pleasant line of thought, and it's rude breaking up came upon him with overwhelming force.

His spirit, for the time, at least, was absolutely crushed.

Like a hunted hart he fled.

As he scaled the cliff and reached the summit he looked back to see who was following him.

He saw the men of the Fairy resting in their boat ; but owing to the nature of the ground he could see nothing of Donald, who was just then engaged in making the ascent already recorded.

" I eould have sworn he was there," muttered Carker ; " but I may have been mistaken. Of late I have had that young fellow on the brain. Of all the false moves I ever made in my life, the worst was smuggling him on board the Water Fiend. I have never known a stroke of real luck since."

He looked about him for some signs of the men who had escaped to the shore at the same time as himself; but they had all gone away in the opposite direction, or, in obedience to amicable signals hoisted by Danby, were making preparations to return on board.

One of the boats had indeed started, for the men knew the nature of the coast, and had no inclination to taste the hardships it would inflict upon them.

As Carker was surveying the scene the form of a man, apparently rising out of the ground about four hundred yards off caught his eye.

The floating handle to save.

It was Donald, who had just succeeded in scaling the cliff, and Carker knew him.

That lithe active form was too familiar for him to mistake it.

With a bitter expression he turned and fled—still towards the ruins of Carita.

The wood on his left he dare not enter. A strange fear of it took possession of him.

Horrible visions of being alone there FOR LIFE uprose before him. He saw himself, a veritable wild man, living with beasts, and almost of the beasts—a monster wandering in the forest, forgotten by all who once knew him.

In times of great mental agony or bodily fear the imagination is very active, and with incredible rapidity scenes of a possible future life alone in such a land passed through his brain.

There was a refuge for him, but he would not take advantage of it, nor could he reason himself out of his overwhelming fear.

So on towards Carita he went—back to the peaceful place he had wrecked.

Silent and determined Donald came upon his trail.

He did not run, but simply walked quickly, with his eyes on the hurrying Carker, feeling, he knew not why, sure of his man.

He was certain that he would overtake him, and then the struggle would be for life or death. No half measure this time. No mercy given or taken on either side.

"It would be a wrong to my fellow-man to let him live," Donald thought, as he flashed his bare sword in the sunlight.

Another half mile of ground was traversed and Carita, or all that was left of it, was before them.

Carker passed the blackened remains of the simple house so briefly occupied by Donald and shuddered. Again he knew not why.

What was there in a few charred timbers to touch the chord of fear within his breast?

When Donald reached it he paused one moment to look at it—wondering what his life would now have been if he had been left there in peace.

Truly, much that was unexpected had happened, and here he was on the trail of a foe to do battle with him unto death.

In that brief moment, devoted to looking at the ruins of his house, he lost sight of Carker.

On looking ahead again he found that he was gone.

Donald ran to the side of the cliff and looked down. No sign of him there. He had not sought safety in that direction.

Breaking into a run Donald speedily reached the spot about the ruins of Carita and eagerly scanned the blackened walls and piles of fallen rubbish—black with the action of fire.

On his left lay all that remained of Captain Frosby's once happy home.

A heap of charred timber as if it had been tossed there in idleness or in sport.

Donald's eyes resting upon it noticed from the ruins a line of bushes ran for some distance parallel with the wood, and it flashed upon him that they might have been used by Carker as a cover.

If so, he must be hiding within the ruins.

If he had taken to the wood the task of following him would be a trying one, but Donald was bent on tracking him down.

First, then, the ruins.

Moving swiftly about, he inspected all the fore part, and found nothing.

On going round to the back he saw the impression of a man's boot on some blackened ashes.

" I have him now," he thought, exultingly.

Carker was assuredly concealed somewhere near.

Now, the ruins of the place here assumed a strange form, the timbers having so fallen as to act like props to a mass of slate and other material which had been used for the roof.

It had the appearance of a rough hut put together for temporary use.

There was even a narrow opening which would serve as a doorway, but it was so low that a fair-sized man would have to stoop to enter.

Donald was certain Carker had concealed himself inside. Indeed, his trail was quite clear, but to get at him required a few moments' prudent consideration.

Such a thing as fear was not in Donald's heart. If Carker were to overcome him his last thought would be simply vexation that such a villain should be triumphant.

Though young and full of life, Donald was not afraid to die in a just cause.

How was he then to get at Carker?

To go up boldly and openly would be to court death, for he was sure to be prepared with a weapon, and would do his best to shoot Donald.

The only thing to be done was to creep up quietly to within a certain distance, and then make a rush.

The thought conceived was quickly followed by the act—a half dozen stealthy steps, and then the rush was made.

As he dived through the opening he received a confirmation of his views. Carker was there, and ready to shoot him down the moment he appeared.

A flash—a report—and a stinging sensation in the left arm, and Donald was upon him.

There was not much room within for a sword fight, but a series of rapid cuts and thrusts were exchanged.

It was blind, furious work, with the defence on both sides necessarily weak.

Donald knew that he received more than one wound, but he did not feel the pain.

He gained his knowledge from the fact of the blood trickling down his face and side, and he could see that Carker had suffered too.

The maddened pirate fought for his life—desperately, fiercely, wildly—and the sight of blood acted on him as it does upon the tiger or the lion.

The fear he felt a few minutes before was dispelled, and in his heart was a fury that took the place of revenge.

Hand to hand and foot to foot they cut, and thrust, and parried within the limits of the hollow in the ruins of Frosby's house.

The space was not more than twelve feet by ten, and

on one side of that was the beam on end upon which the full weight of the rubbish above was resting.

Cut and thrust—hand to hand and foot to foot.

From a scalp-wound the blood poured down, half blinding Donald, who could only dimly see his foe.

In a little while he might not be able to look upon him at all, so he rushed in, forcing Carker's sword upward, and they closed.

Their swords were useless now, and both were dropped. Each grasped the other by the throat and held on, swaying to and fro, until Carker fell against the beam that supported the rough roof above them.

It was driven out of the perpendicular and fell over.

With a crash that could be heard half-a-mile off the mass of rubbish rushed down, burying the combatants beneath it.

CHAPTER XXXVII.

JACK AND INA COME TO THE RESCUE—CARKER'S LAST MOMENTS—TWO STORIES TOLD AT SEA.

HALF AN HOUR passed, and around the ruins supreme stillness reigned; and then a sound in the sea below broke in upon the silence.

In a boat were five of the Fairy seamen, Jack Johnson, and Ina.

The latter could not rest on board until she was assured of the success or failure of her lover's pursuit of Carker, the pirate.

So a boat was lowered, and the party described set out from the ship.

As Donald had been seen moving in the direction of Carita, they resolved to land there and ascend the cliff by the path that was used when Carita was a peaceful little settlement.

They did so, and, arriving on the summit, Jack Johnson and Ina, accompanied by two of the men, looked around them.

It was to Ina and Jack a very cheerless scene—so still, and the mournful ruins of the once happy home a huge black spot upon the landscape.

"Call him," said Ina.

Jack shouted Donald's name in a clear, ringing voice, and the word was echoed far and wide, but no cheering shout responded.

"Carker must have taken to the woods," Jack suggested.

"If so, why did not Donald let him go? The villain would have perished there."

They walked on to the house, and in a mechanical, dreamy way Ina walked slowly round it.

How desolate it looked—black and cold in spite of the warm sunlight.

Jack kept by her side, watchful for a possible foe, with his hand upon a revolver in his pocket and his cutlass loosened in its scabbard ready for immediate use.

They reached the spot where the broken roof had been recently brought down, and then, without any set purpose, they halted.

"Where is he?" asked Ina, impatiently? "Oh! Donald—Donald, can you be DEAD?"

A low moan—it was little more than a sigh of pain—was heard, as if in reply.

The hearers started, and looked eagerly to the right and left, unable at the moment to locate it.

"You heard it?" asked Ina, eagerly.

"I heard something," answered Jack, "but what or where it was I cannot tell."

Again the moan was heard, and this time both detected the direction from whence it came.

"Somebody is lying under the ruins," said Jack.

"It is Donald," said Ina, in a hushed voice.

Jack wasted not a moment in any vain speculation, but calling the two men round to him, he set to work with their aid to remove the *debris*.

Great care had to be exercised; for there was a lot of rather loose stuff that might fall.

Bit by bit they drew away the shattered timbers, until they came to a hand lying crushed between two beams.

"Do not stay here, Ina," said Jack; "it is no sight for you."

"Go on," she answered, in an icy tone, that revealed the terrible anguish she endured.

"It may not be Donald," thought Jack, and in his heart he prayed it would not be. And it was not Donald.

They had come first upon Carker, who was terribly maimed and crushed, but still breathed.

As they drew him from the ruins and laid him upon the sward Ina turned away.

It was a sickening spectacle. Although he had been a remorseless foe, only monsters could have rejoiced to see him in that condition.

"He is not alone," thought Jack, and with an aching heart he resumed his labours with one man. The other was instructed to do his best to revive Carker, though it seemed scarcely probable that he could ever become conscious again.

The removal of a few more pieces of timber brought Donald's head and shoulders into view.

Save for a cut upon the forehead, in addition to the wound he had received from Carker, he had escaped injury.

Several of the pieces of wood having fallen at an angle, he was placed in a comparatively sheltered position.

They drew him out, and at first Jack thought he was dead, so faint were the signs of life.

But as Ina threw her arms about his neck, and kissed him, his chest heaved, and a soft sigh escaped his lips.

With a wild cry of delight Ina clasped him close to her heart, and kissed him again and again until he opened his eyes.

"Ina!"

"Donald!"

It was on this scene that Carker, maimed beyond all surgical care and on the verge of death, looked upon as he slowly opened his eyes.

The soft breeze of the morning, fanning his face, had revived him.

Jack Johnson has never forgotten the expression of Carker's face as his gaze fell upon the lovers. Despite the crushed features, the look of malevolence and impotent hatred and despair was terribly intense.

Speech was beyond him, and with a world of misery in his heart—keener suffering than he felt from his wounds—he made one effort to rise, as if he would tear them asunder, and then fell back—dead!

Jack Johnson drew out his handkerchief and covered the lifeless face; then, turning to Ina and Donald, he asked the latter if he could walk with assistance.

"I can try," replied Donald, with a smile, "but I am pretty well pumped out."

No limbs were broken, and, having got him upon his feet, they led him slowly away out of sight of the body of the man who had been his foe.

On the cliff the three friends sat down to rest, and after awhile the journey down the path on the cliff was attempted and carried out without any mishap.

Great was the rejoicing on board the Fairy when the party returned, and many were the congratulations poured upon Donald on his narrow escape.

They made a couch for him in the cabin—a resting-place for the day, at least—and while he was tended by Ina and Isabel his life was bright as the sunlight on the sea.

Carker was laid in his grave.

"Bitter enemy as he was," said Captain Frosby, "we could not leave his body to the carrion birds of the air and beasts of the forest."

"Assuredly not," said Danby.

"Our work is done," said Captain Frosby, "and now we will spread our wings for home."

.   .   .   .

It was during the voyage back to England that Danby told the full story of his life.

He was the eldest son of a rich man, and descended from a good family, and his home was Mevrill Hall, Leicestershire.

A somewhat wayward boy, and his father being hot-headed, there had been some friction at home, and a false accusation of wrong-doing brought about a climax.

Danby—we shall not change his name here—was supposed to have led a very dissipated life, and he was finally charged with very dishonourable conduct, the nature of which we need not specify.

Hot words ensued between him and his father, and he was ordered to leave his home.

"I will never return until you send for me," he said; "and when you send, you will not be able to find me."

He suspected a cousin of being the author of the foul stories in circulation against him, but he took no trouble to find out the truth.

Determined by nature, he left his home, and, changing his name, went abroad, wandering here and there, and being mostly at sea, soon obtained a knowledge of the management of a vessel.

One day he fell in with Carker in a town on the Chilian coast, and, believing his story about being captain of a privateer, he joined him.

Carker was simply a privateer at the time, and what he developed into afterwards we know. The rest of Danby's story has also been made sufficiently clear in the course of our narrative to spare us any further dwelling upon it.

But there was another story Danby told on board the Fairy on the homeward route, and it was for the ears of Isabel alone. It was the old, old story, and she thought it very pleasant, inasmuch that she expressed a hope of hearing it again and again in the years to come.

What that story was is easily guessed.

CHAPTER XXXVIII.

MR. BASIL BENNETT ABOUT TO ENJOY HIMSELF—A SLIGHT HITCH IN THE ARRANGEMENT—A GENERAL CLEARING-UP.

MR. BASIL BENNETT sat in his counting-house in conversation with his confidential clerk, Jacobs. They were preparing a balance-sheet of the business of the firm, with a view to disposing of it to a purchaser.

The career of the merchant as a business man had come to an end. He was about to retire and enjoy himself.

On what?

On the money that rightfully belonged to Isabel Meriton.

Everything was hers, including the business, which had been the property of her father.

Basil Bennett was his managing man, respected and trusted as a friend.

And when Mr. Meriton, a widower with one child only, found that he was dying, he made a will, leaving everything in charge of Basil Bennett.

"I can trust you," said the dying man, "because you have principle, and I know you will be good and kind to my darling daughter."

Basil Bennett promised to be a father to her, and how he acted the part may be inferred from subsequent events.

The hypocrite had been a liar and a thief all his days. From the first he had robbed his trusting master, and he was on the eve of being dismissed when Death stepped in and saved him.

He took charge of the business, and, having everything in his hands, declared that it was his own by deed of gift. Fortunately he could not touch the bulk of the money left unless Isabel died. Then it would be his.

Too much of a coward to carry out the thought in his heart—to murder her—he did all he could to drive her away and yet leave himself clear of the imputation of being the cause of her rash act.

He succeeded in doing this, and for some time past he believed her to be dead. He was assured that everything was now in his hands, and with a little patience all would be well.

He was in no hurry to prove the will, for the intelligence that he was coming into a hundred thousand pounds gave him any amount of extra credit, and he was now deep in debt.

His purpose was to realise his fortune and leave the country; not for a moment did he intend to pay anyone.

What cared he for the hard things that would be said of him? A private purchaser would take the business, and the creditors could harry him if they liked.

Jacobs was going abroad with him, and the precious pair had laid themselves out for a life of luxurious indulgence in some sunny clime, more befitting the fevered dream of youth than the aspirations of advanced age.

"All is to be settled this afternoon, Jacobs," said Basil Bennett, "and to-morrow we will away."

"Why not to-night ?" asked Jacobs.

"Why in so great a hurry ? Take things cool."

"I've got an idea that a hitch may come in somewhere," said Jacobs.

Barely had the words escaped his lips when the door opened and two men entered. They were very plainly dressed and had an air of quiet authority about them.

"You have made a mistake, my friends," said Basil Bennett, smoothly.

"Not at all," replied one of the men, calmly. "Mr. Basil Bennett, I presume ?"

"That is my name."

"I arrest you on charges of forgery and robbery, and you," turning to Jacobs, "as accomplice."

The two old men stared blankly at the speaker, who sat down calmly upon the table and took stock of the contents of the office.

"Who charges me ?" asked Basil Bennett, in a husky voice.

"Miss Isabel Meriton," was the reply, "through her friend Captain Frosby.

"She is dead," muttered Jacobs.

"Not at all," replied the officer. "She lives."

Basil Bennett got up from his seat and turned a livid face upon the two men.

"If you had given me notice of this," he said, "I would have paid you a thousand pounds apiece."

"That is what you offer us now if we will call again to-morrow ?" said the officer.

"Yes."

"Too late. It can't be done. Captain Frosby and a gentleman friend are outside. Come, get your hat down and let us be off."

Basil Bennett walked across the room to an escritoire, on the top of which his hat was placed.

He took it down with one hand, and with the other open a small drawer.

"I can't go to prison," he said. "I won't !"

Before they could rush upon him he had placed a small bottle to his lips and drunk the contents.

"I have ten seconds to live," he said. "Take that

old rascal, my clerk, to a cell and don't let him out again."

"Why, you—" Jacobs begun; but the rest of the sentence was lost, for Basil Bennett fell heavily to the floor—a dead man.

"I didn't think he had the courage to do it," said Jacobs, disgusted. "Here, take me away. It's a lost game, that's all. Win or lose, it will be the same a hundred years hence."

.   .   .   .

There was a bit of legal work to be done ere Isabel could claim her own, but it was got through at last, and she was a rich woman and a happy one.

While this was being done Danby went down to his old home and was reconciled to his father, who had long known of his son's innocence, and had thirsted to see him again.

He came back with Danby to be introduced to his future daughter-in-law, and was charmed with her.

In due time a wedding took place, and it was made a double affair, Donald and Ina being married on the same day.

Both wives brought their husbands a handsome dower, and in the home selected by Donald some of the grand old armour was placed as a wedding gift from the captain, and it is one of the marvels of the country round.

Captain Frosby wisely decided to have a home of his own, and therein the rest of the armour was placed, a lasting delight to the man who had spent so much time and risked so much in seeking it.

As for Jack Johnson—cheery, simple, whistling Jack—he came back a hero to his long anxious mother, and to all his old friends of the quill.

In recognition of him as a dear friend, Danby and Donald purchased a small but rising merchant's business for him, and Jack, having had enough of travelling and adventure, for the time at least, threw himself heart and soul into it, and is now making money fast.

He is a rising man in the City, and all sorts of possibilities lie ahead of him. Perhaps he may be Lord Mayor some thirty years hence.

Bob Bitters and Mike Barlow, the latter a changed man in every way, started in the boat-building line up the Thames, and they are doing well—that is living comfort- ably and saving a bit for the old age that will assuredly come upon them.

That the married young folks are happy may be taken as granted, for what have they to make them miserable? With youth and wealth, friends, and all that goes to make a happy home. Could they desire more?

If they did, which they certainly do not, they would not deserve anything but the reproach of all honest men. Donald is the more light-hearted of the two perhaps, for Danby is by nature more grave ; but all storms are past, and the current of their lives flow easily. They are as much at rest as a boat in a calm on an inland, tideless sea.

THE END.

Printed by

Sully and Ford,

Plough Court,

Fetter Lane,

London.

THE "BEST FOR BOYS" LIBRARY.

THREEPENNY COMPLETE VOLUMES.

THE WILD ADVENTURES OF
EDDARD & JAM JONSEE ABROAD.

THE WILD ADVENTURES OF
EDDARD & JAM JONES AT HOME.

THE FURTHER ADVENTURES
OF EDDARD AND JAM JONES.

THE SLAPDASH BOYS;
THE Livelihood OF SCHOOL BOORUM.

PLUCKY PHIL FARREN OR THE
MYSTERY OF BRITHWAITE SCHOOL.

HAL O' THE HEATH,
THE WANDERING BOY.

THE BRAND OF THE BLACK STAR.

LIONEL THE BOLD, OR, THE
CIRCUS ARENA ROUND.

VALIANT BOY, OR, THE PIRATE'S
REVENGE.

SIXPENNY COMPLETE VOLUMES.

JACK JAUNTY,
THE HERO OF SEAGULL CLIFF.

DAUNTLESS DONALD DREW; OR,
BRAVE AT RIVER FORD.

BADDLETON BORKETT'S BOVING
SCHOOLBOYS.

THE ADVENTURES OF
BOLD BEN BRERETON AND TINY
TIMOTHY TOPTUN.

OUR BOYS ABROAD;
OR, THE BLACK RANGER OF THE
RHINE

CHING CHING AND HIS CHUMS,
A MIRTHFUL, MOVING, AND
MYSTERIOUS STORY.

JACK O' THE GOLDEN BELT;
OR, STRANGE ADVENTURES IN THE
ISLAND OF GOLD.

YOUNG GRIMM AT SCHOOL;
OR, HIGH AND LOW FOR THE
SCHOLARSHIP.

DARING CHING CHING;
OR, THE MYSTERIOUS CRUISE OF THE
SWALLOW.

GALLANT HAL AND THE CREW
OF THE SILVER STAR.

THE EXILED CAPTAIN;
OR, THE HERO OF EAGLE CRAIG.

DICK STORNAWAY;
OR, A HERO IN SPITE OF HIS FOES.

ONE SHILLING COMPLETE VOLUMES.

HANDSOME HARRY OF THE
FIGHTING BELVEDERE. Vols. I. & II.

CHEERFUL CHING CHING; THE
SEQUEL TO "HANDSOME HARRY."

TOM TARTAR AT SCHOOL. Vols. I. & II.

WONDERFUL CHING CHING.

YOUNG CHING CHING.—Vols. I. & II.

TWO SHILLING COMPLETE VOLUMES.

HANDSOME HARRY OF THE FIGHTING BELVEDERE,
YOUNG CHING CHING.   TOM TARTAR AT SCHOOL.

THE ABOVE WORKS ARE PUBLISHED BY THE
"BEST FOR BOYS' PUBLISHING CO., 17, GOUGH SQUARE, FLEET-ST., LONDON.

www.ingramcontent.com/pod-product-compliance
Lightning Source LLC
Chambersburg PA
CBHW080821250626
47160CB00008B/2828